Daniel Villasenor was born in 1966 and grew up in Columbia, Maryland. He received an MFA in Poetry from the University of Arizona and attended Stanford University as a Stegner Fellow in Poetry. He makes his living by shoeing and training horses in the Southwest. *The Lake* is his first novel.

The Lake

Daniel Villasenor

faber and faber

First published in the United States in 2000
by Viking Penguin, a member of Penguin Putnam Inc.
375 Hudson Street, New York, New York 10014

First published in the United Kingdom in 2001
by Faber and Faber Limited
3 Queen Square, London WC1N 3AU
This paperback edition published in 2002

Printed in England by Bookmarque Ltd

The right of Daniel Villasenor to be identified as author of this
work has been asserted in accordance with Section 77 of the
Copyright, Designs and Patents Act 1988

A CIP record for this book
is available from the British Library

ISBN 0-571-21273-5

2 4 6 8 10 9 7 5 3 1

The Lake

CHAPTER ONE

The long twoheaded shadow their shape cast eastward moved across the marshland of that country as improbable and quixotic as the pair themselves, the lean dark young man and the small boy with the bright red hair. The sun was low in the west and the fields around Florien met the edge of the road and lay out flat and wet forever and gave back the sky between the grasses. The trees lining the slough stirred heavily in the wind. For a long time the man had been listening to the boy who was humming as if he was going to shake. The man's legs were spraddled wide which shortened to his knees the already short pantlegs of his bib overalls and his knees pumped up and down steadily and grazed the plastic grip of the handlebars and the hollow metal on the other side where the grip was missing. He wore an army field jacket buttoned to the chin against the cold and a pair of lace-up engineer's boots. His hands were bare. He gazed into the distance. As if it was coming toward him faster than it was. As if he expected it to be recognizable.

The man's name was Zach. He leaned back until the back of his head rested on the boy's forehead. Look over one of my shoulders, he told the boy, and pick the farthest point in the land and pretend that we're just leaping over it and if we look down we'll scrape our bellies so don't look down and keep your eyes on that farthest point until it is not the farthest and then choose another point still farther, over the other shoulder to trick the shaking. But don't worry Samuel, he said, you're not going to shake.

And then there was glass and minutes later Zach himself began to shake, wobbling the bars. He leaned to turn the bicycle and when the wheel did not come back he had to jam his foot down hard so as not to spill. And he did not curse; he just kicked the stand down and dismounted and turned and held the bike steady for the boy who climbed nimbly down from where he sat under his red hair in that dairy crate they had wedged and bolted to the seatpost and fender behind them. Silently Samuel already had the patch kit out from the torn and frilly basket in front and silently, not looking at Zach's eyes but two feet askance to the left of his ear which was the boy's ruminating wont, he turned to the man with that familiar, that almost permanent expression on his face which seemed to say, *I am too old in my soul and too patient to exhort you or anything to perfection. I am Samuel.*

It was the rear one again and Zach knelt and peeled back the old tire with the Swiss Army driver and inched along pulling it around the rim with the boy kneeling and catching the lip of the rubber to prevent it from springing back. It must have hurt him but he was just humming with his knuckles jammed between the rubber and the steel. Humming the way he did when he was scared or when there was an accident at The Lake or if he was about to start shaking or very much afraid that he would. Zach removed the glass from the tire and Samuel pursed his lips and asked with his eyes if he could spit on the tube and Zach pumped vigorously and they watched the slit in the rubber froth forth and hiss and he wiped it away and placed the patch and spread his thumbs to seal it and they put back the tire in the reverse way with the boy keeping the rubber inside the rim with his knuckles jammed up against the steel and just humming.

Zach inched around the wheel finally overtaking the small fingers and Let's go, he said.

Yes, the boy beckoned, moving his head up and about the way a horse does to warn a challenger, as if to the trees lining the west side of the slough which ran along that road which they had been on for the good part of the afternoon he was saying, Move off, which trees took his gesture into their afternoon light and held it, it seemed, absorbed momentarily in the brief windless repose of their lit barely burgeoning branches as if they would suddenly slam it back upon the two travelers in retribution, this boy's gesture, which Zach loved beyond all reason and which he likened to wilderness, to wind at night or rain on the lake because the boy, like the forces of nature, was entirely speechless. Are you hungry? Zach said.

Are you? Samuel's eyes said.

He was not worried when they approached the store. They had been only a day and a half on the road and already they'd had a policeman pull them over and a busload of children jeering at them for a stretch of nearly five miles and a group of three teenagers firing BB guns in their vicinity and an elderly couple peering at Samuel at a roadside market and comparing him to the drafted image of a lost or dead or kidnapped child on a milk carton. So he didn't even register whether the men on the gallery were whispering. He put the kickstand down and steadied the bike and Samuel climbed out of the crate and stepped deftly down and swept his silent gaze across the street signs blowing in the empty intersection and the half dozen stores of the diminutive town and lastly across the loitering men on the gallery as if he were taking in an altogether new country and they went up the bootworn stairs. Zach asked the clerk if he had any bicycle tubes and the clerk said no. Another man's look must have shot out at him over Zach's head from behind because the clerk who owned as well as tended the store came around the counter and to the front door to see something bearing already a look of comic awe before he even saw what was supposed to be funny. He stood in the doorway of his store expanding and relaxing his suspenders with his thumbs and the men sat or stood where they were on the trodden boards of the gallery and on the steps. The raw late brumal air on them all, roiling them there, not into confusion but focusing them, communal, predatory. There was a storm to the north and the temperature had dropped fifteen degrees in as many minutes. The storm front cut the sky in half almost on a plumb line and it was windy and the clouds north above the awning shouldered like greyhounds, east, against them.

There were seven men on the porch, a few of whom had known one another longer perhaps than Zach had been alive. Another man was coming up from the paddocks visible on the northern flank of a seemingly defunct barn, limping. A few of the men moved slowly aside for him and nodded. One said his name. The clerk didn't nod at the man. He stood in the doorway and looked out at the debris gusting up in the street and then he settled his gaze on the bicycle. He was paunchy, balding, commanding; he had that comfortable haughty bearing of smug men who are admired in but never deviate from their finite realm. He bent forward and looked out from the double doors which were propped open each with a boot scraper. That there's a girl's bike, he said.

It was as if the men had waited for him to speak, to come out and put forth some judgment on the event (on all event) as if they were incapable of opinion themselves; as if if he had come out and stood and praised the novelty of the strangers and their audacious enterprise and asked them to dinner they would have fallen all over themselves to do the same.

Some wind lifted at them then. For a moment no one spoke.

I believe that seat was pink at another time, one man said.

With flowers, said another, bending forward and scrutinizing and then lifting up the tattered basket which did indeed have along its rim an all but completely faded and frayed floral design.

Samuel's hair moved in the breeze and Zach nearly put out his hand to anchor it.

The man from the paddocks looked at the collapsed tire. You need a tube?

Zach nodded at him once.

Go see Frank.

He had one foot raised on the last porch step and his hands rested on that knee and even through his trousers his knee bulged as if it was filled with metal. He studied the pair, one at a time. Turn down toward the bottom after Wheeler's sign where the buckshot live oak's at.

It's a goddamned banana, a banana seat, said one of the men.

Call your girls, Freddie, we could have ourselves a regular Tour de France right down Main.

A growed man on a banana boat with a carrot in the back, the clerk said.

And at that the men roared, those who stood slapping their thighs and those who sat pounding the old porch boards with the fleshy bulbs of their fists. Shaking their heads. But for the paddock man. You can't miss it, he said. He'll have what you need.

He looked at the others and spat and turned stiffly on his good leg and looked down the road and repeated himself. He sat, he lumbered downward with difficulty and braced himself and stretched his leg out in front of him and put his hands on his knee as if to warm it from the wind which was colder now by the minute.

He'll have what you need, he said.

So they rode on, the windblown dust off the road filling their lungs and Samuel's forehead on Zach's back to keep out the dust and the boy breathing the jacket between his shoulders. And Zach was thinking

this is a child and he can hear but he cannot speak or sign in the language of the deaf I am hungry he is hungry we are riding on a girl's bike with a hissing rear tire down a dirt road in Louisiana with eight or more pairs of eyes drilling the backs

of our necks to see a man named Frank who has parts appar-
ently for any device or machine   my knees are coming up and
down like humor and pathos, humor and pathos by turns   do
not intellectualize this   that is not the raison d'être of your
life   the what?   the what?   you are pedaling   it is cold
there is a boy older than you will ever be behind you in a crate

Zach was twenty seven years old. Samuel, he said, though the boy did not speak.

Samuel, what are we doing? I have been sick. You are a child. Do you want to go back to The Lake?

Samuel put one index finger in the blades of each of Zach's shoulders which meant no or you or pedal or good. And they moved on, homeless, ludicrous, hungry and weary, weaving in the cold gloamingdust like a vision, like some warped memory's apparition a chimerical land gives to senility or exhaustion. 'Whither are we moving now,' Zach said, 'away from all suns?' He said it to the air, to no one and nothing at all. He thought of Lazar. That last night in November on the landing of his home, downlit by the porch light and reluctant beyond all measure to leave it, to step out from under it into nothing but a direction called Window Rock, a West, with his wife under the lintel leaning there and her apron still sullied from the sweetbread she had made him for the road, the old man had said, I've never known anyone to trip who wasn't trying to run. And when Zach had lifted his eyebrows at the trite, avuncular phrase, Lazar had said, Aw hell, give me a break for godsake. I've lived long enough on this planet to say anything that sounds foolish enough to be true. All I'm saying is you're not sick. You don't even have a mote of dust under your nails. It's your goddamned birthday. Because dead or alive your blood kin are only part of it.

And he had stepped into his house and stood for a moment and turned and stepped back out to the porch and embraced the young man vigorously like the comrade (or perhaps even the son, this man with only daughters) he had in that short time come to be.

Zach, he had said over the young man's shoulder, you are not sick.

CHAPTER TWO

Zach was a philosopher. All but dissertation at the University of Virginia. When he went to lie down in the road it was early September and already the first molted leaves of the season were awash and clumped in the street rivulets and the air was woozy already with that sharp autumnal afterdark cold which feels on the summer's throat like a handheld knife chafing on a wire. That evening—no, that morning he had rolled up the carpet in his flat against the foot of his makeshift bed and he had lain on the floor on the diagonal and watched the light on the shade and onward across the room and onward still across all the east of the room, fading even as he watched it, turning his head so that when the east wall snuffed to darkness he had traversed, like a starless planetarium's dome, the entire breadth of his room. He moved. He lifted his arm off the floor and rested it down to see if it would make a noise. To see if some cymbal would crash in his mind which would mean a tomorrow and a tomorrow and another tomorrow. No sound. Just the drip of the faucet. It was completely dark now in the room. Just the car wheels' rubber dry on the asphalt but for one diminishing splash from a heavy rain two days before puddled out there in the intersection, that sound too like something

washing over his body in the morning as he lay and then he forgot it for awhile through the afternoon and then by evening the
sound, the puddle, was almost dry and he heard it only faintly
in what he thought was an imagined whisper which whisper
became a voice, a last interdiction against reality—if reality is
one sensual present impeding on another sensual present, he
thought, trying still to hear the puddle splashing under the
cars—and then the voice became some orchestra of voices as if
the linear time past and experience of his life was one increasing
voluminous Voice hoarding an infinite now and he lifted his arm
off the floor and dropped it, over and over again and faster for
sound, all but beating it on the floor—but no sound. He got up
then. He went into the bathroom and flossed his teeth. He had
not even brushed them in three days which he did now after, in
the darkness, not looking at himself in the darkling glass but
some shadow of a head and even the slight protuberances of the
ears, even the mussed not quite cropped but still short hair, just
a shadow, a shade. He was wearing the clothes he had been
wearing for three mealless and sleepless days. And then he did
turn on the light to look, just before he left the room. He stood
squinting a moment until his eyes adjusted. Then he pointed at
himself. Zachary, he said to the mirror. You Zachary. He turned
off the light and stood until even the image of himself which the
retina ghosted before him faded also into the dark glass. Then
he put on his shoes. He bent over and felt the ripeness ascending his back from the motion, the stiffness of the prostrate days.
He knotted his laces very carefully and evened their bows, left
and right. He took off his belt and put on another belt. He
tucked in his shirt. He went to the closet and chose a middle-
weight jacket and then he stood with his hand on the knob for
several minutes. He let go the knob and went to the sink and got
himself a drink of water. He could feel it in his toes as he drank,
the water; he could feel it filling slowly like diminutive reser-
voirs the soft lobes of his ears. Then he walked out of his life
forever.

He went first to the Rotunda on the university campus. He

stood on the grass and studied the buildings, the little rooms along the Lawn, studied the square places the lights made flooding finitely out on the finite grass of the grounds, the circumscribed places. He walked down onto the Lawn. Here too the leaves already lay, the columns lit downward on both sides Pavilion to Pavilion toward Old Cabell Hall; the air was pungent, getting toward cold, that autumn bite of cold. It was after eleven o'clock. It was Friday night. He did not walk about. He stood in what he hadn't even known was very nearly the exact center of the Lawn. There were fires in many of the hearths along the promenades. There were students sitting out in front of their rooms with fires in the hearths and the front door wide open so they could see the homish flames' shadows gamboling on the wall, so they could hear the logs' quaintly burning pop pop pop while they sat outside. Zach could hear the logs. He could hear the students' low polite talking where they sat on their steps or in chairs, their voices charged even from this distance with the sibilant low whispering of the gratefully fortunate, the selfconsecrating and faultless young unmolested and striving and nearly pure in their floating lapse between the naïveté of the child and the true man or woman, the human being contending with humanbeing, the long sightless surge toward the soul—or not, the man or woman who would refuse even the simple and natural accruement of consciousness, who would soon begin to slay, slowly, his or her heart's innocence and dark mystery both until the child was but a memory of a memory and this brief, windless repose, this college, but four all but disappeared years: a few awkward lovers, some forgotten books, and the smell of beer. He could hear them talking gracefully like wind in the grass, their laughter from another world.

He turned. He walked back up Rugby Road, past the beautiful mansions out from whose windows young men leaned and called out to women in cars blocking traffic in the road, or out from which music blared from a propped speaker, curtainless. In one second story window a man sat with his legs dangling over the edge and another stood below him in the yard and threw, from a crate between his legs, ripe fruit upward to his perched partner who then swung at the soft exploding tomatoes and oranges and peaches and nectarines with a baseball bat, a crowd of bystanders shrieking applause if some peel or pulp made it out over the cars, to the other side of the road.

There were parties spilling out of almost every other house and sometimes the revelers—the women especially—called to him (namelessly) from their safe inebrious numbers but he did not even hear them and he walked north until the houses were sparser and the quiet came upon him again and his steps. He continued on Rugby Avenue, walking fast, upright, purposeful. Now the houses were all brick and white trim with broad lawns and even private copses and then whole small plots of wood in between. He passed a lady on the street calling for her cat which cat did show at her summons and the lady's pleasure was all gaudy and disproportionate under the stillness of the night, the enlarging night because he was walking clear out of town now. He passed a couple kissing against the hood of a car. He passed through a group of teenagers weaving slowly down the lane on bicycles, the one in front saying Yo to him as he parted them in the middle of the road like water. And then he was nearly in country. The road was a deep blackness ahead and behind, just a few lit house lights spilling weakly out of the darkness. The trees hanging over, and still. He did not look up for stars. He did not so much as turn his head right or left once but his eyes focused, pierced, and moved on as if they would nail the world permanently into the brain. He passed a cart full of soil with some claw rakes and trowels in it glittering in the light from a garage, some inexplicable hooks hanging from a dormer, a galvanized trash can in which some first of the year's leaves were still smoking. He passed some bags of mortar in stacks by a hole in the walk and some flowers strewn in the curb and then there were no more houses and a threelegged dog came to him out from the shadows, so gaunt that it seemed it could be skewered through its midsection with the not even violent thrust of an index finger. So scared, its tail already way up under its legs, its face shying side to side as from remembered blows. The dog followed him, looking up at him, and Zach did not look down or slow his stride and the dog stayed, halflimping, halfjumping after him. He was on highway 250 now, heading east, walking not quite on the shoulder of the road and not quite in the lane either, the dog askance, slightly behind him. He had begun to taste sweat around his mouth. He reached up his hand and knuckled it across his upper lip and he was amazed at the perspiration (because it was cold; he knew, theoretically, that it was getting cold) and he flicked his thumb across his knuckle to slough off the sweat and the dog leapt away from the action as from a thrown object and Zach stopped suddenly. Go home, he said. Go.

The dog looked behind him and then out into the woods as if he hadn't heard. Go, Zach said again, pointing.

The dog just stood panting. Go, Zach said, louder.

He made a little rush at him and the dog turned and trotted and looked back and Zach rushed at him again and the dog walked, limped in that sidelong jumping action, back into the woods.

Then the road lay out straight before him. Then he walked down it stiffly, no longer fluid at all so that his bones seemed to be strung tighter now on their hinges. Then there was no light at all, but for the few speeding cars. He could hear them coming for minutes before they came. He could hear the pistons slamming under the hot hoods of their passing. He could smell something burning in the air. He could taste something metal in his mouth. He could feel his clothes on his body heavy with sweat. And then he could see nothing, hear nothing, smell nothing: time past and present, the trees, the road, the air, the sky just some tasteless odorless effluvium his body impelled through toward some zenith of its own compulsion, its own design. The road made a bight around a cluster of trees and he passed them and he walked out into the center of the highway and stood looking down at the infinitely black asphalt and because he loved Nietzsche, because when he read him at the very last it was not so much reading as thought itself, his mind leaping, overtaking the words themselves and laying them down in prolepsis as if he was the very generant man himself—because Nietzsche had lain down in the road, Zach felt it as an obligation. Two o'clock in the morning. Highway 250. Nine miles east of Charlottesville Virginia. He lay down in the middle of the road.

And he slept. And when he woke he found himself with saliva all over his chin and his face wet and streaked, and alive. He was surrounded by police officers and he did not know how long he had been there and he could not account for himself at all. He got up and brushed himself off and apologized and walked away and they caught him up and cuffed him and admitted him, later that morning, to the psychiatric ward. And now he wanted his books.

Chapter Three

Michael Lazar had been a psychiatrist for nearly forty years, every one of them at the Medical Center of the University of Virginia. He had no patients but those he chose. He was seventy six years old. Because of his tenure neither the department nor the hospital could have forced his complete retirement even if they wanted to which they did not; he had the alacrity and zeal of a recent postgraduate and the energy of a man half his age and perhaps more crucially that rare blend of irreverence and accountability that is perennially winsome and undeniable.

He had gone to Grady Avenue, where the young man rented a studio, to explain the situation to his landlady and to arrange to have his effects stored. There was nothing on the sallow walls of the flat save two large posters of brushmarked oriental calligraphy, a futon on the floor elevated by pallets with a rolled carpet at its base, a dead plant and a hotplate on a formica desk and papers strewn across the desk and floor. Two bookshelves teeming with books lying open some of them and crosswise others and even one with its cover and half its pages dangling over the shelf edge, all of it a parody of frenzied scholarship. A rotten apple in the miniature sink. The faucet dripping. A bar of soap in the center of a chair. And three oak leaves taped flat to the inside of the eastern window. Lazar perused the shelves and finally chose three books: *Problems of Occidental Philosophy*, *Kant to Heidegger*, and *The Triumph of Inquiry*.

He knocked and he came into Zach's room with the books under his arm. He pulled the chair from the desk and angled it between the young man and the window which shade was shut to the last light of day and handed him the books and sat. He looked at Zach and said, I'm Michael Lazar. I have a lay interest in philosophy.

He sat straight in the chair and his hands did not waver with the weight of handing over three large books. He asked Zach to open a book anywhere and to read.

You've chosen the wrong books, Zach said.

Lazar smiled. A good man can make a bad man decent, he said.

Zach looked at him blankly.

I'm seventy six years old. A good man can make a bad man decent and a smart man can make a dull book read like a tour de force. Put your finger in there and open it up and tell an old man what it says.

Zach began with Hegel and he told about the apparent self-subsistence of finite things and how nothing was real except the whole, not even time and space which were but parts, aspects, lies. He explained that for Hegel logic and metaphysics were the same thing, that nothing self-contradictory was real, even the idea of the universe as a whole, as a sphere of ultimate reality, even such a whole had to have a boundary and thus even this was not the Real, and so Hegel was flawed, he said. He explained that for Hegel relations did not exist, were not real, because they required two and not the One. And anything but the One was a facsimile. He explained that God was the Absolute Idea and that this idea thinking itself was for Hegel the only truth there was.

He talked like this for two hours and Lazar did not speak once. He shifted his position and nodded occasionally at some point he deemed salient. Once he lifted his head as if he heard someone calling for him out on the grounds. He put his hands together and brought the edge they made to his mouth and then he removed them and leaned forward for a time, his hands on his knees, and suddenly he stood up and shook hands and took the books under his arm and told Zach thank you and good-night.

He came every night save Tuesday, Friday, and Sunday, and Zach would read and speak about what he read. And Lazar would listen, never interrupting him save to ask him to repeat some point or to explain the relevance of what he read. At times he said that he couldn't understand the text to his satisfaction and that he needed Zach to clarify it. In truth he could understand perfectly. In truth he could understand so well that he knew that the only medicine for the young man before him lay not in the books but through them.

He began to bring hot chocolate which his wife had made with cream unpasteurized from their daughter's farm in Frederick Maryland. Any food or beverage from the outside was forbidden so he, the tenured psychiatrist, had to sneak it in in an old army issue thermos he had had in Europe in the war. He brought pictures of his wife and children and he talked about them and when he talked about them his voice grew husky with a quality nearly hallowed as if he was making them all extemporaneous and had to coax their shades into reality with his voice. As if their fleshly lives depended on the gravity of his feeling and without that consecration they would vanish as specters and leave him abject and alone.

He cooked well and he brought the contraband leftovers. Thai and Indian dishes and homemade flatbread his wife baked. And always at some point in the evening he'd ask Zach to read, and he listened to him talk about Kant and Heidegger and Aristotle in random turn without sequence whatever or only such sequence as a thumb falls to the pages of a book. Zach would describe the basic thinking of each and the flaws he found there and Lazar thought that the flaws he saw were true flaws and he said so. And when he did put his finger gently on Zach's knee for an explanation as to why this or that point was important it was never patronizing but earnest, even hopeful, as if he might have missed some knowledge in his life. As if the young man might be the bearer of that news.

Zach began to lighten. Over weeks and then months. He felt it rising out of bed in the morning like some balsa wood in the bones, and he felt it performing simple actions, raising his arm to draw open the window shade, tilting his wrist to water the jade plant on the sill, even just turning his head when the wind came in through the window bars they called crazy slats to watch the dustmotes whirl like dervishes in the corner of the room.

They talked more than they read now and often they talked deeply into the night and once they saw gray light through the loose weave of the muslin shade and they laughed and marveled at time. The old man pretended to sneak out like a pubescent boy trysting a girl in a dorm and Zach laughed and he heard himself echo in the hall through the door held partly open and it sounded peculiar. Sounded like a thing breaking out there.

One night Zach turned to Heidegger. Zach had said that but for Nietzsche he admired Heidegger's thinking more than any other but that he was a Nazi and this was impossible to excuse. Lazar, a Jew who had himself fought in that very war and been among the first troops to come across the camps and had lifted from the fetid catacombs his emaciated living and dead brothers, raised his eyebrows once and that was all.

Zach spoke of how according to Heidegger God was withdrawing from Man and that Man could only think of that which withdrew. But Man, he said, had not yet even begun thinking so that we knew nothing of this God who withdrew, who was right now withdrawing. That we could not even stand face to face with a tree because our thinking could never let the tree stand where it stood. And that was when Lazar cut him off mid speech for the first time in two months.

Bullshit, he said.

Zach looked up at him.

Bullshit, he said again, and then he said the word nouns. Nouns, Zach. You *can* stand face to face with a tree.

You're missing his point, Zach said.

No, he's missing mine. I have stood there, all of my life, and not only do trees not withdraw but sometimes they come closer.

What?

They lean, do trees. Nouns, Lazar said.

He smacked his hands flat down hard on his thighs. Damn it, you are not sick. You're not a philosopher. You are dying for things. For the feel of things.

Zach was sitting on the edge of the bed as he always sat and, laid like a kilt across his loins, the book lay open as it always was. Lazar was leaning forward now and he was not calm as for two months he had been the paragon of repose, buddhistic. No matter how true an idea is about a thing it is not the thing. Does New Year's Day 1882 mean anything to you?

What do you know about New Year's Day 1882?

I've done some refreshing. 'I want to learn more and more to see what is necessary in things as the beautiful in them. Thus I shall become one of those who make things beautiful. I want to be at some time hereafter only an affirmer.'

Amor fati, Zach said.

Yes, Amor fati.

You read Nietzsche but Nietzsche—

Lazar held up a hand. Hold on, I'm talking now. I am the senex here and you are the puer.

I don't know those terms.

Good. I'm glad I know something that you don't. When Nietzsche said to live dangerously, to build your cities on the slopes of Vesuvius, to sail your ships out on the uncharted seas, he had to know that one man's Vesuvius was another man's rolling hill.

I don't follow you.

Danger is subjective.

Yes.

17

So he was talking to you but perhaps he wasn't talking about philosophy. Perhaps he was talking about life. Perhaps that's why that is the most famous passage in all of Nietzsche because at the back of it is not the will to power but the will to experience. To live. Because philosophy is your chart, Zach. Your prefabricated shopping mall from which you pick a little Aristotle from this shop, a little Hume from there, some Kant in Women's Apparel, some Rousseau in Sporting Goods, and you sit there in this little buffered eatery of your own making and adjudicate and calibrate and expiate the world's verve. I've sat here for two months and watched you do it.

He was talking about thought, Zach said, quietly.

He was talking about a volcano.

It's a metaphor.

Bullshit, Lazar said. Lava is lava. He was talking about fear.

Zach had his hands over the book as if he was covering the words, shielding the eyes of children from some gruesome event.

He was talking about turning toward your fear. Because the only truly dangerous thing is to try and do what you think you cannot do.

Lazar leaned back and crossed his hands in front of him. Furthermore, I read the gist of him and I don't agree with the man.

Zach looked nearly amused, a layer of amusement over a skull of panic.

No I don't, Lazar said. And I didn't much care for it. You owe me a goddamned night's sleep. I've read too much of the ancient Chinese—no, I've lived too long in the world to think that my will could overpower nature. Or that I could even kill God let alone make him from nothing, erect him. To me that's the height of megalomania. But even if I did agree with him, when that hypothetical demon spoke into that hypothetical ear and said, You will have to live your life again, over and over, with nothing better to hope for and nothing worse to dread in the hereafter, with no hereafter—

Eternal recurrence, Zach said.

Yes, eternal recurrence. And that that will have to be enough.

That you'll have to long for that world's eternal sameness with happiness, even joy. Even that is about the world, isn't it? I can't believe he was only talking about ideas. For godsake he loved Goethe, the botanist. Because isn't that about soil under the fingernails? A plant, watching something, a child, grow? Sunsets, tears, those beautiful leaves you have taped so damned elegiacally on your window? Or a woman, christ, a woman soft under your body on an endless night. And there was a woman.

Lou.

Yes, Lou Andreas-Salome. And they had relations, in the old sense of the word. And he wrote to her—and I know you know this—that her coming just for a three week visit was the best present anyone had ever given him, that her assent was like a birthday in him. She was the only woman, ever, in his life. And she abandoned him later that year. And he never recovered. But for a time she was the world.

That's just it, Zach said. After her he had to create—

Zach, you are not a philosopher. There are people who are philosophers and that is right and good but they are not here in this ward. Let them philosophize. You've thought the flesh and blood world right out of existence. But it does exist. It's afraid you don't exist. It doesn't trust you, and why should it when you've abandoned even your fear? You have to coax the world back. Your life is going to have to become that coaxing.

He reached forward and put his hands on Zach's knees. Risk, he said. Risk is like a root planted in the ground which the world blesses with rain.

CHAPTER FOUR

On Halloween night they got caught. Lazar had spread some densely spiced and seared eggplant on two hospital platters and he had emptied the translucent green Jell-O into the sink basin making a disgusted sound. He had put in its place the mango chutney which he'd brought and Zach had just torn a piece of the flatbread Lazar called kulcha (which he said in mockery of his forebears like a New Yorker saying 'culture,' he a Southerner now for more than forty years) in order to sop up the stewed eggplant when the doorknob jiggled and the door opened and a nurse neither of them had seen before peered in at them where they sat on the edge of the narrow bed, the rich verboten food laid out on the tawdry platters. Oh my god, she gasped, this is not my shift.

Julie, Lazar said, which was not her name, have you got any pomegranate seeds? He said it thickly in aristocratic parody of a British accent.

Oh my god, she said again, and shut the door.

Who is she? Zach asked, through laughter which felt to him exactly like tears.

I've never seen her before in my life, Lazar blurted, himself nearly unintelligible from laughter. What do you think she's doing here?

They laughed all out of proportion, from some mutual contagion that wasn't even sane. Finally Lazar said, Eat, eat, I smuggled this across my wife's porch and you're letting it get cold.

So he could feel the lightness now like a helium balloon up his spine. He learned to judge his will by how high it climbed his back and he attended to this barometer like the private mercury it was. It was late fall in the Piedmont. The colors of the last turning leaves were just astonishing. He looked out the window for hours and he watched the everthinning trees and their final molting leaves like diminutive falling ingles unhurried and ungrieved landing lightly on the lawn. On the benches and on the swept asphalt so carefully poured and smoothed. The people looking both ways and crossing the street with energy and intention. And he found that he could move the lightness up and down his spine of his own volition. He was lying there early one morning listening to the immense sturdy oaks stripping in the wind when he suddenly stood up, held out his arms, and turned a full slow circle in the room.

CHAPTER FIVE

Go on into the refrigerator there. There's a gallon of milk, drink it up. What's left of it.

Zach went over and opened the lid and sniffed at it and Frank looked appalled, insulted, and he said, It's good goddammit, drink it.

It was about half full. Zach began to gulp it down. Drink! Frank yelled, every time he stopped to breathe. Milk spilled down his chin, onto his neck and shirt.

Frank wore a brown T-shirt which hung down around him from sweat and he wore jeans so dirty they matched the shirt almost seamlessly, like a uniform. He had the roach of a joint stuck in the corner of his mouth and it was not lit and looked like it hadn't been lit all day, maybe for days, as if he just chewed it continuously and paced around the rummage, fuming, irascible.

Samuel was picking dainty and slow like some curious animal through the tattered labyrinthine rooms and he was lifting up object after object in the dim light trying to figure their uses in the world.

Kid! Frank yelled, if you get hurt I'll kill you.

The sprawling stead was like nothing Zach had ever seen. It was as if so many wooden rafts resting on a slough had collided and jammed and Frank had built from that vague impression of stability shack upon shack extending backward endlessly. Some of the walls were mere sheets hung on nails or tin sheeting and aluminum siding and particle board and even the remnants of pink insulation actually tacked with broadheaded horseshoe nails into enjambed and welded curtain rods. Along every wall that could support them were meshgrating shelves framed in scrap angle iron and teeming from these were PVC parts and pipe wrenches and elbow joints and saw blades and axles, car parts and vises and clamps and rusted and warped iron stock of every imaginable configuration. There were old sewing machines and vacuums and in one corner an upside-down washing machine with its bottom torched out and jagged upward like some child's rendition of an infernal sun. There were propane bottles rent and rusty and acetylene torches and motorcycle helmets and tractor tires five feet tall leaning against the ghostly forms of three toppled refrigerators, and there were hubcaps hanging by a clothesline from the ceiling and all manner of forgotten discard and not one window among it all. What light there was came from half a dozen reading lamps he had clamped about the place on the random, uneven abutments of the shelves which light gave the objects an uncanny sharpness as in a painting done in chiaroscuro gloom.

Zach was done with the jug. He thought that Frank might have discerned somehow that he was hungry and that the milk had been an offering. He wanted to thank him but for reasons he couldn't name it seemed a ridiculous thing to do.

There's scissors on the bench, Frank said. Have you ever eaten twat?

Zach looked at him.

Stab that jug and cut out an oval the size of a whore's pussy.

He laughed but it was not laughter. What? Zach said.

Do you want a bike?

I have a bike.

Shut up. Cut an oval out of that jug.

And he did. He didn't know why but he did. Somewhere Samuel had stopped moving among the rubble.

Frank had taken the rear tire off the bike and he was turning it in his hands squinting as if he was looking through smoke though there was no smoke.

His hands stopped and he looked up. You don't know much, do you?

Zach didn't say anything.

Your problem's not your tube, it's your tire. You've got a hole in your tire. You could patch that tube a thousand times. Give me that oval.

Zach handed it to him. He shot his middle finger up through the crack in the tread and looked at Zach and wiggled it, smiling, in a pornographic gesture, and then he wiggled it faster and made a woman sound and laughed which was not laughter. He slid the plastic oval into the inside curve of the tire directly where the hole was and then he slid the inner tube into the crease keeping three fingers then two then one on the oval until the tube was in place. With his other hand he worked the pump six times and then removed his hand completely and turned to Zach and said, Pump it up.

When Zach had finished pumping he slid the tire between the forks and centered it and tightened the bolts and looked at Frank and called for Samuel. He felt the boy's head on the small of his back. He had no idea how long he had been there.

Not a good idea to leave this time of night, Frank said.

We better be going. What do I owe you?

Shut up. Not a good idea. There's bus seats in back. They'll do just fine.

We ought to be moving on.

Frank looked at them. He made an exaggerated forlorn face and reached into his pocket and took out some money and looked at it as if he was sad for it. He looked at Zach and then at the boy and back at Zach. I'll give you a dollar each if you'll stay, he said.

We should be getting on.

Shut up, Frank said.

November 15

Two shoes at the foot of the bed, a sink, a window, a curtain,
four walls, a notebook, a pen, a man, a room around the man,
a world around the room, a list, a list around the list? Just
a list, a

CHAPTER SIX

Michael Lazar had told Zach to take not a single book and to keep not a journal but, daily, and without expounding upon it, a simple list of things. Why? That's just words, Zach had said.

It was late. It was their last clandestine meal in the ward. They'd eaten the samosas and the green curry and laid the plates aside (in addition to the ecumenical food Lazar had begun even to bring his own ceramic plates in a padded knapsack [he rode his bicycle the nine miles in to the hospital and home in the dark with a flashing indicator behind his seat and one pinioned between his handlebars, right down the center line of the municipality roads because he said that he could be seen better that way, and he shut the flashers off and the headlight too for the last silent and nearly sightless two miles of country road that led to his house], those too made on the wheel by the hand of one of his daughters), and Lazar was stroking the hairs on the back of his knuckle which circumscribed a small aberrant bareness and he was abstracting upon it, telling Zach he needed to make the lists. He held up his knuckle and looked at it and turned it toward Zach and said maybe.

Maybe? Zach said.

Maybe, Lazar said. Maybe I should let one of these finger hairs grow long and lay it over the bald spot. He grabbed the tip of such a hair and tried to maneuver it.

Crosswise, like the other prune faces in this department with their godforsaken three foot long piece of hair plastered over their domes so that I could hang them by it. Put them out of their misery.

Zach just looked at him.

Bullshit, Lazar said suddenly, glaring at the young man. Words? Words? The words are children at the things, Zach, pets even, scratching at the door, waiting to be fed.

Pardon? Zach said.

'Pardon.' If I'd been as polite as you when I was your age I would be dead. They are. Just scratching. You've got it all wrong, your manifest brilliance notwithstanding.

He made a little flourish bow with his hand, circling downward. Zach smiled. Shook his head. Tried to grow serious, then outright laughed.

The words come looking for the things, not the other way around. They're hungry, they want to live. They're beautiful as ballerinas without a score, words. But don't mistake them. The world is not—the world is made of soil, and sunlight, and rain, and spit, and semen, and salt tears, and blood. Give me your hand.

Zach held his hand out and Lazar took him by the wrist and with the nail of his thumb he raked a mark across his palm. That.

He did it again. And that. A word can't do that. Only a shovel or a nail or a log or a flame can. Or a woman. A woman's heart can do that. Her teeth can do it too, in fact they should.

Zach looked at him.

A good woman has sharp teeth.

Zach raised his eyebrows.

A good woman is always more than one woman. She's at least two, three or four if you're lucky.

He leaned back and appraised Zach with obvious roguish pleasure.

Something tells me you didn't get a fair hearing on the birds and the bees and it's too late for that now but let me give you the all but dissertation version. Most men have it wrong. They look for a woman who is one woman, or one who thinks she is. That's an assbackwards way to fall in love. After a year the man needs to divert himself with the world's width and the woman grows more and more neurotic trying to remain the one woman that he married because she thinks that's what he loved. That's nostalgia. What did Shakespeare say? 'Melancholy is the midwife of frenzy'? Something like that. Well nostalgia is the midwife of divorce. And pretty soon they begin to hate each other because the man thought when he married her that she was all the world he needed and the woman gave up the world—the worlds, that is—in her in order to marry him because that's what she thought he wanted and now she wants—understandably, I'd say—some recompense for the sacrifice meaning at the least fidelity and probably a slew of mail order material goods and he, after all, he wants the world. Go figure. But that's the way it often is. My wife could pass for Quaker by day but in bed she's terrifying, she's a sorceress, always has been. And that's the way I like it.

He laughed. He grabbed Zach's hand again. Words, he said. The words look at that. They say: scratch, mark, wound, gouge, what else? I don't know, the hell with it. The point is they're drunk. Do you see?

Perhaps, Zach said.

Perhaps? Perhaps? You need to see. This you need to see. Listen. I said a minute ago that the words are hungry. Maybe in your case it's the other way around, the things are hungry. I can see them, all gaunt and blown up against a flat brick wall by the wind of your philosophy, breathless. I can see them. There's a hubcap, there's a chest of drawers, an axle, a wedding dress, a little dirty at the hem with some joy on it where she danced, hmmm? And the mere wake of you flattens them on that wall. And they're calling out to you. Because the words need to be filled with the things. I'll grant you the paradox. I'll grant you that the words almost live when there's enough life in them. I'll grant you that they get up off the flat page a little bit and try to walk, try to dance, and then fall down like malnourished kids. But there's never enough life in them—never. Even Shakespeare ought to make you get up at the theatre and go home and do something about it and before the end of the third act too. And I don't believe that the purpose of life is to fill the words. The purpose of life is to love the world so much that the words, if they must come, come because they can't resist you. Do you see? You don't get to heaven on a word. Or a deed. Or even faith in the streets of gold. Not by my lights, anyway. You get to heaven by participation, courageous participation, maybe even by default of the very doctrines themselves because most of the doctrines tell you a thousand and one ways how not to be here at all, who knows. Every man, every woman starts out as a little vertical piece of earth and the world lifts at it and plunders it and cuts streams and valleys through it and pours molten lava over it and bakes it and rains on it and blows it to pieces and plants it and if you have something to say about that that would explain and justify it then maybe you're just not in it enough to be awed by it and if you have something to say about it because the sound of your joy and travail makes a word out of a moan then maybe you're a poet. But the saying of it comes after, or during, not before. Because we're in debt to that before, to all the befores where the life was before the words. Every time we pick up a hammer and a nail there's a dead man in it who built a lean-to out of the weather in Wyoming in December or a farmer in Latin America someplace on the back of a mule-drawn cart broken down with a town's vegetables rotting in the sun or a Mennonite right over there in McGaheysville this minute saying no to some nigh useless particle board siding and still fashioning his house with his hand. I'm tired. It's late.

I see, Zach said.

Make the lists. Say the words outloud and love them, but out-live them. Say them for the way they finish into a thing. Say the word 'wood' and love the 'd' in it, love the way it sounds like an axe thunking into a log.

I believe they're going to put you here in my place, Zach said, after I'm gone.

But Lazar didn't laugh.

Listen to me. You're going to have to just hold things. Just sleep with them. Maybe for a week, maybe a whole month or even a year. I mean it literally. Put a bicycle in your bed if you have to. An ironing board. You think people think you're nuts for your time in here wait till they see you walking down main-street arm and arm with an iron skillet or a hacksaw, or sitting at the Boar's Head Inn with a velvet napkin on your lap sere-nading a sad umbrella across the table. You have to fall in love. Speaking of which.

And he'd gotten up then and pulled from his pocket a scrib-bled address and directions and an invitation to dinner with a couch to sleep on afterward.

My wife would like to see this man I keep talking about.

Then, for the last time, he walked out of the room, home.

CHAPTER SEVEN

So in the evenings Zach and Samuel would find some suitable place to camp, a park or a school field, a wash or some woods along the road. Nate had given Zach a mini propane stove and after they'd unrolled the plastic tarp and laid out the sleeping bag they shared Samuel would explore the perimeter around and Zach would warm up whatever canned contents they'd bought in the nearby town. After dinner they'd gather wood for a fire and Samuel would sit staring into it with great seriousness and Zach, by the light of the glancing flames, would write the things that day which he'd observed:

February 23

Sun on the tips of a flower I don't know, dew too, a baker standing in his doorway in the actual town of Bakerton (made me laugh), eggs on Samuel's breath when he burped, a kid cursing at a can he was kicking, two horses in a field looking in opposite directions resting on each other's bodies, a semi's wake opening what looked like pollen from some roadside flower, the guy in the passenger seat flipping us off, his red hat, a cramp in my left calf, a civil war–type fence in Longley, a

woman also in Longley slowing down and shaking her head at
us, the old hands of the clerk at the store, his sad eyes, the
woman on the porch with her cigarette ash as long as her un-
smoked cigarette, Samuel suddenly wheeze-laughing about an
hour after lunch, beans and pork, what looks like cattails but
probably isn't, huge live oaks, purple sky, sudden cold air, my
legs nearly on fire, fire smoke thickening my hair, black sky,
the first star, first planet I don't know, Samuel's hair in the fire-
light, Anna.

And it was not rare: Samuel, wrapped in Zach's motheaten surplus wool sweater, got up from across the fire where he was sitting staring into the flames and took the pen from Zach's hand and took from his lap the blank book in which he'd been writing and flipped to a clean sheet and ripped it out and wrote on it, all in capital letters, ANNA. It was not unusual.

Do you miss her? Zach said.

Samuel shrugged.

I miss her. Samuel, what is it to miss? I miss her.

CHAPTER EIGHT

It began with Zach's mouth. Or perhaps before that. Before The Lake, before Anna, on a bus ride from Charlottesville to New Orleans. Three days before Zach was released Lazar had walked into his room in the ward. It was early morning. There was sunlight on the white walls and on the door that opened and on the man Zach had never seen before in morning light. He was brushing his teeth. Lazar had knocked lightly with the tips of his four fingers and opened the door and just stood there. Finally he said, I've heard.

It's true, Zach said. Yes. On Monday.

Monday.

Yes.

Zach was talking to him in the mirror, his mouth full of paste.

Were you going to tell me? Lazar said.

He spit. Yes, of course.

When?

On Sunday.

I don't come Sundays.

I was going to call.

Oh, I see. Where will you go? Back to school?

No. I don't know.

Lazar stepped into the room and shut the door. He put both hands behind his head and his lips moved for a moment without sound. Are you sure? he said.

Yes, I'm sure.

How do I know?

What?

If you're ready.

I don't know. We don't know. I have to go.

Sit down a minute, Lazar said.

Zach spat in the sink and ran water in his hand and cupped it into his mouth and dried with his sleeve. He turned around and looked at the old man.

if I lie down here   each car out on that road not even a sickle anymore   even you cannot hold me good man   and I'm wrong to want that   that is the first lesson   and unwarranted kindness   is the only thing   if I heal if I praise   my hands are still blue with the ill guest, with winter   but if you run well, Nietzsche said, if you run well   four nights a week for how long he's come   and I have never thanked him   you have never once thanked him   what does he see now how can I thank him   I'm leaving I'm really leaving   leave that leaf for the next man   and the next man? And the next man? Donne's poem about the bell tolling   if you are insane I am insane?   if I am insane you are insane?   don't say anything   sun through the veins of the leaves   the beautiful dead skins of the leaves   look at his hands not even shaking   good good good good good   pacing out the future   good good good good good   the juvenile joke about taking one O out of good and you had the divinity   god in subtraction like that what eyes I have never seen such eyes   did you believe that such harm could come to you simply on the broad back of thought?   did you? did you?   be quiet and thank him   did you? did you?   that he would hold me?   that he has held me   don't say anything that would make him ashamed of you

god the sun as if indeed he brought it   the sun, I say, sincere,
the sun   don't be so eager   he'd never believe he saved your
life   you Zachary   you thank him you

and sat on the edge of the bed. Lazar squatted against the closed door. Seventy six years old and squatting on his heels like a countrybred farmer. I could not figure it, he said. Have you not heard from your parents?

Thank you, Zach said.

Pardon?

I have not heard from my parents since I was seventeen. You know that.

Yes, I know that. Nor have they heard from you.

Zach looked at him.

They know you are here. I could not figure it. I've done some looking. I've pried beyond, way beyond my legal and probably my moral bounds. Zach, he said, sit down.

I am.

I know you are. He looked squarely at the young man's face. Your parents are not your birth parents. You're adopted. I figured you had to know.

Zach was watching the ceaseless sifting of motes in and out of the shafts of light

even that is a journey which is light   a death which is shade
which is shadow

and then he was thinking nothing at all.

Your dad was a Dutch jewelry trader on the Zuni pueblo in Arizona and your mother is half Navajo. His name is Wyn Vanderwagon. Your mother is Loretta Begay. I don't know much more. You are not Irish. Nor are you Italian. I could not locate either one of them, but there are records.

He made a diamond with his hands and looked through it at the linoleum and then he looked up at the man who was sitting on the bed with a look of inscrutable interiority that can sometimes be seen on the faces of the blind.

Perhaps I should have told you sooner. I don't know. You were four years old when you were adopted.

Zach felt the warmth, the long exhale in his groin. It spread down his thighs and soaked his jeans and he could feel it exactly like hot air leaving a pent lung. The two men sat there in the rising ripe stench of urine and neither of them moved. I'm sorry, Zach said.

Don't be, Lazar said. I know where you need to go.

All right, Zach said.

CHAPTER NINE

By the second week in November when the bus left Charlottesville proper the fields were covered with first snow and lit lightly in the dusking and the sky was evenly the color of a pigeon's breast. To the west a line of magma veiled in the trailings of the front diffused and gave the various copses across that farmland their lines backlit in that immense whiteness. He could see the fading barns and the silos of extinguishing farms where the cows congregated around the spilled alfalfa and he could see where their breathing plumed. The soft mountains in a dull greengray against a barely lighter, grayer sky. He made it a study to trace the difference between sky and escarpment below it until one became the other completely and then he looked at the place where the difference had been. Much later he woke and saw snow in the headlights. He slept again and when he woke light was flooding through the windows and he sat up blinking in the brightness.

Across the aisle and a seat ahead two girls sat together bathed in morning light touching each other along the whole length of their bodies. Their skin was the color of milk chocolate. They stared together at some fixed point in the landscape that never fixed for the traveling. They looked to be twins about thirteen years old and their kinky hair was pulled up and back and braided identically, one with a yellow and the other with a pink barrette, and even seated they had about them that rangy delicacy which foals possess where clumsiness is some ultimate modesty approaching grace. Zach looked at them for a long time. They did not move at all or speak but once the nearer one lifted her finger where a lash had loosed and removed it from about her eye and held it suspended and examined it and then put it deftly on the seatback in front of her. She felt Zach's gaze and met it for a moment and looked away out the window.

In Blounts Creek North Carolina they pulled into a filling station with a convenience store that looked to have been converted from a two car garage. Zach bought a loaf of bread and a can of sardines in tomato sauce and a clear soda called Teem. He took a section of coffeestained newspaper from the lone table and walked outside and brushed the beaded rain off a railroad tie and lay the paper down and sat. It had rained through the night which storm had been snow to the north and the tie was soaked through and the wetness came up through the paper but Zach took no notice of it at all. The driver passed the time with the store attendant and he seemed in no hurry. They stood off to the side and they laughed loudly and pounded each other on the back and finally the driver said, All right Bill, I'll get with you, and the two men shook hands still laughing. Zach swabbed the last juice from the can and twisted shut the loaf and stuffed the butt end of bread in his mouth and joined the small queue where they were shifting impatiently. The driver stood on the landing and made one last quip to the attendant and then he ducked in and said, All aboard and the passengers shuffled on silently, like prisoners called back from a brief blip of recreation in a yard.

They rode all day through New Bern and Havelock and Wildwood and the sun did not break once and the rain came down in a fine ceaseless mist. Zach opened his window and leaned his face out the crack and left it there and squinted out at the land. The air was cold and fresh and wet. The country was rural and spotted with crude leaning cabins, smoke spiraling from the chimneys of every one. For the most part he saw no one but once he saw children in slickers and rubber boots running after each other in a yard and he saw also a group working in a pasture fixing fence in the sleety rain. There was an older man and three younger men and a young woman. The woman picked up a handful of mud and slung it at the back of one of the younger men who was hammering down a post and he, blind to the sally, ran after the wrong one, brother or friend, and tackled him in the mud and all were laughing at the mistake. He got up and ran after the woman and he caught her and tackled her too and they fell and she began to hurl huge handfuls of mud at him and he pinned her down and kissed her on the mouth. Zach craned his neck and looked back at them as they faded and he saw the older man turn and rest his forearms on a freshly driven post. He leaned there and it seemed to Zach that his body was a burden to him and he seemed to take in all that land and rain and Zach thought that he saw his face grow stony. He settled back into his seat and lifted the shirt away from his chest and bent his head and wiped the rain from his face. He slept.

When he woke it was to the smell of Nacho Cheese Doritos. Behind his ear a man was saying, Would you close that damn window, this aint Florida.

I'm sorry. I fell asleep.

The man was sitting behind him and he reached over Zach's seat and offered some chips. When Zach took one he stood up and came around the seat and said, You mind? I'm goin crazy not sayin nothin. It's goin on a day and a half now. Where you goin?

Zach moved over and the man sat down.

New Orleans on this bus. Then Arizona.

Nothin like rain to make a poor country look the worser.

It's awfully wet, Zach said.

It is. Where you goin?

Zach looked at him to see if he was joking but he wasn't. New Orleans, he said. After that Arizona.

My sister lived in Darlington. Bout three hours down the road. You know where that's at?

No, I don't.

It's an hour out of Florence. Nothin there but bingo. She played bingo. A mean bingo.

He laughed and his laugh was fraught with phlegm. Lived all alone with a big woman. For sixteen years. Hell. I'm goin to her funeral.

I'm sorry, Zach said.

The man looked out the window at the rain. Hell, you're a young man. You married?

No.

You aimin to get that way?

I don't know.

You better know one way or the other, son. Dastardly women are drawn to indecision like a fly to shit. It's like they know you'll think about em if you don't know what to think of em.

Zach looked out the window. I'm not sure what you mean, he said.

Hell, it don't matter anyway, the man said. It don't matter anyway.

The man spoke loudly, as if declaiming to the whole bus. He had a two week beard with false cheese hung in it and he smelled like food chemicals and morning breath and wool from his sweater which took the edge off the other stenches. He tilted the bag toward Zach and Zach looked at it for a moment and took a chip.

I feel sorry for them, the man said. A woman that lives alone can go crazy. A woman who lives with another woman goes insane. My sister was married in '52 but her husband got drunk and shot her cat. She didn't take well to that. She carried on for a week and he said he'd shoot her in the foot if she didn't quit her carrying on. I'm not sayin it was right to shoot the cat.

He paused as if he was weighing something in his mind. He shouldn't have, he said, finally, but he said it without conviction as if the jury was still out on the question. He looked at Zach for input on the matter but Zach was still looking out the window.

She hitched all the way from Barnwell to Darlington. That took some balls, a woman alone and all. I'll give her that. She moved in with that big social worker woman and never moved again in her life. For awhile Billy came around drunk and shouting for her and she would stand out there on the porch with a shotgun I know she'd never fired in all her life and probably didn't even know how.

He shook his head and crammed some chips in his mouth. A woman alone loses her purpose, he said.

He shook his head again and fell suddenly sad and was silent for awhile.

I thought you said she lived with another woman, Zach said, after a time, but the man didn't seem to hear.

Then he sat forward and made a sudden chopping motion in the air with his hand and blurted: She don't know how to concentrate on the least thing. She talks to herself and doesn't eat nothin and stays up late and reads and gets up early and talks to plants. What is that? Hell, last couple of years townfolk told me she didn't even sleep at night. They said they seen her out walking under the full moon with her head tilted up at it and her gullet quivering in the light. That's what happens. A woman needs a man to keep her powers about her. I couldn't do nothin for her. You hear what I'm sayin? I couldn't do nothin. What would you have done?

Zach kept his eyes on the withdrawing land. I don't believe I know the situation enough to say.

Hell, it don't matter anyway, the man said.

Then he galled. It's in the goddamn Book. A woman bears child. She stands by her man and shows him who he is lest he forgets. She can't take her own life. God Himself said it. They don't know what they're doing. Look what they've done.

This last piece he said loudly, he yelled it, as if this cardinal law was in jeopardy beyond all forbearance.

A woman sitting a few seats back whom Zach hadn't noticed stood up clutching the seatback in front of her and told the man to keep quiet. She said that he belonged in a loony bin. Then she sat down.

The man turned around. Ma'am?

Leave that young man alone, she said. She stood again. You don't know anything about women. Probably men neither. Surely not God.

The man looked sideways at Zach. He ate a chip. Zach turned and looked back at the woman. She was older than the man by about ten years, mid sixties perhaps, and she had a mottled shock of gray hair like some desert bush. She was gaunted and lined and weathered and her posture was shot but her eyes glared brightly and they had behind them a clarity and that clarity was levity.

Men are good for nothing sacks of biology, she said. If there is a man anywhere that does a woman any good I've never met him and I never will. A woman needs to leave at least one man before she knows what she's capable of. Why when I was young I turned every head on Hegenburger Avenue and I never looked back and that's why I turned them.

She looked at Zach. Don't listen at him, she said. He talks about God like he knows. God is most likely a woman anyways. A woman men have been covering up all these years. Why else do you think Jesus had long hair?

She paused on account of the profundity of that remark. As if she was surprised at her own powers of deduction. Then she thrust her head toward the man. He's just like all the rest of em. He's jealous because women already have God in them. We can make life. From nothing and nine months we bring it into the world. What does a man do? Nothing. Drinks himself stupid and shoots up house cats.

She began to hum a strong melody to herself that could have been religious. She was still standing. Anyway, she said to the man, you talk loud enough to wake the dead.

She looked at Zach and her look was nearly professorial. I'm telling you, she said, Men are scared. They're scared of women, God incarnate.

Then she sat down.

A thin longlegged man with short dark hair in the front seat turned sideways in the aisle and looked backward at the three of them. He had a mustache that looked nearly wet with fine grooming. He wore a rich suede cowboy hat and he took it off and held it delicately over his abdomen as if he were protecting a wound. He cleared his throat and began to speak very quietly so that Zach and the man and the woman leaned forward out of their seats in order to hear him and he spoke with an accent that could have been Mexican or more probably South American. None of you know anything about God, he said. He whispered.

Even swiveled as he was he sat ramrod straight and he turned his hat slowly in his hands as he talked. You don't know about God because you don't know about death. You have fear but you fear the wrong things. You have fear because you have not come to terms. When a man and a woman know death they breathe life into each other. Death is all around like a handsome groom, like a young bride.

What's that? the Dorito man said. Speak up, chief.

He looked at all three of them in turn. You do not understand. You have not come to terms. When a man and a woman come to terms they have no problems. They breathe life into each other unheard of.

He said this last sentence with great emotion and he fronted himself in his seat and put on his hat. No one spoke for a while. The Dorito man said, Well, and got up and went back to his seat. Zach looked out the window. It was full dark outside. The storm had scudded east and the night was brilliantly clear. Lights from farms near and distant hovered in a staccato frieze and those far away met with the horizon and joined the stars pooled in the vales of the hills so that it was impossible to tell the difference between them. One of the foalish girls began very quietly to sing. She leaned her forehead on the back of the seat in front of her and she sang softly in some private language and the travelers looked out the windows at themselves, at some third person handing up out of the motile dark their own known scars. She brought the whispered notes high and out of tune and low again and rough as if she were with her song tracing some ever changing terrain which accessed both posterity and yore. Zach put the heels of his hands together and lay his head on his crossed thumbs and he felt the speed humming under his feet and the blood in his brow and he spoke to whatever power there is. I can't, he said. He whispered it.

November 18

The man ahead's naphtha neck? the liquid downward sip of his
coffee? the? the? look out the window now, all window now, the
uprising of mist? the cantankerous little earthbound vapors
refusing to land? all through the clouds there what narrow hurts?
what anorexic striations of light? Of umbra monumental? light
pith and airy? the back of a bus seat, the telescopic vinyl? the
map-like grief-like stress lines of vinyl's sham? a bus window, the
steady lionlike roaring of the traveling under my feet? the pocked
wall of that steel-colored horizon? a list Zachary, the light just
pushing down through the folds? the folds so folded? the folds of
the clouds like the soul on the verge of? on the verge of verge? a
list, little barn out there on your little raft of green idea? the
lascivious thumbprint of god that says, barn, field, gate, light,
light? the light now like some string instrument outpouring

*through the slit? the myriad lumens in their frenzy to be known,
seen, popular? the slit, as they say, in the heavens? the light like a
muscle spasm, a helpless origin, a regretful action in its seething
assembly of what, grace? the music pushing back up? wanting to
return? return into what? return into wanting? a store called
Store, the sign for New Bern—32 miles, the upswirling of? the
dank effluvium of thought in this slipstream of its making? Peter
saying to that biblical heckler, I didn't know him, I never knew
him, you Peter you, write a list, crying like no other man*

CHAPTER TEN

When he arrived at the bus station in New Orleans he made the mistake of not purchasing a ticket for the next leg of his trip. He was exhausted and there was all manner of commotion at the counter and he had a six hour wait in any case so he slept, his bag on the seat beside him. And when he woke the rucksack was gone along with his money, Lazar's seven hundred and fifty dollars which was to stay him until he made Window Rock Arizona where his real parents might live, where, apparently, he was born. On his person he had only what change he'd crammed into his pocket from a fifty dollar bill. He wandered out into the streets of New Orleans altogether without intention. He counted his money as he walked and put it back in his pocket. He took it out and counted it again and put it in the other pocket. He divided it in half and put it, equally, in both pockets. He began, lightly, to mumble to himself about his situation.

Two and a half blocks north of Jackson Square, on Dumaine Street, several men of a desultory air sat leaning against a wall and slept or stared out unblinkingly. A crowd of tourists passed through them ceaselessly like fish through a futile net. A few of the homeless didn't have shoes, or had one shoe. A couple, a man and a woman so thick with sun and grime they looked ruddy and genderless, like hermaphroditic twins, rifled through a tattered bag and argued venomously about the contents of a pint sized plastic container. Zach crossed the street where there were only a few men sleeping curled up embryonic with their hands between their knees and the volatile couple followed him as if he might be a witness to their squabble or more as if they were players in a roving drama for which he was now their chosen audience and whose undivided regard they needed in order to be.

He sat a little way from the others in the northwest nook of a low dividing wall which jutted out perpendicular to Dumaine and faced south and he leaned back and closed his eyes and turned his face toward the sun. Using the wall for leverage he lifted his body off the ground, shimmying up, and right then left he put his hands in his pockets and fingered his bills and his coins. The seams of the pockets cut off the circulation to his hands. He had just counted his money and yet he'd forgotten already how much he had and he fingered it awkwardly for the size of the coinage and the thickness of the paper wads. It seemed he could not think clearly at all. He was very tired. His hands felt dead, devoid of all dexterity. They felt like two dead animals he held in his hands. He pushed his head back on the wall and the warmth came through his skull and he felt transparent, the harder he pushed the more so. He took his hands out of his pockets and clenched and unclenched his fists weakly and raised his arms and looked down the length of one and then the other and he expected them too to be bloodless, diaphanous. That they weren't seemed a joke. He looked at the soft web between his thumb and index finger. The smooth palm, the smooth pads of the fingers. Those are no hands, he said to himself. No hands.

All around him was inchoate motion. There were the trees of limbs and the leaves of car horns and the smell of shit and piss from Nichols alley and the ponds of silence in between, barely, and in the brief ponds first and then on the conveyance of the other din he began to disappear and his life began to play out in his mind, to unravel in scenes random and continuously, like a line drawn by a snared fish that through the slight and shifting angles of its sidling brief prisms of luminescence blurted and extinguished so that he asked himself if he was indeed crazy, if he was young, if he was old. If he was at all. And he saw a hill. And he was frightened because he saw the hill only in great despair and it was something of hope and health and continuity and it was dangerous that he saw it because it meant that things were very bad that he saw it at all and when he had thought of it in the ward he felt like his skull was a glass vase so that he had to set himself down upon his own thoughts very carefully and he hoped painfully for a visit from Lazar at those times and he was afraid now that he was again that weak and he said no aloud and no one noticed at all because it was nothing to talk to oneself on the streets. And the hill was all of a soft green, and then it wasn't at all, and he remembered in his youth sitting in a curtilage with a woman late in her life whose dress opened in the wind exposing her clean and wizened bosom and a goat she had brought him stood on a red paintchipped wooden stool so that he could drink its hot milk and how she had looked at him when he swallowed, in the last few years of her life, licking her own fingers of the whey and smiling at him kindly. He saw himself clear his throat and raise his hand in a seminar room as a seventeen year old firstyear liberal arts student at the university and end an argument on the distinction between knowledge and being quoting Levinas that in the realm of truth being was the otherness of thought and became, with true knowledge, the property of thought. It was an early evening class and he remembered now that afterward he had walked to the Rotunda and stopped suddenly and felt through his body the duskblueing smoke of the distant Blue Ridge Mountains moving toward his marrow like an almost vanquished drumming and another man, a student coeval, stopped and looked where he looked and they didn't say anything. And he saw himself turn and extinguish the drumming, just by the slight turning of the head, and the feet followed, and the torso died and the heart closed and the silent gift of the other bequieted consecrator was expunged as easily as saliva touched to the tips of the fingers snuffs out a flame. And along the flanks of the ghetto of a city the name of which he could not recall he remembered a boy stumbling down the street in the rain with over his shoulder a huge garbage bag, and the two boys' eyes had met, and he had looked back through the rear window straining to hold the eyes and the boy had stopped his weaving walk and put down the bag and the car had turned down a side street and broke their gaze. And in a restaurant of a St. Patrick's day he remembered looking out the window and across the manmade suburban lake where through the multiple reflections of the lounge's glass a highway touched like a parabola the purloined sand of the shore and he saw a silent car crash in the instant of its occurrence, the literal pileup and then the flames in their silent combustions as car after car folded inward upon the heap, and for a small time no one had seen and the facile drunken gaiety of the adults around continued on to crescendo in counterpoint to the suffering until someone noticed his transfixion and followed his gaze across the lake and began to scream. And finally he saw sitting in the lobby of some tropicalized hotel his father smacking his knees talking with other men whose lives were only money and he saw the golf club turning in his hand as he reached, not even delicately, across their group's mirthless mirth to poke with the out-stretched driving iron the buttocks of a Filipino maid leaning over to water a plant and he saw the silver gleaming in the mouth of his head-thrown-back cachinnations and he saw him turn and see his small son where he'd come from the room up-stairs where he was staying alone. He saw his father look at him across the portico—the fake fish in the pools and the fake ferns in the breeze that was even to this boy's sense and sadness al-ready elegiac, the scent of life unattainably fresh and true—and turn away. Just turn around. And the breeze blew the plastic ferns. And he knew. He wanted to tell someone. He didn't even know what he knew, but he wanted to tell it: that he was alone, would be, before, now, and ever, or that the bones behind the faces he saw ceaselessly in the world did not caress the world well or that the eyes did not well recommend the thoughts or that no matter how soft the air was falling on soil or surf or stone there would be someone trying to buy it. And that the only consolation for this was the articulation of it. And so he had stood and examined the human life there in the hotel for one last someone to tell it to before he began to try to say it to no one at all, not even God. He had stared into the selfsame recesses in the bones, the pools of the eyes. And nothing veneered upon nothing. And a woman, a worker at the resort, had come to him then and very kindly put a hand on him and asked him if he was lost. He saw himself look at her now as if there in the streets of New Orleans he was her seeing his boyself, his look imploring for grace or perhaps simply searching for just one thing in her face, in her countenance of kind and vacant succor, that might stop his look from passing all through her and the walls of the faux antiquated place and the falsely promised hale air he breathed and the turning world itself. The look had terrified her. She blinked. She looked away and turned, too, and left him there. So that he knew. And the green hill rose again before him now, with the soft crabgrass and the smattering of dandelions and the shadows of the cumulus and the almost blue tints of the spears of the blades stirring in that posited scape. And the homeless couple there in the street argued about the last glop of gumbo in the cup and the woman banged her shoe on the spit-strewn concrete and said something to Zach that he might watch, watch, watch them, her exhortation but a scaffolding upon which his daydream briefly surfaced and submerged. I am beyond even sleep, he thought.

On the east side of the street the limbs of the citizens still churned to and from the marketplace. Again he looked from that blur to his own body before him. And his forearms did transluce on his thighs. And a girl named Tristen of his youth came over the green hill in his mind. So long ago. And very softly she said his name. He saw her mouthe it. The fruit of her mouth out of which the softness came. Softness out of softness. The whisper like a divine thumbprint planting him into the soft earth there and telling him to be. Zachary Thaddeous Brannagan. And that was joy. He saw himself turn and run down the hill and home on the broad swath of the asphalt with the applause in his chest and burst into the door where his mother lay on the bathroom floor comatose in one of her innumerable withdrawals. And he heated the stew and cut the bread and put the pills in a saucer and brought them to her tilting back her head to drink and not even looking at her as she swallowed. And refrigerated the remainder in a bowl for the father who might not come home at all. And that night he read as he always read. And the words with their powerful reckless wings took him. Now in the street he could not remember where they took him. For the thousandth time he asked himself where they took him. He saw himself in the Bloomingdale's countrified twin bed with the book nearly as big as his twelve year old torso and the flashlight upturned in the bound crevice of the spine, the room dark, the words lit and he, a little man already, thinking *I am a little man already*, proud even, thinking and already proud of it that his thoughts could not be held to the page, that the world could not accommodate his world. World, he thought.

He looked up. Across the street a man was adjusting a letter on a sign. He climbed up the ladder and tilted it a few degrees and climbed back down. He looked at it and then walked farther away and turned and looked at it again and then looked away altogether and whirled suddenly upon it as if his senses had been dulled with the looking and he needed some subterfuge to see freshly. Then he climbed the ladder again, adjusted the letter and arched backward, appraising. He climbed down and paced out a small distance and turned and leered at it again and then gave up on it altogether and folded the ladder and carried it inside. At a table in front of the café a couple was sitting with coffee and the paper and a man came down the street selling carved wooden instruments out of a canvas rice

bag and he stopped at their table and the couple examined carefully the gourdlike flutes and the tambours and shook their
heads no very kindly and he made a gentile bowing gesture with
his body as if to say, Are you sure? consider again their great
and singular beauty, and they shook their heads no and smiled
shyly and the man bowed again and moved on, singing. A
woman came out of the café door blinking in the sun and dried
her hands on her apron. She stood facing southwest with her
eyes closed, rubbing her neck with her fingers and turning her
head in slow heavy circles, pendular, toric; then she went inside.
When the sun fell behind the buildings it was cold. He found a
table under a gas heater on the veranda of a restaurant and he
sat looking out onto the street but the proprietor came out immediately and told him he had to leave unless he ordered something and to keep warm he walked the streets of the Quarter
and he inhaled the air aromatic with baking bread and rich coffee and malt and the fried seafood and the Creole spices and the
battered beer and then it was eveningdark and the lights of the
shops came on and the very air was charged now with a quality
at once viscous and quick with undulant proximity and the
streets were suddenly crowded again and the people cloistered
in animated groups under lamps or couples walked along on
each other's arms and no one noticed him at all as if he was indeed floating withal in a netherworld with the living and breathing populace like a river he could reach his hand to without so
much as disturbing the flow or even dampening his fingers.

That night, with a black man named Carver and a boy who
couldn't have been more than sixteen and who had tight curly
brown hair which was balding on his dome, he stole fruit from
the French Market, the three of them crawling under the locked
canvas open air tents and toting the pilfered goods in Carver's
ramshackle threewheeled shopping cart and breaking open the
huge melon on a comealong behind a filling station off St.
Charles, the partners eating the oranges peel and all, peels first
as in some timeworn observance of epicurean discipline, and
leaving the melon rind be. Eating on hubcaps and an oil drum.

I aint eatin that shit, Carver said, pointing to the carcass of the melon. Aint nobody that hungry.

When they'd finished eating they were silent and it was just cold and dark and even the cars on St. Charles were scarce and there were no stars for the lights of the city. Carver and the boy stripped and hosed themselves down with the shop hose and Carver produced a bar of soap from the rear pocket of his polyester pants and they passed the soap back and forth in the cold air and made inarticulate ecstatic sounds to keep warm and to quell and humorize their poverty and invalidity naked and exposed under the whole night and Zach stripped as well and they handed him the soap and the hose and he scrubbed his entire body, hair and all, and rinsed well and shouted obscenities into the spray and the three of them stood cursing the cold and jumping up and down in the lot behind the station drying as much as they could with newspapers from the trash before the wind came up quick and they had to put on their clothes. Then they slept. Wrapped like sardines in Carver's two blankets in the gutted hull of a Dodge Dart. When he woke they were gone and he woke all curled up around his own body and there were flattened appliance cartons atop him where the blankets had been and he thanked them in his mind profusely and he felt as if he had known them all his life and he wanted at first only to find them and then his head cleared and he spoke to himself and he thought of Lazar.

He slept all that day. In what sun he could find, moving when he got cold from shade and sitting against another sunny wall and sleeping. Afternoon found him on Barracks Street in the sun and he slept and he dreamt of Virginia and the Blue Ridge Mountains but they changed as he dreamt and the carpet that covered them removed like so much dandruff blown forth from a norther and they recessed and reddened and coarsened and when it began to snow in the dream there was nothing but land divided by horizon and then sky and a young Navajo girl with flat black hair and a wide reddishbrown face on a small motorcycle was dragging a dead animal on a long rope through the snow and the ribbons of redrock unfurled along the distanced cliffs and the sky was a low blanched endlessness and he waved at her and she waved back at him and they were very happy to greet each other in the snow but he did not remember this dream.

When he woke there was a hat on his head and an orange in his lap. He looked up into the thin, studious face of a man in his late forties, early fifties. You have clean hair, the man said. He was smiling.

What?

I'm Father Michael. Are you on the streets?

Zach looked around him at the sea of legs churning toward the market. Yes, he said. I think I am.

The man was dressed in black and white in the manner of the clergy. He leaned down not unkindly and held out his hand and helped Zach to his feet. He took back his hat, slapped it on his knee twice, and put it on. Follow me, he said.

CHAPTER ELEVEN

He stood in line for nearly two hours. The queue itself bent twice along three city blocks and the line led up to a towering old edifice the walls of which were failing fairjointed stone of rough faced masonry from the early part of the century. Midway up the façade two huge windows were covered with bars which seemed not so much to protect the glass as to serve as struts reinforcing the frame. The entire structure was original stone down to the cornices and the gaptoothed fishscale roof. In the crumbling anteroom of the shelter two men wearing clerical collars were sitting behind a foldout table of fake wainscoting. One of the men was handing out a small pile of sheets while the other collected ID's from those who had them and directed those who didn't to stand to the side. The third was counting the men out loud as they passed through the second set of doors. When he approached the registrar Zach looked down at the table. No tree has that grain in all the world, he thought.

The men standing in the wing stood as beeves stand, in a quality supplicant and patient, and in exact contradiction to the victorious whooping of those who were admitted and had cradled in their arms a set of clean sheets. He saw that they held also little transparent Ziploc bags of toiletries with diminutive tubes of toothpaste and likewise a tiny toothbrush and a pack of vitamin pills and a razor.

You don't have an ID? the priest said. He was studying Zach closely, incredulously, studying his thick cotton flannel shirt and the perspiration on his face and his new dark jeans and studying his loafers. Zach thought for a moment that the man had dropped something but he was only looking under the table at his shoes.

I was robbed.

Where?

The bus station. I fell asleep. I was on my way to Arizona.

And how did you find out about us?

Father Michael brought me.

Of course. The man smiled, thinly. On Dumaine, yes?

Yes. How did you know that?

Father Michael is our resident apostle. He goes fishing on Dumaine. And you have nice clothes.

They were a gift.

You have nothing with you?

Everything was in my backpack. I have twenty-eight dollars.

I see. That's enough for a hotel.

I know. I have nowhere to go tomorrow. Or the next day.

You're planning ahead?

I guess.

That's unique here. You are alone? There's no woman with you?

Sir?

This is a men's shelter.

I'm alone.

I'm sorry, the priest said.

Zach looked at him.

About your bag, your backpack, he said. Not that you are alone. We are all alone.

He leaned forward and held Zach's wrist delicately and studied his watch. As if he simply wanted to know the time. He brought us in alone and He takes us out alone and inbetween He is our company and our only confidant and the mirror of our sickness so that we might come to Him and He is the bones of our hope and also the rungs of our despair.

He finished speaking and let go of Zach's wrist and looked up at him a moment and extended his own hands forward, palms down on the table and looked at them as if he had lost a ring recently and was checking to see if it had arrived, magically, back on his hand. He had not been shrill. He had spoken quietly, nearly suspirant, and he had met Zach's eyes as the evangel does but not with the evangel's exhortatory glare. He had faded bluegray eyes and he sat slightly stooped and had about him generally that tired nearly offhand manner of those who have spent their whole lives serving and do not begrudge the service, in fact see no other life and know without pomp or regret that they will have no other, but have also seen pass before them such manner of human suffering and depravity that God no longer asks them to be gentle or exhilarant but rather to be stern. As if to cajole the human world with too much softness or delight might be the wrong preparation. For such a God.

Be careful here in New Orleans, he said. And inside as well. Follow those stairs up to the landing and Father Michael will give you a sack for your clothes.

Zach looked at him blankly.

You'll have to wear a smock.

A smock?

A smock. It's the rule. It's the top sheet in your pile. With the hole in it. You'll give your clothes to Father Michael and you'll wear the smock. Follow those stairs up to the landing.

Thank you, Zach said. He turned toward the doors.

Where are you from? the priest said.

Virginia.

What were you doing there?

I was studying.

University?

University.

I see.

He looked momentarily interested, a flicker of it. He smiled, if you could call it a smile, the corners of his mouth turned up so slightly they looked like two dapples of pale light glinting off the cursory ripples of a current, and Zach thought he was going to ask him what he was studying.

The stairs are through there, he said, gesturing with his head.

The landing was no more than the first broad turn in the stairwell. Men were taking off their clothes and putting them in the white duffelsacks Father Michael held open, himself arching backward for the stench, labeling them with black marker on a sticker and hanging them from hooks around the perimeter of the room. Swaying and rank in the dim grated light the bundles gave off vaguely the impression of hung meat in a slaughterhouse. Gave off a correlative of the deaths that are permanently in the clothes of the homeless, the myriad deaths: the children abandoned and the loves lost and the parents lost or dead and the experiences bygone, some rich and true as any to be had, with no currency, no one or place to absorb the telling, shucked there, dead all, their occupants numb as newborns and equal now in their nakedness and all gone up the stairs.

And now their brief euphoria was gone. On the landing the men were quiet, subdued. As if the truth of their weakness and decrepitude was there unavoidable in the raw bodies themselves. They covered themselves awkwardly with their hands and with their postures, bending over their shrunken muscles and gnarled genitals and the swaths of aberrant balding on their chests and the lesions on their thighs. They turned the corner to climb the stairs like so many scuffling apparitions, barefoot, silent, besmocked, uniform to a man and clutching the little transparent bags of toiletries exactly like geriatric women on a shopping spree holding their purses with that desperate quality of pointless possession.

Zach took off his clothes. His own youth and relative vigor embarrassed him. He could feel the men's eyes on him

just a boy then   as with trees, I said. Sunset.   Terra, terra mother looked at me scared and forsaken   god the infinite terrible memory   does memory abase every moment?   even here in this filth I should be glad   I should put my hands on my torso and turn around naked in the world   and be glad   how could you have forgotten this?   don't you see that health is music and you are music   lymph leave me, blood come back, nothing novel   a leaf drifting in a word as gorgeous as Shenandoah is not a curse   make me hale   in the great Russian story when the young student finished telling the already griefstricken mother and daughter the tale of Peter and he went home, went on, and the revelation was his, what felled him after? and after? light come through the window on these stricken men?   body, my host, my guest   demented cello of the platelets dying haven't even   I'll be quiet now, all gratitude   look at them look look that is suffering that   lift a glass, toast them   at an angle   now not a sound in the room   make me hale   that is suffering   you, wholly impregnable by grief?   there are others oh many   put your hands on your torso and turn around naked in the world   let them look   why go on this way   everything is music   remember that forget the other kind of memory sublimate the referents to the now   stop talking this way   if you could just live   sublimate the referents to the now   stop talking this way

and it made him feel insubstantial, perforated. Father Michael was watching him as well. He was smiling. The smile was a strange smile, sincere and empty at once, as if the genuine man had suddenly left the body but the skin and the countenance entire still remembered him. Zach put the smock over his head and bunched his clothes into the sack the priest held open for him.

Fine, Father Michael said.

Wait, Zach said. He reached in the duffel and pulled the fourteen dollars out of each pocket of his jeans and folded the two wads into one and put it, along with two dimes and some pennies, in his toiletries bag.

Fine, the priest said again, that same smile—kind, glazed, civil, empty.

He climbed the stairs and on the next floor he went through a door which opened onto some bleachers which in turn tiered downward onto the huge sunken expanse of a swimming pool. The floor was cracked in broad faults and the walls were shivery. There were more than a hundred cots spread out evenly in the basin and more than a hundred ghostly forms some lying on the cots some walking about gesturing to themselves or to strangers like prophets mad or valetudinarious scholars exhorting in some perverse portrait of The School of Athens. Some were crowded in what had been the diving well and where once was a springboard now was erected a television screen and the laughter of the men watching some sitcom drifted incommensurate and terrifying up the huge vaulted failing space and gave the impression so vividly of a purgatory that Zach almost sat down.

Another priest, not much older than he, was sitting at a desk at the top of the stairs which went down to the pool. The priest told him hello and said that he had to find a cot and after that he had to take a shower. He gave Zach two green three by five cards, each laminated, with the same number, 117, and told him to put one of them on the cot and take one to the shower room and to carry it with him at all times.

Welcome to the Inn, he said. He smiled. He was young and buoyant where the others had been stoic if not grave.

The Inn? Zach said.

That's what it's called. It used to be a YMCA. This was the pool. He turned and gestured to the huge, obvious space below like a realtor.

Yes, Zach said.

No lap swimming! he said, and laughed.

Zach walked down the steps preternaturally. So much like his own shade descending that he was not even afraid.

He had seen the two men watching him in the shower room as he put his toiletries bag under his smock and he had seen them after watching him from across the pool. They were in the section marked 3ft. and he was in the 5ft. section. Inbetween the milling smocks he could see them sitting side by side on the same cot, staring at him. Not talking, not moving at all, with a quality grimly patient, only their heads coming up out of the smocks, the heads so markedly different, like two discrepant vegetations out of the same glacial topography. One had a fat pocked face with a wide nose and a wide flaring beard which Zach had seen him hack at with his razor in the showers. The other was thin with long stringy hair that came down both sides of his narrow pointy mute face making him look rather like a wan female addict in need of a fix.

He got up and walked toward the deep end and the television and he turned around and they were watching him and he walked back toward the shallow end and up the jerryrigged stairs toward the bathrooms and they were watching him.

He lay down on his cot. He got up and went again over to the deep end where the young priest was now supervising the television crowd. The young man was leaning back in his chair and he was watching the show. Zach asked him for a pen and a piece of paper and the priest hesitated for a moment and then tore a sheet from the pad in front of him and handed him a pen from his shirt pocket all the while keeping his eyes fixed on the television screen. Zach went back to his cot thinking that he would make a list. He could not.

November 20

As easy as this is, as easy as this is

He held the pen very tightly, poised and motionless above the piece of paper as in some pose of artistic disconsolation. Cousin, a man said, and squatted beside his cot. Is that a diary?

He was a lithe black man with hair graying at the temples and his brow was furrowed deeply. The rest of his face was soft and smooth and his eyes were huge and clear and beneficent so that his head entire bespoke some kindly invertebrate. His brows flittered up and down seemingly of their own accord. But his voice was smooth and his breath was rhythmic and long, like a yogi's. His smock of issue was far too small for him, for he was quite tall, which made him look like he was wearing a women's simple cotton shift.

Sort of, Zach said. I make lists.

I want to show you something, the man said. Have you ever heard of the Reverend L. L. Langstroth?

Zach shook his head no.

Do you know anything about bees?

Zach shook his head again.

Look here. The man opened a handwoven, dogeared leather bound journal and displayed for Zach a charcoal pencil sketch, finely wrought, of what looked to Zach like two dresser drawers with a large square wooden hood that came down over the stacked structures.

The year is 1851, the man said, squatting, his eyes bright, looking up at Zach.

The Reverend has been studying the Huber frame hives for ten years. And the man has a revelation, the Reverend L. L. He realizes that Huber's mistake was to duplicate nature too closely. Huber was a Swiss naturalist, we're talking the late eighteenth century. He looked to see if Zach was following. You with me? he said.

See in nature the honeybee leaves a two bees' width gap between combs. And I mean a two bees' width. Bees are exact.

That precise space—he held up his hand and brought his index finger slowly toward his thumb—lets them work on both combs at once without knocking into each other, but it's still close enough so they can connect the combs. But then if you want the honey you've got to cut the comb, and you ruin the whole thing. So L. L. is bad. He knocks everybody out. He builds a hive with only a quarter inch spacing between drawers. That way the bees won't build more adjacent comb, they'll move on to the next drawer and start again. So what? you say. He looked at Zach. Say it.

Pardon? Zach said.

Say So what.

Zach smiled. So what, he said.

So now the beekeeper can smoke out the bees from a particular drawer, get the honey, and slide the comb back in later just like it was your underwear and socks. He looked at Zach who was smiling, nodding his head.

But there's a problem, the man said.

What? Zach said.

The queen.

The queen, Zach said.

Absolutely. See the queen looks for empty comb to plant the larvae. You know what larvae are?

Babies.

Right, babies. But the workers, they look for empty comb to store the honey. So there's a conflict of interest, dig? Again he looked at Zach before he went on.

Yes, Zach said. Dig.

The man shuffled closer in his squat and put his book on his knee and drew out the pencil from the spine. The queen, he said, almost collusively, is bigger than the workers. What our man L. L. didn't know, and what yours truly does know, is that all you have to do to keep the queen out of the top drawer is fashion some vertical wire struts like this—he drew, quickly, with flourish—too narrow for the queen, wide enough for the workers. Money, the man said, and shut his book.

66

You're a beekeeper, Zach said.

Am I a beekeeper? Cousin, I got the finest farm in Louisiana, right there in Baton Rouge.

Zach thought to ask him what brought him to the shelter but he had already gathered that there was a code against the question, as if any other inquiry was fair game but to have to answer to that would be to sever some final cord to the world.

Let me tell you about bees, the man said. We aint nothing compared to the bees. Have you ever heard of a cat called Aristotle?

Zach felt a single hard thump in his chest. I know about Aristotle, he said.

Even Aristotle had them wrong. He was the world's authority on bees for almost two thousand years. His trip was he had trouble with women. See the bee world is a women's world, there aint no doubt about it. You got your workers and your drones and your queen. The drones are the fellas and all they do is mate and die, that's it. They can't even sting. And there aint many of them to begin with, like one for every thousand worker bees. All the worker bees are female. They do everything. They feed the larvae the royal jelly which produces the queen, and then they feed the queen that royal jelly her whole life long so she can fertilize ad infinitum. You know what that means?

Zach just smiled.

I said ad infinitum. The queen is—he paused, searching for how to say—colossal. They groom her and build the hive and get the nectar from flowers and turn it into honey. Aristotle couldn't deal. He saw all that industry and he thought it just had to be men. So for two thousand years that's what everybody thought. He shook his head as if he couldn't couch perennial human stupidity.

And the queen, lord. The queen is mean and sexy. Like Catherine the Great. Have you heard of Catherine the Great?

Zach had to laugh. Yes, he said, his hand over his mouth.

She's sucked up enough sperm from those drones to last for years. And if she's the first one born look out. She eats the other queens before they're hatched. And if one comes crawling up out of the cell she'll kick its newborn ass. She'll eat its head right off while its eyelids are still covered with wax. I've seen it. I've seen it myself under plate glass and it is something to see.

He reached into his toiletries bag and took out a bottle. It was capsules of Royal Jelly Elixir. He popped one in his mouth. You want one? he said.

No thank you.

The man looked at Zach, those large, dark, beneficent eyes. You think I'm crazy, he said.

No I don't.

Bees, the man said. They delight me.

He rose. He leaned down and held out his hand. It was cracked and smooth at the same time; the cracks recessed and the surface above them downy as silk. Jamal, he said.

Zach.

He opened his book and took a clump of blank pages in his fingers and ripped them out so that the glue still held them together and handed them to Zach. Keep making them lists, he said.

He turned and began to walk away and stopped and turned around. And another thing. That Swiss cat Huber? The naturalist?

Yes? Zach said.

That brother was blind.

CHAPTER TWELVE

They took their meal in shifts according to the number of their issue and they ate in the canteen. A line of men in blanched jerseys and shower caps slopped potatoes and an unidentifiable strip of meat under a gummy dark sauce and pale corn and pale peas on a pale excoriated plate and the last man, looking in the eyes of each of the men with a kind of opiated ogle of omniscient love, said, Here you are, and put a Hostess Twinkie and a package of saltines and a small carton of 2% milk, at precisely the same angle, on every tray. Zach sat at a corner table where there were just two men sitting directly across from each other, leaning forward so that their foreheads were not more than two feet apart, earnestly discussing something. He sat at the far end of the rectangular table. He was not hungry until he took the first bite. Then his mouth filled with saliva and he began shoveling in the food without breathing. He told himself to slow down. Eat as if you are not going to eat again for a very long time. Chew. Eat like you have diminutive teeth.

That he might slow down he made it a point to listen to the two men. They were talking about a machine. They leaned together and spoke with an air of almost combative import. Their plates were all but licked clean and in the residue of brown sauce one of the men was slashing a design with his hairy index finger and the other man way saying, But professor, the disorder of the universe would be much reduced. Without a localization of energy. Professor, what holds the sodium carbonate in the machine? What prevents it? If there is water through the cracks then you have a polarity. Professor, what's to prevent it?

It can fly, the other man said, bluntly.

But an H_2O molecule is polar.

It can fly.

Show it to me, Professor.

The man looked suspiciously across at his partner as if he didn't trust his intentions, didn't trust him with the secret information. All right, he said finally, turning his plate around and holding it up.

I want you to see the sun, he said. He pointed to the dripping gravy. We've got eight minutes. Eight.

He put the plate down and held up eight fingers and stretched them toward the other man's face. Eight.

That's not a lot of time, my brother.

I said eight. If we go longer than that the hydrogen to helium balance will fail. Then the earth as we know it is fucking fuck fucked. Fucked, he said, and slammed his fist on the table and flushed with an irreferable anger.

The sun is ten million degrees, he said, under his breath, with his teeth clenched.

The other man shook his head very seriously. Then he just resigned. His whole body bent forward and he rested his hands on the table, palms upward like an exhausted beggar about to keel. I give up, he said. I give.

The man he called Professor slammed his fist down again on the table and said, Ah ha! Ah ha!

You win, the other man said. You win you win you win you win.

Zach took a bite of the meat and chewed and looked around the room. An old man at the next table was peering deeply into a dogeared book. His hair was nests of hair. Dirty manganese and past shoulder length, and balding about the dome which surface he traced from the bridge of the nose to the base of his skull with the index finger of the hand not holding the book as if he was repeating his own surgical cross-section ceaselessly. In the corner of the room a huge fat man was swatting at insects which weren't there and he was swatting them across his body, shoulder to shoulder, right hand to left shoulder, left to right, and sometimes freezing in the middle waiting for them to land with his arms crossed as if he was holding himself at bay, the steaming food untouched before him. At the same table another man who must have been near seventy was lifting his fork slowly to his mouth and his hand was quavering so violently and increasingly as it approached his lips that he took the bite, finally, with preemptive predatoriness as if the potato or meat on the tines was some quarry trying to evade him. Yet another was seducing the air beside him. With varying tacks he was trying to court a female ghost at his elbow and he was fielding a myriad of rejections from the invisible girl and he seemed to find his own refusals amusing and he seemed inexhaustible. He'd turn to the air beside him and say, Why don't we . . . you know . . . why don't we . . . why don't we . . . and then he'd wait the proper amount of time for her imaginary response and then throw back his head with laughter and say, No no no no, you don't know what kind of man I am, you don't know who you're dealing with. And he'd begin again: Why don't we, err . . . why don't we . . . how about it if we . . .

But mostly the men just chewed woodenly, in silence, trying not to make eye contact with each other for shame. And they seemed sane enough. They seemed embarrassed. They seemed like they wanted to eat quickly and fall asleep. Occasionally he did make eye contact with these men and they nodded a brief fellowship based doubtlessly on varying degrees of cogent vitality or the intimations of it. As if viability, as if the world itself, the world above and outside, was a singular quantity which one approximated or did not. Which one achieved or did not (and that by some blindly administered law of Chance), the succeeding human family 'out there' like begetters, progenitors of the continuing ranks and the black sheep—the lost and the broken and the hopeless—forever awful in front of their predecessors' time like gawkers before a monument behind glass uneroded after centuries of weather. And it seemed to Zach terrifically odd that under any other circumstances this could be a locker room or a group of political refugees or an assemblage of unhoused townsmen at an elementary school sitting out a tornado. Because the human face in its myriad forms and expressions was not as traceable to human trait as ease would have it. And what was sagacious wrinkles in one was affliction in another. And the eye and the spine which ought to tell whole chronicles of a man told nothing. And the blink of an eye was a career. And a lifetime of transformations was the palsied lifting of a fork.

Suddenly he realized how tired he was. He finished everything on his plate and then he crumbled his crackers in the gravy and smashed them to a fine powder with the back of the spoon and ate that as a gruel. He was about to gather his tray to rise when a man whose face was covered with festering lesions sat down and looked at him and handed him his Twinkie. San Antonio, the man said.

Pardon? Zach said.

The man's pustulous face broke into a grin. San Antonio, he said again, and handed Zach his milk.

It's all right, I've eaten, Zach said.

San Antonio. He handed over his entire plate, crossed his arms at his chest, and began to cry.

Zach looked at his face. He was blubbering openly, quietly, and tears pooled down his cheeks and lips and into the open wounds and he was wiping them away and saying, San Antonio, San Antonio, and small flecks of loose flesh were abrading from where he wiped the sores and he flicked these off his fingers like dead insects out behind him and his whole body was rocking on the plastic schoolchair as if only the motion kept the silence. He began to heave more emphatically still and still in almost total silence and then he picked up the salt and pepper shakers and began to profusely spice his empty tray. Zach got up. He walked around the table, first with the man's Twinkie and the milk and then he reached over and set the plate back down on his tray and sat beside him and said, Eat. Please.

He handed him his fork. Go ahead.

And the man did, happily now, repeating his one phrase between swallows. Zach stayed with him until he was done. When he'd finished there were only a few men left in the canteen. Zach got up to clear his tray. San Antonio, the man said.

All right, Zach said, softly. All right.

The old man was still reading at the adjacent table. He had moved directly under the light and he leaned ever more increasingly into his book as if the light was dimming, which it wasn't. Zach walked the long way around his table and cocked his head and saw that he was reading *King Lear*.

Chapter Thirteen

The canteen was adjacent to the entrance on the first floor and walking back up the stairs Zach paused in the landing. It was almost evening. He was nearly the last one out of the cafeteria. High above the two windows let in the golden light and the meshgrating inside and the vertical bars without focused the gloam in patterns on the opposing stone wall. There were two windows and they were each ten feet across and fifteen feet high at their points and they were Palladian in design with pointed stone arch heads and antiquated glass that made the light look fluid in its passage through. The dust lit up in the traversing sunbeams and flowed slowly upward in its soft gyrations on the draft and Zach stood there in his smock. He stood barefoot on the ancient stone floor and he let the light break down upon his shoulders until the hall was as dark as if someone had slowly dimmed a bulb.

He walked up the last flight of stairs and opened the door and looked down into the pool. Most of the men were in their cots. The lights above had been turned out and only the lights in the sides of the pool which had at one time been for underwater vision were on and they cast a sallow glow across the depression so that it looked like an excavation, like something being exhumed. From above it looked like some scene of terrible vastation, the priests walking about with flashlights checking for life and the limbs writing in the dim light but they were only dreaming or tossing insomniac and for the second time he descended those stairs.

He had to cross the pool to get to his cot. He walked through the forest of prone men who stunk yet even after their mandatory showers. Many of them were talking to themselves, haranguing. Some were snoring loudly. One man grabbed his leg as he came near and laughed as Zach yanked it away. He saw his empty cot from some distance away and already it seemed to him a place, a veritable destination. He took from the toiletries bag, which all the men toted around like purses, the green laminated card and put it, along with the one on his pillow, under the cotspring. He folded the plastic bag about itself and put it under his pillow. Then he sat. He put his hands on his thighs. He lay on his side. It seemed he lay with an infinite heaviness. The ticking sagged and the spring groaned. He turned once more and lay on his back with his arms flat down by his sides, his back nearly touching the floor. A man yelled six o'clock and the pool lights went out shortly thereafter and the small emergency lights went on above on the high walls. There was a brief flurry of grumbling protest and then it was absolutely silent for a few seconds before the coughing and snoring and the low vicious mumbling began again.

He lay awake long enough for his eyes to adjust to the darkness and then he looked around at the sleeping men and down the length of his own form in the sacking and then he lay his head back and was asleep.

When he woke he had slept so hard that he had no perception of time or place and he even stood up with a kind of urgency as if he had somewhere to go. He sat down. There was a foul taste in his mouth. In his sleep he had broken into a sweat and his smock was damp. His hands were tired and he realized that he'd been clenching his sacking in his sleep. He looked about him at the snoring ghostly shapes swagging in the ghostly cocoons of the cots and at the achromatic walls of the ailing pool and he could not believe where he was and he thought briefly that he was yet dreaming, that he was, after all, still in the ward. And then he remembered them. He turned slowly and looked out across the pool. He saw the swollen face above the apron sheet and the corrupted beard and the formless outline of the man entire, motionless, sitting, staring out or sleeping in the pale darkness, and as if he knew, had known it all along, he turned his head slowly and looked down the length of pool and saw the raised apparitional and thin figure, sitting, staring out or sleeping, and he lay down. Now his heart was outsized in his chest. His breath was loud and saliva began to form in his mouth. He pushed his head back into the pillow and felt underneath it the toiletries bag in which he had stupidly cached his paltry change and he cursed himself. He lay breathing. He put his hands behind his head atop the pillow and laced his fingers. He looked at the ceiling and said *ceiling,* said *windows, stone windows,* said *bleachers* and *breath, morning,* and he closed his eyes.

He woke to the sharp crack and the crunching by his right ear. He smelled the breath moldy and rank and he turned quickly right into the full filthy width of the hand which covered his mouth and nose both in its grip. The man whispered in his ear, That sound's the razor coming out of the razor. You make noise we'll cut your throat.

Zach lay still. The man took his hands, one at a time, from underneath his head and gently laid his arms crosswise on his chest as a pallbearer might rearrange the jostled limbs of a corpse.

We want your bag, the man whispered, almost apologetically, in his ear. Lift your head up, pretty boy.

He did. He felt the bag sliding out from under his pillow and he watched the swollen fingers open it and he watched the bent figure sifting the bills and the eyes squinting like two gashes in that brutal, humongous face. Shit, the man said.

He looked down at Zach and shoved his head hard into the pillow, his thumb in one eye socket and his pinkie in the other.

Willy, he said, and his voice sounded oddly childlike, querulous.

How much? the thin one asked.

Twenty eight. But he's so pretty.

Don't worry about it, Mull, the one called Willy said.

He's just so pretty.

Don't, Willy said.

Willy, Willy, Willy, Willy. Oh Willy.

He stood and he looked away. He looked sad, as if he was watching his only love leave him forever down a straight, flat road. And Zach did not sense or see him turn and he did not see his arm come slashing back around. He saw instead a single flash of white light like a synapse splitting in the brain the second the razor sunk into him. He thought at first that maybe he was just scared. That in fear maybe he had simply sucked in too much cold breath. Because the first sensation was wind. And then he felt the pain and the laxity there and he reached up and felt the clean draping flap of his mouth hanging down and the hot blood pumping out and *do not cry out* and it was as if he could hear the blood now running its rapid course down his chin and *do not move.*

There were people who could have taken care but he just lay there a long time without moving. The smell of sick and drunken men all around. The coughing and the snoring and the phlegmatic breathing all around. He lay very still. What is this, he thought, but that you are still alive. He lifted his hands as if he had never seen them before and they were covered with the blood of his own circumstance and he began to laugh. His mouth had begun to clang now (later he would remember it as a tolling), the blood pumping loudly and in absolute silence. He laughed. From some ancient loneliness he laughed and he felt clean and he felt license. Beyond license. Because there was nothing he wanted to do or prove or shatter, he felt liberty. He laughed and the laughing hurt and he continued on insane in the laughter. Finally he sat up holding his mouth and he had one thought only which was that he needed to get to the landing and put on his clothes.

When he walked outside into the street it was raining. Mists of vapor in the streetlights. The boardgame emptiness of the predawn streets. His face was tired from shock and laughter. The rain was weirdly warm, warmer than the air it seemed, and he walked with his face turned upward to the mist, the pain not so sharp now but dull and throbbing, the blood all but stopped, just lightly leaking. His mind was oddly keen and he walked with great purport, his neck arched back and his mouth turned upward toward the rain, like some exotic homing bird in a ritual of spring. He walked into the bus station and up to the counter. He held his mouth in his hand and just stood.

Can you talk? the clerk said.

I need to take a bus towards Arizona. He slurred.

Arizona? What you mean towards?

Yes.

You needs a hospital is what you needs.

When is the next bus? West.

West? West? The clerk turned to the wall behind where was posted the schedule and he turned back around and looked at Zach.

The 313 goes to Natchitoches. At five forty.

How much?

It's a thirty two dollar fare. And beyond that the rates go interstate and rise.

I don't have any money.

Huh?

I was robbed. I've been robbed twice.

He studied Zach. Why'd you ask me how much?

Zach didn't say anything.

You has, the man said.

What?

Been robbed. You went and stuck your lip on someone's

knife. What you need is a hospital. That shit's wide open. You need some thread, and quick.

He reached for the phone. Zach leaned forward and would have held back the man's wrist if he had not snatched it away. Don't lean on my counter, man.

He looked with disgust at the blood prints Zach's hands left on the counter. Zach glared at him. I just—

Some stitches, the clerk said. I aint callin the cops.

No. Don't. Just let me ride to Natchitoches.

What the hell you want to go to Natchitoches for? Natchitoches is north besides. Northwest.

Please, Zach said.

The man shook his head. All pity and cool bewilderment and reserve. He took his hand off the phone and reached under the counter and handed Zach a roll of paper towels. He looked at his mouth. He reached down again and handed him a key. Clean up your face, Slim. And your hands. And don't leave no blood in there, hear? If you fuck that bathroom up you aint gettin on that bus.

Thank you, Zach said. Thank you very much.

Chapter Fourteen

The dreams he would remember began on the bus. In the first dream he saw a storm all self contained on the rim of the world and lightning within it encapsulated and all around only blue sky. And he felt his heart beating dark and correlative to that distant finite squall, louder in his chest so that his bones rattled with each beat more inconsolably and he became aware that his joints would unhinge from their sockets and this awareness in him was fear so that he knew he needed to fly; in exactly the way the terrible machinations of cog on cog need oil his body needed flight. And then there was a sensation of speed with the earth just below him, his knees scraping the tips of the interminable sage, dense, rainedupon, pungent, and the sharp wetness cut him in beautiful calligraphy across his legs and he saw that the wetness was words. *Words,* he said, and began to laugh, and even sleeping he felt the great wind of the wound in his mouth and then the laughter was not his anymore, abrogated by and swallowed into the immense land and sky all around and he was limping across a vast mesa toward a group of Indians standing around an old red pickup truck and they were spitting from so much laughter and one of them pointed toward his approaching diminution, all dusty and lame, and said Donkey! Donkey! and they laughed and spat and kicked at the dirt with the toes of their boots and then a herd of horses came thundering from behind, nostrils flaring and snorting, all muscle and speed and unified rage and wind, and ran over them and through them so that they did not exist at all.

When he woke he knew immediately that he had to get off. His mouth was clanging horribly. He was dusted from dream and nauseous from he knew not what but that motion appalled him. He stood, shakily, and walked to the front of the bus. The next town, he said to the driver, what is it?

Marjolaine. We're here. Just after the bend.

Can you let me off?

What about Natchitoches? Vince said to let you ride to Natchitoches.

Marjolaine's all right.

Marjolaine it is, the driver said, shaking his head and speaking in that counterfeit jaunty tone of complete incredulity which abnegates all responsibility. As if the world was infected with a weakness, an arbitrariness alien to him. As if there was nothing to be done for it simply because he had his post, a single, finite, known place in a padded chair from which he observed the participants of the world through his window as a child might observe the inane and pointless industry of a single ant.

The bus came around a curve and there were churches on both sides of the road. The marquee on the lawn of one said, For God So Loved His Son He Gave Us Marjolaine. Zach was holding onto the grips, one in each hand. He looked down at the passengers. They were looking at him with a kind of sated abstraction, as if they were looking not at a face but out a window at a puddle forming in rain. He had the sudden freak sensation that they might be dead, swaying as they were in their seats. When the bus stopped he climbed down into the lot of a filling station and retched.

There was only one island for gas upon which stood two archaic fuel pumps. The doors hissed shut and the bus went on. A boy was sitting on the curb in an oversized worn indigo shirt and over the breast pocket in cursive embroidery it said *Joe*. He was scooping some of his purple snowcone onto a tortilla. Zach stood up and spat and wiped his mouth on his sleeve. Do you work here? he said.

Yes.

I need a hand.

You do, the boy said. Dad, he called, here's a man, he needs to go to The Lake.

The man came out from the garage and looked at Zach. He had on bib overalls and an engineer's hat. He looked to be in his early to mid forties. He was lean but strong, the strength seeming to pool down in his hands in a weighty and capable heaviness which hands were darker than his forearms and plumply veined and from his wrists down it was hard to tell whether the cargrease on them was suntan or the suntan grease. He was a little above average height, lean but not skinny, and the hair under his hat was brown, almost ochre about the ears where he'd started to gray, but it looked more gold than gray, as if he'd just come from under some fine confetti at a parade. His eyes were soft gray. And impenetrable. Kindness for sure, but recessed, as if the amicability in him was reserved, and that with an intricate lock. He put his grease covered hands in his pockets and came closer. He looked at Zach's face, at his mouth, leaning forward and darting across his countenance as if he was looking at the brushstrokes of his own work on a canvas. He took off his hat and ran the sleeve bunched around his bicep across his forehead and turned around and walked back to the shop and rolled down the garage door and turned the sign to Closed. Bobbie, he said to the boy, get on up in front.

Zach climbed up onto the flatbed. They drove over roads degenerating from asphalt to gravel to washboard to gullies and finally to mud, all the while his mouth like a rock clanging in his mouth and the hay particulate in the truck flying up about him and the smell of it and the smell of the mud and the cold clean rushing air and the sky. At some point he fell asleep despite or because of the pain and he woke to the feeling of the cab window opening along his back. He moved aside and the boy thrust a cold orange soda from a cooler on the seat through the opening and Zach took it and drank from the good side of his mouth and it stung and it tasted unbelievably good. He had not known how thirsty he was. A twangy music came through the window of the cab. He drank the can in breathless gulps and handed it back through the window. The boy took it and tossed it on the floor in front of him and with his small flat palm to the glass he shut the window and the twangy music was gone.

They were heading into fringes of forest. They crossed over a bridge that was nothing but wooden planks laid upon and interwoven into a hammock of rope and he felt the truck dip a good foot and a half before they climbed the other side. The forest began to deepen and then momentarily they crossed another bridge just like the previous one only more shoddy and compromised. The truck swayed for a moment in a dull vertigo before they crested out on the bank and the woods thickened and the road narrowed and then he began to see cattails and the water increasing by degrees of width and silver and he began to see all manner of fowl in the actual lake.

They passed to the west of it. In the gloaming it looked like a burnished smooth salver handed up to the sky. Only then did he realize that a whole day had passed, that earlier he had slept deeply on the bus and long and now it was evening already and the sky without so much as a glimpse of horizon was streaked across with those seemingly sourceless castings of coral and fuchsia like so many soft phalanges of another world.

They left the lake and made a sharp turn around a cluster of oak and he saw the heads of two deer and the broad tawny flank of another disappear into the deciduous spatulate leaves of the undergrowth. The truck stopped and he swung over the side and brushed the hay off his pant legs. He looked around and saw that there was a house and he saw that on the porch were children. On the grounds around too. Maybe a dozen of them. Some with braced legs being pushed in carts by those with healthy legs, some with scoriations and pus oozing on their skin playing checkers on the gallery, some with black cloth patches over one or both eyes being led about or swinging alone from ropes tied to the thick branches of the trees. A pair tossing a foam rubber football, the one with stubs for arms letting it hit his chest and fall to the ground and kicking it back to the one with arms who picked it up and threw it back at the first one's chest. And all around only silence. Only wind in the trees. So that it seemed he was beholding this place from without. From without language and without mortal time and without suffering, and that these were the peaceful avatars of these very maimed and stricken children gone to an afterlife.

She's in the house I'll bet, the man said, and drove away.

Zach watched the truck as it disappeared down the road. The boy had turned in his seat and he watched Zach out the rear window until they were gone.

He walked toward the house and when his first footfall hit the steps a darkhaired boy with metal braces standing on the end of the porch on one leg as if to flaunt his handicap struck his foot down on the metal brace once and the children stopped playing. He looked at Zach with eyes vaguely oriental and with a stillness Zach had seen only in pictures of the mystics and the starving. Until then the children hadn't so much as looked at him. Or they hadn't looked up. They stopped throwing and stopped swinging and chasing and now they looked at him of a piece, as if amongst themselves in that silence they were reading his heart's intentions as herd animals read the portents of wind.

Under the lintel of the front door a girl of about ten was standing with her arms stretched across the jamb. She was standing with matronly authority and a long string of drool was drizzling out of the corner of her mouth and she made no motion whatever to wipe it away. When he stepped forward he heard voices inside. The girl did not move at all. He lifted her hand very gently and turned through the doorway holding her hand all the while as in a dance and then he replaced it where it had been on the jamb. She never even looked at him.

He was in a kitchen of sorts only it was as long as the entire house was deep and there were two low tables dressed with brilliantly starched sheets. All around the room were shelves with hundreds of jars. To the left, at the far end a veritable wall of windows let the last fleeting western light onto the figures there: a woman's back was bent over a boy whose legs were the shape of two boomerangs facing outwards and she was putting needles in his feet and he was saying, Why if you can eat chocolate with peanuts can't you eat chocolate with garbage beans?

Garbanzo beans, she said, laughing, And you can, you can, who says you can't?

Humans! the boy said. But they're hard and they're for humans! giggling now and moving his head from side to side, and she said, Now you're being ridiculous, laughing. Hummus, they're for hummus. Lie still.

Her hair was dark and thick and it was braided nearly down to her waist. Zach made a noise with his throat and she said over her shoulder, Shut that door, Jonah. He made the noise again louder and she turned. She colored. A deeper color. A deeper color than she already was from the sun. Oh, she said.

I'm fine, Zach said.

He held up his hands as if he was under arrest. What am I doing here?

That's what you tell me, isn't it? She brushed hair from her face and it fell back and she blew at it and it fell back again and she just left it there. The prone boy was craning his head upward the better to see but he had a milky film in his eyes like the scum in the stagnant alcoves of a pond and he seemed to be having a hard time placing Zach in space. The woman had a needle poised in her hand as if she might commence a symphony.

Yes, Zach said. But the children. Who are these children?

Her eyes narrowed and she turned profile. They are my charge.

She turned back around and looked directly at him. What do

you want? If you are from the city come back with an order. I've been through this before.

He stepped forward. Look at my mouth, he said. I think I am here to see you.

She looked at him and then she looked at the floor somewhere between them. As if some shadow was moving there. As if some authority on the subject of his probability lay conspiratorially in the worn boards. She looked up. I cannot help you but I can probably fix your mouth, she said.

CHAPTER FIFTEEN

Samuel's hair lapped at the fire and the fire lapped at Samuel's hair. They had declined Frank's bus seats and rode the last hours in the dark with not so much as a fingernail of moon to blanch white the lines along the middle and flanks of the road. At a convenience store in a town called Pelt Zach had bought a loaf of bread and some bananas and some peanut butter and some chocolate chips and they were knifing the butter and passing it back and forth near the fire and dipping it hot into the chips and smearing that in turn on the bread and eating the bananas in mouthfuls in between. Already his legs were getting stronger. He could feel the muscles jumping in their minute charges under the denim of Nate's bibs and he liked the feeling. He sat spraddled and massaged his legs and looked from the fire to Samuel and to the fire again. Then he lay back and watched the woodsmoke disappearing into the stars.

Earlier Samuel had wheeled the bike so that the rear tire was in the light of the fire and with the screwdriver of Zach's pocketknife he had for nearly half an hour prodded the plastic oval of milk jug through the slit in the rubber, looking up from time to time in perplexed wonderment which was not admiration for ingenuity but a kind of nonplussed disbelief that he had not thought of something so simple himself. Now he was staring into the fire with a quality of intense sobriety particular to him. He was sitting crosslegged and erect and the alertness of his gaze and the sacrosanct posture made it seem that he was himself making the fire and burning the logs and blowing the wind across their whole diminutive enterprise.

Samuel, Zach said, do you believe in reincarnation?

Samuel looked up at him slowly and shook his head no.

Do you know what it is?

Samuel shook his head no again.

Zach thrust a stick under the log and stoked the fire. It's the belief that we live over and over again but in different bodies until we are wise enough to not have to learn any more from life and then we—I don't know, exactly, but we don't need a body anymore. We disappear.

Samuel looked down at his own body. Then he looked at Zach.

There was a great Samuel once, Zach said. In Israel. He was a seer.

Samuel was still sitting in that crosslegged posture, still sacrosanct, the flames flickering across his expressionless expressive face. He studied Zach.

The people sinned. They wanted a king. They weren't supposed to want that. But they wanted to be like all the other nations who had kings who fought battles and Samuel tried to warn them that it would be trouble for all of Israel but they didn't listen, they just wanted a king. The Lord was Samuel's friend. Samuel spoke to the Lord and told him of the trouble and the Lord told him that bad things would happen but if they had to have a king he would provide one and that man's name would be Saul.

Samuel had hardly moved from the posture but his eyes were suspicious in the firelight and his body leaned slightly forward with the listening.

Saul came to Samuel at the gate and said, Where's the seer? and Samuel said, I am the seer, go up before me to the high place. So they went to the high place. And Samuel made Saul king of Israel. He poured oil on his head. He took Saul to the people and said, Behold, the Lord has set a king over you. But they didn't believe him. So Samuel told them all to stand still. He told them they would see a great thing. It was wheat harvest day. Samuel told them that he would make thunder and rain to punish them for asking for a king. Then he asked the Lord to make thunder and rain and the Lord made it. It thundered and rained. And all the people of Israel feared Samuel and the Lord.

Samuel got up and took the thermos from the basket and poured some water into its lid and walked over and handed it to Zach and squatted in front of him and watched him drink. When he was done he went back and filled it again and came back and gave it to Zach and squatted and watched him drink again. Zach handed him the empty cup. I don't know, Zach said. It's just a story I read a long time ago in the Bible. I don't know what it means.

Chapter Sixteen

Zach stood there in the kitchen with the woman's back and the boomerang legs framing it and he moved the better to see them. He watched her turning the needles forefinger and thumb in the boy's feet while she sang softly to herself or to the boy. Apart from their breath and the low song she sang the house was silent. But more the vast night around was silent. And even more it seemed to him that the earth was silent, that if he made the simplest sound, the mention of his name for instance, it might interrupt the natural flow of the world. He stood in the silence and listened to their breath and song and he watched the lamplight play on the sinew of her arms as they moved in patient dexterity along the misshapen limbs of the boy and he had the strong desire to run. A longing for the feral. A desire to run through the dark woods leaping creeks and logs in the sloe colored air and plunging into the sloe colored lake and planing off what skin in that black silky water and calling out to whom?

I'm Zach.

She did not turn around. Let me finish Edmund's treatment and then I'll look at it. Get a basin down from the cupboard—don't touch the inside—there above the sink and fill it with hot water. Put in some squirts of that antibacterial soap on the counter and wash your hands in the sink first and then wash your face around the cut in the basin and take a towel—the cupboard to the left of those jars—

Those jars? Zach said. There's jars everywhere.

I'm pointing, she said. With my elbow. Those jars. And some of that Betadine solution and set them on the table. Grab the scissors too, on the sideboard. Anna, she said.

He looked around the room for another person. He looked at her back, at her shoulders. What color her skin would have been was a paler strip where her tank naturally fell. As if she wore nothing else ever but tanks and perhaps too her pair of man's jeans which were bunched with nothing but a cotton rope through the loops. I'm Anna, she said.

She looked outside. Shit, it's almost dark. Could you call them in? Tell them to shower and to meet in an hour in the reading room.

Who? he said, and immediately he knew she meant the children and he felt ridiculous for asking. Can they shower?

What?

Alone. Can they shower alone?

She turned and looked at him for a long time, holding a needle in the air as if it was something she was deciding whether or not to pin on his chest, like a boutonniere. Again she blew at her hair but what aberrant hair there had been she had put behind her ear and there was no hair to blow. They shower in pairs. Some of them wash each other, if that's what you're trying to figure.

He walked out to the porch and looked out into the darkening. He could not see a single child of those he had seen before and he could not find his voice, whether from the pain in his mouth or the wind off the woman he couldn't say. Come inside, he said to no one, as if his mouth was full of crackers. Nothing, not a sound. He held his mouth that the crack not split wider when he shouted and he yelled, Come inside and shower! and the burn tore down the corner of his mouth and opened along the chin it seemed and still nothing, only silence. He turned and was about to walk back inside when he heard a shrill warbling from above and the body of a man suddenly fell on him as in ambush and he jumped sideways and yelled out and warded the body off. Only it wasn't a man but a boy, nearly as big as a man but certainly a boy with eyes set so wide apart they were almost on the sides of his head and a mouth nearly lipless and stretched straight across so that his face looked like a planet seen in a scope. Boom! Boom! the huge boy was saying where he lay on his back on the gallery boards and he stood up and began to pummel Zach's chest with some invisible mallet in his mind and then he stopped suddenly. He looked at Zach and made a face tragically sad and said, almost in tears, I'm sorry, I'm sorry, I thought you were Bomber Man.

Bomber Man? Zach said.

The boy put his arms completely around him so that Zach could barely breathe. He held him tightly and said, Huck, Huck, Huck over Zach's shoulder and then he released him, abruptly, as if he was healing the man, casting off a spell or a pestilence. Zach held the boy's shoulders and looked at the blubbering, sincere face. Go inside and shower, he said.

That's cool Huck, shower.

Huck? Zach said and he heard laughter and looked up. They were all standing head or chest high nearly disappeared off the ledge of the gallery, their faces beached up out of the darkness like so many masks bobbing there looking at him where he stood barefoot with his pants rolled up to his knees. Then one by one, as if in some preordained order, they came up the ramp and for the door, jostling and pushing each other and looking at him as they passed through, some demurely, some directly, some quick and indifferent after like does checking the momentary flicker of the underbellies of leaves in the wind. The small drooling one who had cut such a matronly figure in the doorway grabbed his hand and kissed it and then bit him hard on the thumb and squealed as if she herself had been bit and ran through the door. To each one in turn he said something about a shower and a reading room and when they had all filed in he went inside and said to the curve of the back and the redbrown shoulders still bent over the boy, This is an orphanage.

No, she said, without turning around. It's a disco.

She smelled like leaves. Like autumn leaves in retrograde somehow toward summer. Like fresh leaves burnt ahead to fall by that same summer sun. He was sitting in a woodframed wicker chair with a fringy hole in the seat and she was sitting on an identical chair only she had turned it around and straddled it. She was leaning forward with her elbows resting on the backrest and he was already squeezing, whitening his knuckles on the struts of her chair by the time she said, Here we go. She lifted the needle out of the Betadine bath and threaded it and tied the knot and cut the excess and breathed in deeply and put it through his mouth. The cut was a little over an inch long and it ran at an angle form the corner of the right side of his mouth halfway to the line of his chin. He was looking at her throat, the wide fine V of her collarbone and he began to configure it into a formation of scudding fowl and then he was simply trying to break the chair in his grip. She was saying something but he had no idea what she was saying.

And then he could hear again, her long slow exhales which smelled like rain on those selfsame leaves and her voice coming back from a distance. Coming back with a quality of softness alighting. Her mouth open ever so slightly and her dark hair falling about it against her lips which were a little dry from concentration, billowing there from only her breath and touching down and billowing again and his own torn mouth not more than a foot from hers so that he began to breathe as she did or she as he, as if she was sewing not by surgical thread alone but by some shared conveyance of air and *do not look into her eyes*.

She held the thread in one hand with her knuckles against his mouth and reached for the scissors and placed them on her lap and then tied it off and snipped the end and leaned back holding the struts of the chair and looked at her work. She let out a breath and wet her mouth quickly. I've done better work.

Can I see? he said, but he couldn't open his mouth to talk properly.

There are no mirrors in the house.

She stood and took the Betadine bath to the counter and closed the lid and turned on the water in the sink. You sound like a caveman, she said.

And suddenly he felt giddy. He though of Lazar and the nurse and the pomegranate seeds. Antidisestablishmentarianism, he said, though through the tightness of his lip it sounded like nothing at all.

What?

Antidisestablishmentarianism.

Am I established for terrorism? What are you talking about?

She held her wet hands in the air and turned toward him cambering as a horse does over a high stall wall and her neck was long in the posture and her braid was unkempt and her hair was all about her. What are you talking about?

He just sat, not quite smiling, callow, indefensible. She dried her hands on a towel and shook her head at him and walked over to her chair where she had placed the scissors. She reached for them and he touched her wrist and leaned forward and looked at her with a counterfeit urgency. Anti-dis-establishment-arian-ism.

And now her face clouded. She bent forward and looked closely at her work and looked back into his eyes and turned around and took a crayon and tore a corner off a placemat from the table across and handed them to him. Write it, she said. She rested her forearm on the chairback and held out the palm of her own hand for a stable surface.

He wrote the word. She turned the paper in her palm and read it several times, slowly. She looked up at him and read it again yet slower and back to his face and read his face as slowly and looked it seemed through the very sockets of his skull to a place in or behind him, a humorless place where perhaps she saw the image of herself as seen from without where she was abject for shame of her lack of formal learning on the whole and the look on her face was fear. What is that? she said, trembling.

A word. The longest word in the English language. He felt sick. He tried to enunciate clearly.

A word, he said. He felt sick. She considered him in such stillness. Like a genius piece of statuary upon which moods do change and play. Because the fear was gone and then it was pity and then it was anger, though the face never moved, never changed. Don't laugh at me, she said, finally. I thought you were in pain.

I am in pain.

Maybe, she said. Maybe.

She moved quickly now and opened a cupboard and grabbed a pile of linen and whirled around clutching the cotton to her breast. There is a room up the stairs, three doors to your right.

She threw a set of sheets in his lap. He gave her a confounded look. Your bed, she said. I'll need two weeks. I need to put calendula on that thing every day, twice a day. And then I'll have to take out your stitches.

What can I do? he said. To pay you.

She looked at him and blew at her hair. Don't ever laugh at me.

November 21

The light on the lake when we passed, the weeds or something, grasses or plants out of the water, red, the man who owned the gas station—his eyes were gray, he didn't even say his name, and true, you didn't look at him enough, you should have looked at him more, shut up, you should have, you were in the back of the truck, how could you have? true eyes? as simple as this is, a list, red, the boy had the same eyes, dark red where the shade was under the trees, and very true those eyes, very? umber on the water, under the trees, the sad trees, the trees, trees, just write a fucking list, trees, tree, a tree, how can it be this quiet? with all those kids, Anna's voice before down the hall to the children, soft, unmaternal, un-, un-, something so soft in it and endless and soft in it and yet somehow unmaternal, the thread in my mouth, the pain in my mouth, like a little heart, my mouth, pump pump

pump, little school desk, little chair, bare window, wind on the bare window, my bare feet on the floor, a yellow raincoat in the closet, a little desk, wind picking up outside, what am I doing here? what? Zachary, a root in the ground, he had good eyes, like Lazar's almost, and the boy, a little desk, you write a bad list Zachary, indeed, antidisestablishmentarianism, jesus christ Zachary, her hair turning when she turned, red water at dusk, it was the stillest water, on the water was so flat, flat water, still water on the water, still water, still water.

CHAPTER SEVENTEEN

The room he lay in was shaped like a trapezium as if it had been made from a larger room on one end and a closet on the other. There was nothing in it but a bed and an old school desk and a child's chair. The wood boards of the floor were warped and the windows shivered in the wind. Deep in the night the rain came driving against the glass like so much sand come scouring. He lay awake fingering the nub of thread in his mouth and listening inbetween the driving pulses of rain to his own breath and the woodmurmuring of the old house. He felt something and he thought that it might be peace. He marveled at the simple fact of dryness on such a torrential night. As if walls and windows and a roof were of a bounty beyond reckoning. If peace, he thought. If peace is an invitation to sleep and to rise and to give thanks without knowing whence or why or wherefore.

He woke early in the morning and pulled on his clothes and went quietly downstairs to the kitchen. He looked at the rows of shelves teeming with jars and he walked closer and read them and but for a few in fifty he had no idea what he read: Astragalus and Celandine and Fennel and Wild Yam and St. John's Wort and Valerian and Ginseng and Echinacea Angustifolia.

Kava and Hawthorn Berry Extract and Bugleweed and Motherwort. This was one shelf. He pulled the Motherwort jar down and looked behind and there were half a dozen jars with names unpronounceable, all with labels facing, and he put it back and turned the label exactly as it had been. It was then he realized the meticulousness, the complete order of the kitchen. Each jar had behind it a row of jars containing other substances and each row had a certain color to the label as if to designate a subgroup based on some likeness. There were immaculate white towels piled in front of each shelf and there were cotton balls and gauze piled in jars all along the counter and sponges unwrapped and wrapped both in stacks and another jar full of cellulose material cut in all manner of triangles and squares.

He moved to the next shelf and read along the row: Aconite and Barberry Root, Night Blooming Cereus and Chickweed Herb, Alfalfa Leaf, Usnea Lichen. He reached up and pulled down a jar labeled Passionflower and opened it and breathed it in. He sat at one end of the largest table (there were three tables, all with placemats depicting fires in trees and monsters and oceans and stars and all manner of animals real and imaginary and somewhere in each fabulous landscape a child's name) and looked about at the room.

The southfacing window which had been added along the whole length of wall had panes of different thickness and quality as if they had been salvaged from many houses or a junkyard. Dangling from nails in a two by four across the top casing hung plants, herbs, upsidedown in clusters like inverted feral bouquets. He recognized dandelions and nothing else among them. A rude shelf—a two by twelve braced across stacked cinder blocks—ran the length of the window and on it were jars of oils, each of a different color, with leaves or roots or flowers or sometimes the plant entire set to soak in the sun.

In the northeast corner of the kitchen stood what looked like a bookcase and a dresser set which had actually been sawed in half vertically and set at ninety degrees to accommodate the angle of the room. On it were blocks of beeswax stacked and more

Betadine solution in rows and a number of bottles called Ever-clear and rolls of tape and countless empty jars and tiny empty bottles with dropper lids. Next to that and inbetween the cabinets that ran the length of the counter was a battered armoire and he opened it and instantly smelled raw alcohol. In the darkness of the cabinet he could see more dishes and jars with herbs soaking in the spirits and he shut the door and turned around and she was standing there barefoot in the clothes of the day before and holding the jar he'd taken down and she said, It does the opposite, if you're wondering.

He was looking at her feet, at her right foot. There were marks across the instep, three distinct and raised darknesses like stigmata. What?

Passionflower. It calms you down, puts you to sleep.

Oh, Zach said. He heard wheezing and he looked to the door and a small boy with hair so red it seemed improbable turned and bolted across the porch and down the steps and into the trees across the drive and was gone.

I would like to work, to do something in exchange, Zach said.

We're putting a wall in, I am, in the reading room. I've got the top and bottom plates cut out but I'm thinking of doubling the top plate so you'd need to match that cut. You could cut the studs to length while you're at it. It'd be best if it was done to sixteen inches on center, it would save wood and it's plenty strong enough even with that sag in the ceiling. You'll have to mark the studs on the sides so we can nail true. Use the crow's foot and set the first one at fifteen and a quarter for your measure so that we'll be flush with the wall covering when we go to nail, and set the others at sixteen and multiples so on down the stud. There's nails in the shed. For the top plate to stud I'd use two sixteen-D nails crosswise, that's all you'll need, but for the headers I'd use both toenails and face, just to be sure. Use your plumb bob to plumb up to the top plate to figure where you are.

She sighed, lazily, as if she were bored and trying to figure what to do with her day. The joists are shot, she said. It's like the hull of a boat in there. I would—

I was foolish to joke yesterday, Zach said.

I would jam it up under there with a jack when you've got it all nailed. Then we'll probably have to use the eight pound sledge to bang it in. Toenails for the rafter to plates. Face nails for the braces. You were, she said.

She looked at him and nearly smiled, a condolatory smile that had no condolence in it. There's a mule. The stall needs mucking. I need some manure in the astragalus beds. You can do anything you want. You can turn soil in the hothouse. You can pick shiitakes off the logs.

Good, Zach said. Who was that?

What?

The boy.

Oh, she said.

That hair, Zach said.

Yes. That's Samuel. He's curious. He was outside your room last night, standing there. He was listening to you breathe.

How do you know?

I saw him.

No, how do you know he was listening to my breath?

She looked at his mouth as if she too was wondering what that expiration might tell about his heart. Because he changed his breathing. He was breathing with you.

I see.

No you don't.

I think I heard him on the boards.

Maybe.

What do you mean maybe?

She placed the jar of passionflower back on the shelf and stood with her back to him.

Don't pick him up.

Why?

He'll scratch your eyes out.

All right, Zach said.

He likes you. I don't know why. He doesn't talk.

Chapter Eighteen

The Lake was a forty acre piece of land on the southwest tip of the Kisatchie Forest. To the north the hills began to rise gradually toward Salt Peak which beetled due south out of the dense pine and could be seen only from a distance, like a bent thumb stuck out of a bush. The lake itself lay along the eastern flank of the tract, seventeen acres of pooled runoff from Old Salt Creek, and ran southwest to northeast roughly parallel to the old logging road that expired at the property. Jacques Beauchamp (midway through his eighteenth year he had begun to call himself Jack) had purchased the piece in 1866 when he was only nineteen, anticipating the spreading of the railroad and the imminent (the urgent, the suddenly necessary) boom in the lumber industry after 1865 and he studied the plans for the line and chose a plot of land near enough to be practicable and far enough, he surmised, to give himself and his yet nonexistent conjugal family some bucolic remove and good hunting right out their front door. He built the house himself along with two skilled ex-slave brothers named Moses and Swell, twins, and the brothers stayed on the property and built the barn and the outbuildings and also the first ad hoc whiskey still in the nook of what they called, for reasons which no one was able to discern, Barely Knee.

The house was a finely wrought (that is, in 1866 it had been finely wrought; now it sat crumbling and warped and paintless) two storey Greek Revival but with a broad full-façade gallery in architectural homage to his French Colonial forebears who had settled and established themselves in central Louisiana long before the Purchase. It had a hipped roof and a simple entablature above the plain doric pillars and a front gable canopy window with six-pane glazing which looked out isolate over the gallery like a watchful eye. Eight rooms and a spread kitchen with a broad stair and a balustrade.

And for a time he'd been right. He stabled fourteen mules in the barn and for nearly ten years they were integral among the beasts of burden transporting materials for the Texasbound south and west forks of the line. But then the railroad expansions were done and no town grew up around the now obsolete mill adjacent to The Lake on the southwest tip of the Kisatchie. Moses and Swell migrated north for work in the large booming cites. The mill closed down. Jack sold the mules and moved to the tiny town of Marjolaine and married straightaway and started a contracting business. The Lake lay fallow with the house cankering in the woods for forty years until Jack's grandson John began to make whiskey on the property in 1917, himself living in Marjolaine and still contracting in the family name and making forays out to The Lake for whiskey runs (and sometimes just to be alone and hunt). In 1922 he got caught. First by the local sheriff who did nothing but fine him lightly (the two of them standing in the Marjolaine courthouse and laughing about it and throwing down the gauntlet, as it were, for a subsequence of hide and seek, and the judge stolid but amused as well) and later that year he was caught again but by the federal agents this time and he served five years. When he was released he wanted nothing to do with whiskey. He reinstated his business and developed the reputation as the finest and most accountable builder in the area and with his son, Cass, who by the age of eighteen was already a journeyman prodigy and a maverick as well, he built probably a quarter of the new houses in Marjolaine. By the late 1950's the town just had little need for more houses. John retired and Cass switched to electrical work and in the end even worked for the bureaucracy of the state which he had no taste for and perhaps to spite the begrudged necessity of government regulated employment he quietly and efficiently reinvigorated the whiskey business out at The Lake and taught his only son, Lance, both trades. In the fall of 1962 they went fishing—that is, they took sixteen cases of whiskey as far as North Albany to sell and they brought their rods and caught some fish in the meantime. Coming back over the pass they cut through Robeleine to avoid a norther and Lance, who was then eighteen, saw a young woman of definite Spanish descent in the passenger seat of a beatup dark green '58 Ford pickup truck with Louisiana plates sitting in the lot of a general store and he slammed on his brakes. His father, who was asleep in the seat beside him, woke up and said, What?

We need gas, Lance said.

We filled it in Omeleine.

There must be a hole in the tank, Lance said.

The father followed the son's gaze where it had not so much as blinked lest it lose even for a second sight of the woman. Oh, he said, I see, and went back to sleep.

Lance got out and stood at a respectful distance and told her that she was the most beautiful woman he'd ever seen in his life. She told him to climb a tree. All right, he said.

He started to turn back to the truck and then he stopped. I'm afraid of heights, he said. How tall are you?

She just looked at him very sweetly and rolled up her window.

But he found out her name was Anita Chavez from the store manager and he came back every few weeks, making the hour and a quarter drive after work, and called her from the store (calling no fewer than nine Chavezes out of the directory and crossing them out one by one until an actual Anita was summoned to the phone). And eventually she'd see him and soon after they fell unrestrainedly in love and two years later she was pregnant and he married her. Anna was their daughter. Anna Beauchamp.

CHAPTER NINETEEN

Zach ate with the children. Scrambled eggs and fried onions and cheese in whole wheat tortillas with salsa and a fruit shake she made with half a dozen kinds of fruit and milk that was very cold and came in unmarked glass jars. The children looked at him over their glasses when they drank and then did not look at him at all. He made as if to pass the salt to the boy next to him but the boy put it right back in the center of the table without using it. No one spoke at all. He looked for the redhaired boy named Samuel but he was not at breakfast. He went out after behind the house and the morning was fresh and clear. He surveyed the property and walked it to the woods' edge in four directions and as he walked he moved his arms in large circles in the air like a man in a sanitarium. In the eastern alcove, in between the house and the barn which ran perpendicular to each other (from a northerly vantage like an inverted T with a large gap in the joint of it) was what he surmised to be an old corridor storm shelter, but as he walked closer he saw that there were chickens. In the western bay there were neat rows of herbs and the lightframed plastic hothouse and the fallow garden plots in dislimned columns as if they'd just been picked clean and salted with manure and left for winter.

By mid morning he'd mucked the stall and swept the floor clean to the corners and laid down fresh shavings on the boards. All the while he worked the mule stood looking at him askance and curling back her lip and lifting her head and unpeeling her gums and Zach, who'd never really looked at a horse let alone a mule, thought that she was actually making faces at him. She'd never smelled anyone like him before and she was no doubt trying to make sure he was what she thought he was but it made him embarrassed and he turned around finally and said, What are you looking at? She sauntered off like she'd been wasting her time anyway and he laughed and bent back to work.

He cleaned the stall like it was a room in a house. Like guests were coming. He even cleaned the dead bugs off the hanging lamp and the pussy willow nests of flies between the ceiling boards. From the manure pile just outside the paddock he made three trips with the wheelbarrow to the herb beds. For all her discourse on carpentry Anna didn't seem to mind the sad shape of the paddock fence and he nailed the loose boards at their joinings and he nailed some where the boards were not loose at all. Two of the older boys named Neil and Raoul had been watching him for most of the morning and when he went to the shed they trailed behind him, and when he put a brush each in their hands they looked at it and turned and followed him like he was some Nazarene. They were both afflicted with the same random convulsions and their brushstrokes were irregular and spotty but they tried to touch them up as they went along and they worked seriously. The three of them were just coating the last section of fencing with a compound Zach had found in the shed called Steel's Wood Protector when she came up drinking from a large glass of water which she handed to him. Tom Sawyer, she said.

She was wearing a hat with a broad brim and she dipped her head down to hide her smile. He took a drink. It was falling to pieces, he said.

She looked at his clothes. Doris says to tell you Nate's got clothes. Says for you to take the motorbike into town to get some clothes. Doris brings some groceries and the milk. Nate brought you. From the filling station. Can you ride a motorbike?

Yes, he lied.

Me and Samuel will be turning soil in the hothouse when you get back. If you want to help. The bike's behind the shed and the key's in it.

She looked at the fence and said thank you under her breath but he'd gone back to work and he didn't even turn around.

He wheeled the bike as far as the bend in the road where the trees thickened again and where through the underbrush the lake was barely visible from the rise in the road. He turned the ignition to where it said On and pushed the button that said Start and the bike lurched forward violently and died immediately and fell to the ground. He picked it up and looked at it like he might reckon with it. He did the same a second time. The bike lurched again and fell with a terrible inert sound and the boy came out from somewhere among the trees and squatted by the bike and put his hands on the bars and looked up at Zach for help. They lifted the bike and Samuel kicked down the side stand and put his left hand on the clutch and pulled it in and looked at Zach. He looked pointedly down at his foot and he stepped on the gear shift and pulled the clutch and released it and made the noise with his lips of the motor downshifting. He pulled the clutch again only this time he put his foot under the peg and flicked it up and made a higher pitched sound and thrust his head downroad indicating to Zach that he wanted him to wheel the bike forward. When the bike was rolling at a fair speed Samuel ran around in front of it and squeezed the right handlebar lever and the bike stopped. He made the forward motion again and ran alongside and stepped on the little platform near the right foot peg and the bike stopped again. He turned and ran down the road and leapt over the gully that separated the drive from the woods and disappeared into the trees.

Zach fell six times in all, once at nearly twenty five miles an hour into some sedge when he got cocky on a curve and once when he thought he'd understood how far to lean in accordance with his speed. Once when he downshifted twice by accident and suddenly released the clutch and the bike nearly stopped dead and he went over the bars. He fell on his shoulder and he stood up and extended his arm and rotated it and it was fine and he laughed out loud and then was silent a moment and then all of a sudden he whooped at the top of his lungs and looked about him like a man just emerged from the depths of cold water.

Before he got to town he'd broken off one of the rearview mirrors and he'd burnt a hole in his jeans and seared the skin on his left calf. A little over an hour later he made the shop and Nate smiled which he had not done the day before. He handed him a rucksack not unlike Lazar's and said, There's two pairs of bibs and a pair of jeans from before you were born and some shirts. They're not pretty but they'll work. I reckon you'll want to make your keep out there. He scrutinized Zach's feet. There's an old pair of engineer boots that might work. You got any underwear?

Actually no, Zach said.

Actually? Nate said.

I don't have any, Zach said.

Nate went into the house which was adjacent to his shop and in a moment he came out with three pair of underwear and some T-shirts and handed them to Zach. I've never given another man my underwear in all my life. Tell Anna to send back Miriam's canning jars with Missy when she come with the groceries.

Thank you. Do you have work here?

I reckon you'll be busy enough out there. Till that thing heals.

Naturally, Zach said.

Naturally? Nate said. He looked at the young man like he was some kind of experiment.

Me and Anna's old man, we were like brothers, savvy?

Pardon?

You don't understand what I'm sayin to you?

I'm sorry I don't think I do.

I'm talking about that woman. Her old man, he's passed.

For a moment Zach didn't understand and then he said, I'm sorry to hear that.

Don't disturb her unless she wants to be disturbed, savvy?

I have nothing in mind, Zach said.

I know it else I wouldn't have sent you out there in the first place.

Zach put his arms through the straps of the pack and swung his leg over the bike and started it up nonchalant and habitual as if his whole life had formed him to it. You look like a fish that swallowed a line, Nate yelled over the motor.

I know it, Zach yelled back. He gunned the engine and flipped the gears one two and three and sped off down the road.

CHAPTER TWENTY

That night he had the second dream and the second dream was rain. He heard it driving and relentless on the roof in his sleep and then it was on no roof but smacks of it on the dry suntamped plain laid out endlessly before them. He was walking with the redhaired boy through some distance all disappearing in rain and the light of the day was folding back like a curtain let from one horizon to another and they loved the rain and they were not cold and their clothes were drenched and the boy opened his mouth to let the rain in and Zach saw that he was eating the rain and it gave him strength to see the boy so nourished and he knew that they could walk that way for as long as they wanted to and they would not grow weary.

He woke to a knocking at the door and he called out Who is it? and it was Anna. She said that the wind had blown the tarp off the hay. He dressed in the dark in the new old bibs and Nate's thick wool shirt and went downstairs. They pulled on the rubber boots by the door and went outside in the wet and streaming dark and Anna pointed and yelled over the din of the rain, It's in the barn.

They tucked their heads for the wind and rain and walked by the chickens so tidy in their wooden box stalls, in their dormed houses, and the barn loomed up like an ominous wall of thalassic sky, a huge window into nothing but the punishment of weather. It was an old pole bank barn of local pine and it ran perpendicular to and behind the house, jammed into the side of a hillock on its north end where the land already began to rise in repeating and ascending hillocks toward the arête of Salt Peak. Trees had been cleared for a pathway to the north entrance but the path was gone and scrubbrush overcame an entire third of the structure from the hill houseward and foliage grew over and into the roof itself and hung down from out the torn rafters and within like vines under a rainforest canopy. The structure had remained intact at all simply by virtue of the stone retaining wall embedded in the hill which had kept it standing for the better part of a hundred years. Through the sleeting gray wall of rain it looked like a listing ship; he could see it lean and return on the wind, as if it was exhausted, as if it wanted to lie down but was afraid of what it might crush beneath it. Only a third of the pine boards were intact and as they approached he could see the pale planed rainslicked poles inbetween the slats rocking three feet off their moorings with the gusts of wind. The structure was nearly thirty feet long and when it swayed it swayed broadly all of a piece which further gave it a navicular attitude.

They walked in. He saw the tarp flapping in the wind like some sail gone mad atop its canting hull. The sky through the flayed open roof and the rain nailing into the blown canvas and the sopping hay the hard smacks of which were so close and constant it sounded like one long thudding drifting more or less intensely on the blasts and lulls of the wind. Anna looked up at the sky through the roof, squinting, the rain hammering against her face. Zach watched her profile out from her slicker hood and then he watched the walls of the structure sway. He felt the earth under him move. He looked down at the mud and then back at the walls. He didn't know if he imagined the feeling. Is the ground moving? he yelled.

No, that's the walls. She leaned into him so he could hear her.

That's just the walls. You're already walking on the hay and we haven't even climbed it yet.

They stood there for several seconds watching the walls of the barn cant and right. Then she walked over to some nails on the wall and took from them four hay hooks and handed two to Zach and kept two herself and just walked up to the stack of hay and as if she would punish it she hurled the hooks into the bales and began to pull herself up. She thrust the hooks right then left, hanging in the air for a time until her toe found small purchase in the crevices, until she made the top and sat and looked briefly down at Zach and swiveled her body and swung her legs around and disappeared. Zach threw a hook into the hay and it just bounced back and he looked at it and placed the curved point around the highest baling wire he could reach and began to pull himself up. He looked for another such wire and could see none and he felt himself about to fall. In desperation he hurled the hook into the packed bulk and to his surprise it stuck. He began to pull himself up, hand after hand. He made the top and hoisted himself up and stood and looked up through the roof and down at the barn around him. He could barely see for the contrast between the sky and the darker recesses of the barn, for the shifting shadows the nightlit doglegged edges of the opening cast about the gutted infrastructure. He splayed his legs for balance. The stack was definitively shifting under his feet. I'm over here, she yelled.

The wind blew hard then and moved him bodily and he squatted and fisted some protruding wire.

Where?

Turn to your right, then look straight ahead.

He did. He saw nothing. Then his eyes adjusted and he saw that she was straddling atop the far corner. She had a rope coiled in one hand and with the other she was gathering the tarp into her body. He walked slowly over to her, bending, making his way over the swaying, his arms outstretched now to the sides as if he were walking on a rope, and squatted in front of her. She looked up at him. Rain! she yelled.

Rain! he yelled back.

Grab this corner, she shouted, and walk it diagonal back the way you came.

He grabbed the end and began to walk backward, watching her, or the figure that was her, dim. Then she disappeared. She fell. As if a trap door just opened beneath her, she was gone. He stood for a second with the rain pummeling him and pummeling the grass and the remains of the useless roof, and then he scrabbled to the edge and searched blindly with his hands for the hooks and found them and turned his body, stomach to the stack, and drove the hooks into the mantel of hay and began to descend. Midway down a hook caught on a baling wire and he hung there for a moment jerking at it but his own weight kept him from lifting and releasing it. He looked down the ten feet to the ground and just let go. He landed and rolled. He ran around the far side of the stack. She was standing there in the middle of the strewn and broken bales with her hands on her hips, looking at it around her like the last earth of an island upon which she was marooned. Like she was gauging how long she had before the sea encroached upon her altogether. She didn't even look at him. She knew he was there. She just knelt and felt about for the hooks and found them and started climbing back up. More hay chafed and she fell again, only this time she landed on her feet and backed into Zach's upheld hands. She tried again. Zach came up behind her and made a leverage with his interlocked fingers and pushed her up and she swung the hook into the meat of the hay. She hung in the air. Hold on, Zach yelled.

He quickly piled two of the fallen and intact bales on top of each other and stood on them and further pushed her foot upward and she sank the hook higher and hung again and he repeated the process, lifting her, she hanging in the air while he piled more bales for stools and thrusting her upward on some perfect and unspoken timing, as if he could feel each time through the soles of her boots the tightening of her thighs themselves which signaled she was going to leap. Once more! she called down to him.

He pushed her hard. As hard as he could and the bales crumbled beneath him with the force and he fell but she rose upward as upon a lift and swung and caught the hook and in a motion she curled her body over the ledge and disappeared. He kicked the hay from about him and stood looking up at the place. He thought that she might come crashing back through. He waited. But she didn't. What he saw was only her head extending over the lip, in darkness. He couldn't see her expression. He wanted very badly to see her expression. He looked up into the rain, all but shut his eyes against it. He could feel the drops driving on his sutured cut, on his teeth, even in his throat where his mouth opened slightly for the uplooking. She seemed to be examining something, looking for something. Zach looked down about him among the tumbled hay. What are you looking at? he yelled.

You, she said. Here's a rope. Use the hook and the rope.

What?

Use both the hook and the rope to climb. Wait ten seconds till after you've got it so I can walk to the far end.

She let down the rope. When she saw that he had it she disappeared and ten seconds later he felt a tug. He began to climb. He was halfway up when he fell. The hook just loosed out of the hay. With his left hand he hung for a moment on the rope and then it began to slide through his wet palm and burn him and he swung at the hay with the hook in his right hand but he couldn't get a purchase and he dropped to the ground and rolled. He stuck his palm in the mud to cool it and wiped that hand across his slicker. Again! he shouted. He felt the pull on the rope. He climbed. Again midway the tenderloin grass gave way and he began to fall backward. He threw the hook down and caught hold of the rope and began to heave himself up. He felt the rope give way toward him and he thought for a moment she was going to drop him or come down upon him but then it stayed. He climbed hand over hand and crested out and swung over and rolled onto his back. He rolled over to her where she was sunk in a recess she'd made by removing one of the bundles. Sitting down in it with her feet braced up against a wedged bale and the rope turned twice around her waist. She had removed her hood. Her hair was plastered across her face. In her mouth. She was soaked through. So was he. He sat up and took off his slicker and flung it back behind him but the wind nearly carried it out of the huge jagged gap in the west flank of the barn. It caught around an isolate bare pole, a pole from which the siding had been ripped long ago, and hung there whipping in the wind in a kind of pent desperation. Like it wanted to be let go, released. He shook the hay from his fingertips and sloughed the water off his face and pushed back his hair and rolled again onto his back and looked up into the rain and shut his eyes against it and just let it pound on him. Let it pound on his cut where the pain felt good and cathartic of what he did not know. But very good. But that he loved it. He wanted to yell something through the blasted roof but he didn't know what he would say. He turned, shielding his face with his cupped hand, and looked at her. She looked away. She stood, bending over, and began to turn her body unraveling the rope and when she was free very carefully they walked back to the corner, getting on their hands and knees at the last where the surface had fallen away entirely and the avalanche had made veritable loose leaf out of what remained. She gathered the tarp as before and he took hold of the corner. Look, she yelled, making a looped knot with the end of the rope and turning it over and making a mirror image of the same knot and fixing them together and unraveling it and making it again.

She looked up at him.

Again, he said.

She made the knot and looked at him.

Again.

She made it again.

Again, he yelled.

She did. Good, he said, and began to crawl toward the far

end, the canvas ripping out of his hand so that he had to hold it with both hands and shimmy backwards in a near squat, twisting side to side on the balls of his feet, the wind whipping at him and at the heavy canvas as if he had done something to it. As if it wanted to dash him to the ground.

When he made the edge he stretched the canvas and looped it around the corner. He watched the flurry of her hands as she made the honda in the rope and she threw her end toward him and it fell short and she coiled it back and doubled the honda to weight it and tossed it again and it landed a foot from his chest. She was squatting now, watching him. So still. Watching him so seriously where he bent with great concentration and made the knot well, her hair still plastered across her face, not even wiping it away the better to see. He slid his end through the honda and threw it back and it landed where he wanted it to and she called to him to pull it as tight as he could and he yelled What? over the driving rain and she called it again and he did with all his strength there in the dark as if something of greater consequence depended upon it. Then she tied her end down. They stood and shifted to the other diagonal. Without saying anything, just got up and traversed like next partners at a country dance. He walked carefully back across, sinking sometimes to his knees and again squatted in front of her and gathered the flailing tarp into his chest and found the corner and walked it back. They pulled it tight across and tied it down likewise. Then they looked across at each other. Done! he yelled.

Mine too! she yelled back, and swiveled and disappeared over the edge.

Once on the ground they didn't even look back at the stack. The wind was blowing so hard now the groaning of the barn was audible above the gusts and the rain both. They began to walk toward the house, to lean toward it, and then the weather seemed to further increase as if incensed that it had not foiled the human beings entirely and they leaned almost twenty degrees into the gusts and walked on and then they heard the crash. The crashings, the vertiginous dissembling sounds of structure collapsing. They stopped of a piece and did not yet turn around, wondering perhaps if it was distant thunder. She put her hands on her hips. I hope it did, she said.

What? Zach said.

I just hope it did. I'd just as soon as it would.

She turned around and looked at it. But it was still standing. Only the rafters that remained on the south side of the roof had collapsed and fallen part way inward. The new shards of upriveted corrugated steel flapped against the fallen trusses as in a maniacal newfound freedom and made a metallic clapping and scraping sound that seemed demented, like it begged for something or someone to extinguish it, to finish it out of its misery. She stood looking at it with a kind of disgust as if it was a demolition site and only one charge had blown. Then she walked toward the paddock stall. Zach stood and watched her. When she came out she was leading the mule. Zach looked at her but didn't say anything. He did not even wonder at her to gauge the sense in the situation. He did not think wherefore the mule. He did not think about sleep or chill. He was only standing in the loud mud with a woman and a mule. A mule that without her familiar lean-to would barely stand in such a wind. She was shifting her body, looking behind her as if she was sure she was being stalked by a demon which she couldn't see. The rain came down in flat ceaseless smacks on her chestnut back. She pawed at the mud and looked up and around and whinnied and when she turned around toward the house, bending deeply at the neck, her upper lip curdled in the wind and her mane and forelock hair even wet as they were blew back behind her off her face making her look severe and skeletal as if she were some original and terrible orthogenesis of the mule from which the current species derived. Anna handed the lead rope to Zach. Hold her. If she tizzies just let go some play in it. But she won't. She's older than god. And darling.

What? Zach yelled.

Darling, Anna yelled.

Zach stared at her.

She bent her head, laughing. She looked up. Not you, she yelled. Jenny. The mule. She's darling.

When Anna came back from the shed she had a full face work horse collar and leather lines over her left shoulder and a harness equipped with a hip drop assembly over her right and two coils of quadruple ply webbing around her neck. She walked up to Zach and leaned her body and the collar slid off her shoulder and he took it in his free hand and then she turned her body and shucked off the lines and he held those as well and then she hoisted the harness up again on her shoulder and took back the collar and put it around Jenny's neck. The mule stood completely still now as if the harness and labor apparatuses somehow rendered the weather benign, inconsequential. Next she lifted the right hame high and looked, peered into it it seemed for the driving rain and opened the harness and laid the hame over the mule's back and secured the hame straps right and left above the crest and under the neck and slid the brichin down her back and over the dock and flipped the tail out from the leather in a gesture not unlike a girl impressed with her own ponytail. She secured the breast strap and the belly band and buckled it into the billet and slacked it and pulled the pole strap through and snapped on the quarter straps one to each side and then she went back to the shed for the bridle. When she came back she opened Jenny's mouth with her thumb and bridled her and attached the lines and finally, with a Conway buckle and a hip drop ring she attached the webbing to the tugs. Then she stepped back and looked at the mule. Jenny was looking at her. What? she said. You're a mule.

She walked her toward the barn, only this time around to the west side which way the structure was leaning. They turned and stood and faced the façade. The three of them there like travelers who had come a long way through weather to see a monumental thing and this is what they saw. With the webbing unspooling over her shoulder she walked toward the north end of the barn and climbed up the retaining wall and through the hole in the siding and squatted on a girt, facing inwards. She jumped through. She wrapped the webbing around the brace beam and the top plate and what rafters were intact and reachable and she also took it four turns around the horizontal girt on which she'd been squatting. Then she climbed out dragging the end behind her and when she reached the mule she shucked the play up through her loosed palm and just put the end of the nylon in her teeth without even looking at it or so much as holding it out for the rain to wash it off. She was just shy of length. Back her, she yelled to Zach.

He looked at her. Stand in front of her and pat her on the neck and walk forwards, she said.

Zach did this and to his surprise Jenny just stepped back straightly until he stopped walking. She attached the other end of the webbing to the tugs and turned and looked once more at the barn and then she looked down at the water flowing all around their feet, around Jenny's hooves. They were nearly in a pond of it. The rain had not let up, had in fact increased since they'd begun. Anna looked at Jenny and then back at Zach. She's retired, she yelled to him, over Jenny's withers.

She rested a hand a moment on the mule's sopping neck. Then she took a line in each hand and letting them run through her palms she walked behind the mule and evened herself with the traces and took up the belly in the lines and yelled to her over the rain, Move out.

Jenny moved forward. At first she could not find purchase in the mud and seemed merely to paw and sink but then she dug in and seconds later the webbing tightened and what was left of the barn began to rip. It sounded horrendous, like an orchestra of bones being ripped backward out of their joints. Anna walked behind her talking to her. Then the whole north end of the roof and siding cracked and fell with a noise louder than Zach would have expected. A great, awful, resigning noise. It came ripping out of itself, the frame eaves and the fascia boards and the headers, and then the whole structure followed easily on the wave of it, nearly as soft and compliant as the interstices of the moss and mold which had glued it together. She halted the mule and turned and looked at the heap of fragmented wood. She smiled. Or he thought he saw her smile. He saw something lift slowly the length of her face. Then he turned and walked toward the other end of the barn.

She took Jenny's face in her hands and gently shook her muzzle and blew hot air into her nose and ruffled her drenched poll and smoothed back her mane. Her own hair was about her face flat as wet paint and she did, finally, wipe it away. Forgive me Moses and Swell, she said.

But Zach didn't hear her. He was already looping the second coil of webbing around the supporting posts and the rafters on the south end. Using the zee flashings and the skirt trims for leverage, he'd climbed the far post and was hanging from a rafter, one foot looped into the loft joist. When he'd made several turns around the brace beams and the still intact horizontal girts and rafters he hung out in midair scissoring his legs for the freedom of it and perhaps to vaunt over the storm and the night and all barns and all weather and then he jumped down and rolled over his shoulder in the mud. He looked aground for the end of the webbing but Anna had already shucked it through the mud and she was already tying up to the mule. Then she drove her again. This time when Anna heard the cracking she turned to watch it fall but Jenny stopped too and the barn hung in unbearable suspension on nothing it seemed but the memory of itself. Good mule, she said, under her breath. Then she shook the reins once and called Move out and walked the barn down until the crashing ceased into the steadiness of rain.

Inside they wiped their faces on the dirty towels hanging in the hall. She said she'd put on something hot to drink and he said that would be good and she asked that he look in on the boys and they went upstairs and changed into dry clothes. When he came back down he saw that she had put a bottle of cognac on the counter by the stove. She had put two ceramic bowls next to each other on the only round table in the room. She was standing at the stove watching the heating milk and slowly rubbing her hair with a towel. She heard his feet stop and spoke as if to the wall above the range. Once it's wet it molds and Jenny could colic on it. It's ruined for the mounted now anyway.

She spoke softly, almost in a whisper, as if she were apologizing for the fate of weather. Zach nodded though he was behind her, though he had no idea what she was talking about. He pulled a chair from one of the low tables and pushed his fist into the wicker to test its strength and turned it toward the stove and sat. He still had a towel around his neck himself and he wore another of Nate's wool flannel shirts and Nate's ancient jeans which were a few inches too short and he was barefoot and he leaned forward with his forearms on his thighs.

The mounted? he said.

The national forest's horses, she said, stirring the milk. That's Nate's hay. Was. He feeds the police horses with it in the winter. He comes every six weeks and hauls it out to the old mill where they stall their horses. They're picky though. That hay on top is shot. The alfalfa might be all right though. It's hard to tell.

She stuck a knuckle into the pot and tasted it. I'll have to see in the morning. He's not going to like it at all.

Zach came up next to her and stood watching the milk and held his hands near the gas flame as if they were cold which they were not. You didn't make the rain, he said.

She looked deeply down into the saucepan. I love rain, she said, as if she was speaking to the milk. I do.

When the milk began to boil she poured it into the bowls and they sat and she opened the bottle of cognac and he saw that it was new. She blew at the milk and swirled it around the rim to cool it and poured generous splashes into her milk and handed the bottle to him. He had not had alcohol since before the hospital ward and he looked at it a moment. He poured generous splashes in his milk and she got up and brought over some ground cardamom and some cinnamon and he shook those also generously in the hot milk. She drank once and put more liquor in her milk and they listened to the rain. It slashed against the mismatched panes and they listened to the wind and to the branches of the trees thrashing on the roof which sounded like grandiose blind mutes exercising an angry braille and for a long time they didn't say anything. He finished his drink before she did hers and she offered some of her own and he said no. He looked into his empty cup. Why did you tear down the barn? he said.

I don't know.

He touched her arm and rose and said goodnight and went up the stairs.

CHAPTER TWENTY ONE

Early in the morning Jonah fell. He heard it still asleep and he thought it might be Anna knocking again but it was the boy's metal and limbs banging down the stairs. He heard the moaning and then three brief sharp wails and then the moaning again and then the rapid feet down stairs and Anna cursing a boy named Chris for letting Jonah come down alone. There was a strain in her voice that he would not have imagined. He pulled on his shirt and his overalls and went down and knelt beside her and helped her lift the boy all metal and brace and warped legs and they laid him on one of the dressed low tables in the kitchen. He was mumbling something about a third time and his eyes were darting about as if he was watching some insect in the room and Anna was stroking his head. She took the brace off the left leg which had bent backward forty five degrees at the femur, a few inches above the knee. Zach watched her carefully as she undid the straps and he took the brace off the right leg likewise. Anna told Jonah to close his eyes and she maneuvered his legs gently, supporting them from underneath, and laid them flat, propped at the sides by pillows, and now he was moving his head back and forth like a blind person listening to an unwelcome music. A music that he couldn't get out of his head. Chris was sitting on the bottom of the steps banging the side of his head into the wall. Cut the show, Anna said, and go find Samuel.

The boy got up and ran out the door. Jonah asked if it was broken again and Anna said that it was and he asked if it was a bad break and she said that it was. He began to moan again and to slur something about it being the third time and Anna said, I know, I'm going to tan his hide.

Put a hand on him somewhere, she said, turning toward the cupboards. Zach held the boy's tiny shoulder and collarbone all in the palm of his hand. When she came back she had some arnica pellets in a paper cup and she opened his mouth and with her finger lifted his tongue and poured in the pellets and told Jonah to keep them under his tongue until they were gone and then she began rubbing his leg very gently with arnica oil telling the boy all the while that he was a knight, that he was a knight in shining armor. Zach still held the boy's shoulder. Anna scratched an itch on her temple with the back of her hand and looked at Zach. His bones, she said. He has the marble bone disease. His bones are chalk.

Zach nodded and looked at the boy. Jonah was looking at Anna. He was looking at her very seriously with a haunted all-but-breaking stoicism. Anna went to the sink and washed her hands and came back to the table with ice and a rag and an Ace bandage. From the dining table she tore off the corner of a plaçemat as she had done two nights before. It seemed to Zach a long time ago that she had torn it. She took a crayon and wrote a name and a number on a piece of paper and handed it to him. Zach couldn't read it and he handed it back without saying anything and she penned it very slowly and handed it to him again. He still had to concentrate to decipher the name. He looked at her.

You said you were looking for a good deed, she said. Most times I have to wait two or three days when this happens until somebody comes out with milk or groceries. He's in more pain than it seems. He's just thinking he may have a while of it so he better not even start carrying on. What day is it?

Zach didn't know.

Catlin'll reset it anyhow. The nearest phone's at Zippo's Mart at the exchange. Or Nate's.

Is there gas?

You rode it last.

I don't have any money.

She looked at him doubtfully. There's gas in the shed.

She turned back to Jonah. He still looked at her but now his eyes were calmer and he looked old and wise. She kept her hand on his forehead and turned to Zach and said, I don't either.

What?

Have any money.

He looked around the kitchen at the fruit teeming in baskets and the two commercial juicers and the jars with uncountable medicinal herbs and she looked at them too as if seeing them anew. They pay for everything, she said.

Who?

The people whose children these are. The people who know but won't tell whose children these are. The people who are ashamed because they're ashamed of these children. The people. I leave everything on the cork hanging on the door. Lists and instructions and bills and it gets done. By somebody. I don't even shop. I don't have a car. I've never even driven one. Half the time I don't even know who brings the groceries.

You never leave here?

She was stroking Jonah's head and then she quit. How could I?

Somebody could stay with them.

Who?

How would I know? Somebody.

Nobody would.

She began again to stroke Jonah's head. She looked at the boy. She looked across the kitchen at Rene who was sitting at the table and had very quietly put a scoop of chocolate ice cream in a bowl over which she'd poured orange juice and sprinkled loose parsley flakes from the spice rack and she was stirring the concoction and staring into it like Narcissus into the pool. Why would anyone want to?

By now most of the children had come down from their beds and they were standing around silently picking sleep out of their eyes and looking quietly down at Jonah. Some were sipping juice to which they had helped themselves. Anna laid the thin rag around the swollen, bluing break and placed the bag of ice on it and wrapped it around quickly and firmly with the elastic bandage and elevated the leg on a pillow. Chris came in with Samuel and Anna said, Chris, goddamn you, what the hell is wrong with your head? How many times do I have to tell you? You are his legs. You are his legs. Samuel, hum to him, hum to Jonah while I go outside and hang this boy from a tree.

Zach thought that he ought to be going to town to make the call but he was riveted on the boy. Samuel moved slowly through the small group and they opened for him like he had been summoned from some great distance to perform a rite. He looked at Jonah and put a hand on his wrist and assembled himself and Zach thought for a moment that he was going to pray. He began to hum atonally and the other children stood around in a reverence of which they were not unaware. Jonah looked peaceful and no one moved. Zach felt some sadness that was also a great clemency rise up in his own chest and he had no idea from where the feeling came. Everyone stood stock still until the boy stopped humming. Then Zach walked outside. It was wet and there was no wind and the sky was perfectly blue. All manner of strewn foliature lay about the place from the storm the night before. He looked across the lot and he saw Anna bent over the boy Chris talking directly into his upturned, streaming face and then he saw her look across at him. He swung his leg over the bike and started the engine and then he saw her pick the boy up and hold him in her arms.

He sat the bike and watched her carry the boy back into the house. Then he cut the engine. When he walked back into the kitchen the children were scattered, sitting at tables some of them and others were pulling food out of the refrigerator and the cupboards. Samuel was sleeping on the boy Jonah. Or at least it looked like it. His head was turned to the side, resting on Jonah's stomach, rising and falling with the breath. Anna thought she was alone, that is, she thought Zach was gone; her back was to the door. She was speaking very softly into Chris's head, mouthing the words upon his actual hair, and the boy was nodding with great earnestness as she spoke, pulling a clump of her hair in the fist of one hand as if to emphasize the listening. She set him down and pushed him away gently and she looked at Jonah and Samuel for a moment with her hands on her hips and then she opened the refrigerator and began taking out eggs. Why don't I just take him? Zach said.

She turned around quickly. She colored a little.

It will save the doctor the trip. Four trips, if I can count correctly.

Anna studied him. She looked at Jonah. Samuel's eyes were open. Jonah's were still closed. Catlin'll never come out here. He sends somebody.

It will save somebody four trips.

How would you get him there?

On the bike. We could splint his leg.

That road's going to hurt like hell.

It's the same road.

That's true. You would do that?

It's my idea.

She looked at him. She looked at Jonah. She looked at Samuel who looked at her and nodded. All right, she said.

She went around to the back of the house and returned with an array of plank boards and Samuel came from the shed with some bungee cords and ropes. They laid one board up under the leg and the other alongside and strapped them tightly and then they picked Jonah up and carried him out of the house, one on each side with Samuel semaphoring them toward the motorcy- cle as if Anna and Zach and the suspended boy were castaways lost at sea and he was reeling them in with glowing lights in his hands. They sat Jonah on the rear of the seat. He looked like an ornament. Even in his pain he seemed to enjoy the process. Samuel went again to the shed and came out with more rope and began to mummy his leg and Jonah laughed and then his face went blank with pain and then he laughed again. Samuel stepped back and looked at the wrapping. Crossed his arms like an artist before a mural, like he was haggling an aesthetic. Then he unwrapped him and rewrapped him and walked around looking at the bike and the perched boy. Anna and Zach were watching him. He held up a finger. When he came back he had a floating life vest. He lifted it up to Jonah and the boy put his arms through the holes and Samuel stepped back again, mulling. Then he held up a finger. Zach and Anna looked at each other. When he came back he had a red bandanna. He couldn't reach. He made the motion of tying it around his own head and then handed it to Zach and with his jutting chin he indicated Jonah. Again Zach looked at Anna. Anna looked at the ground and then back at Samuel and shook her head. Then she walked back into the house.

Zach tied the bandanna onto Jonah's head and swung his leg through and started the engine. Anna came out of the house again and ran down the steps. She stuck a piece of paper in the front pocket of the field jacket which Zach wore, which was hers, which had been her father's, and buttoned it. Here's his home number too, in case it's a weekend. I don't know where his office is. His name is Catlin. Robert Catlin. He won't charge you. You may have to wait all day but he won't charge you.

I'll see you, Zach said.

He gunned the throttle and Samuel stepped back and saluted them with an exaggerated officialdom and then he fell down on the ground laughing at his own theatrics for exactly three seconds of outright hysteria and Jonah laughed and Samuel stood up just as suddenly and patted Jonah's back reassuringly like a father at a station sending his son off to college. Zach put the bike in gear and lifted his feet to the pegs and Jonah put his arms around his waist and held him very tightly and they sped off up the road. Samuel's face grew serious, almost severe. He watched them until they were gone.

They stopped at the filling station at the exchange and Zach called the office. It was a Thursday. The secretary told him to hold the line and then she came back and gave him directions. Twenty five minutes later, his face numb from the wind, he pulled into the gravel drive. The office was near the center of town, off the old square, across from a Kroger and a laundromat, in a brick building with paintchipped wooden pillars upon a foreshortened porch which was more than a landing and less than a gallery. He waited seven and a quarter hours. He told the boy whatever stories he could think of. He told him about Virginia. About Virginia in the fall. About the Shenandoah at dusk, at dawn. He told him about the life cycle of the leaf and then Jonah slept and Zach even nodded off for a time. At a quarter to five the secretary left and locked the door behind her and turned the sign to closed and opened the door back up and looked at Zach and said, He'll be out in a jiffy.

Five minutes later a shortish, bespectacled, silverhaired but not old man came through the lobby door and said, Jonah my boy, where've you been all my life? I don't believe we've met, he said to Zach, holding out his hand. Catlin. Doctor Catlin.

Zach.

The doctor had a sturdy, middleaged, well kept handsomeness; his hair was of that perfectly combed and stiffwedged quality as if some newfangled aerodynamic flying toy had fallen on his head. His hands were fleshy and pink, his eyebrows long and steelcolored and curving and his countenance was one of subtle but effortful tolerance as if he spent much of his life accommodating people's underachievement. He stood looking Zach over. He pursed his lips and drummed his fingers on the side of his thigh. He had the seemingly sourceless and perennial nervous habit of some men in all walks of life whereupon but for when they are actively working or talking a thigh is always shaking or they are chewing gum or drumming their hands so that when his fingers ceased on his thigh his jaw commenced and when the jaw ceased he smoothed out his unwrinkled overcoat and then his thigh shook anew and the cycle began again.

I appreciate you doing this, Zach said.

Surely. He looked at him again. It's nothing but my Christian duty, aint that right Jonah? You live here in Marjolaine?

No sir. I'm—

I didn't think so. Didn't think I'd seen you before.

He looked at Jonah. Well, son, old hat, aint that right? He ruffled his head.

Jonah turned away slightly, not entirely impolitely, but enough so that the gesture ceased and he nodded once in the man's direction without any expression at all. Let's get to it, the doctor said.

A half an hour later Catlin came through the door and sat. He'll need to stay supine a piece before we move him. He doesn't feel anything at all now anyway. I gave him a tinker of morphine.

He began filling a pipe and lit it, sucking at it loudly, squinting, looking up at Zach and waving the match in the air to cool it and placing it gently in the ashtray on the coffee table. He put up his feet. So where'd you say you were from?

I'm from Virginia. Charlottesville.

Charlottesville. They've got a dandy medical school out there. Dandy. So how is it that you come to know Mr. Jonah? You know Doris?

Doris?

Miriam then?

No, I haven't met anyone named—

How is it that you know Jonah?

Zach looked at him. There was a tone, an unpleasant imperativeness not even quite below the surface of the interrogation and Zach thought that perhaps it was a cantankerousness simply native to the man. I'm staying out there in the Kisatchie at the place called The Lake.

The doctor put a cupped hand to his ear. What's that?

I'm staying out there with the kids at The Lake.

Catlin swiveled in his seat, turned his knees the other direction so that he looked at Zach now with a sideways squiz. You're staying out there? In the bottom? You're with that woman?

Anna?

You're staying out there with the Beauchamp girl?

Is her name Anna?

Yes it is.

Then I am. I mean, I'm just staying in the house. She sewed up my mouth.

I see that, Catlin said. I mistook you. I thought Doris had mentioned some swarthier kin. You're living out there?

Until this heals and she takes out the stitches, I guess I am.

The doctor looked at him and his eyes narrowed, for the smoke or not. You're living out there?

Zach just looked at him.

Are you now, Catlin said. It's just I haven't heard of anybody living out there in all my life.

There's a lot of people out there. There's eleven children out there. And Anna.

That I know son. That I know. You don't have to come all the way from Charlottesville Virginia to figure that out though, do you? to tell a man who inhabits his own darn forest now, do you?

Pardon? Zach said.

Catlin pulled on his pipe and looked at Zach apologetically. As if his own acerbity was a necessary and distasteful pharmaceutical the doctor had himself prescribed for the young man and just administered for his ultimate good. Or more his look bore an altogether moralistic patience as if Zach had needed a kind of lashing in order to come into his own rightful moral bigamy that he might thereby fraternize with some of the grit of the world, which, the doctor's haughty and removed patience seemed to imply, was what it was to be a man.

What did you say your name was?

Zach.

I mean, Zach, we all know that here in Marjolaine. It's just nobody's ever lived out there. Are there eleven of them out there now?

Yes.

Any niggers?

Pardon?

Does she have any more niggers out there?

Zach looked at him and then he looked at the wall across. There's a boy who looks half black whose name is Wah—

The mulatto. The mulatto boy from Bayou Saint John. He still out there? I'll be darn. Let me tell you something, son. That's no place for a righteous man. You ought not to be out there at all. I'm just telling you as a good Christian. You ought not to be. Folks don't even talk about the place anymore. People always said Lance Beauchamp was a nigger lover but he was a heck of a hand at just about anything and he'd help a fellow out, from horses to our Lord's own trade, and he served up the devil's own I'm told better and cheaper than anyone this side of the Sabine though I myself don't partake of drink so I can't rightly say but the town looked yonder over their shoulders like a good Christian ought sometimes out of his duty to protect his ways and his folk. But sometimes it just happens. The other day I was watching something about it on television where a girl in Wyoming, the valedictorian of her high school class, walked out one day in a snowstorm and made her way buck naked to the barn and started eating grain right out of the tubs and just froze to death, her hand still in her mouth. Her parents thought she was up the stairs at her homework.

He shook his head as if he felt sorry for the world. The devil has his ways. The town said she just went crazy when he died.

Who?

Beauchamp's girl.

Anna?

That's right. We heard she went and lived with a nigger

woman in the Saint John. And when she came back she had that half nigger boy with her like she was its flesh bearing mother. And for a time we thought that she was. We darn sure thought it could be. But he was too old, by just a hair now mind you— he made now an infinitesimal measurement between his fingers—and it didn't figure. But you would have thought she was by the way she took him into that house, that cursed house because the devil already'd been living there in more ways than one I declare. And started putting needles in him and singing. Standing over him and sticking him with needles and singing nigger songs and the house all full of nigger herbs and nigger potions from top to bottom. Out there all by herself and wouldn't even come to town for groceries. That's what the town told.

That's acupuncture, Zach said.

I don't care what in damnation you call it, it's nothin the good Lord was meant to look down upon and see and condone with His own hand. Least of all on a nigger.

For a moment, for a quarter of a moment, the men looked at each other. The late afternoon light was straining at the shut blinds. The doctor smoothed out his jacket, relit his pipe, and looked up at the clock. And then he looked across at Zach and assembled his expression into patience, into compassion, and spoke to him as to a child who had to be convinced of the body's need for vegetables.

I know what you're thinkin. I can see you are an intelligent young man. I know what you're thinkin. You don't have to be Albert Switzer to tell what you're thinkin. I can see by your face Virginia already borders up on Canada. Don't it? You're not from these parts, son, and you wouldn't know a damn thing about it. You wouldn't know a damn thing about the nigger. You think it's wrong of me. You think I should just serve every hurt or sick man woman and child and woollyheaded charity case that comes across my door. Don't you. I did once for that mulatto out of my Christian duty but let me tell you something. A Christian is not a Christian without foresight, you might even could call it clairvoyance. For instance Jesus. When he gathered the men to fish with him for the souls of men, you think he really needed those men to save the world eternally? He was God. Those men were just men. So why'd he gather them? Why'd he make them fishermen of men? Because he knew a man could only come to a man, not to a God. A God was too much. The people needed to grow into the light of the Lord slowly. Jesus had foresight, see. The people weren't ready for God. So he picked his seedlings and said, Follow them, learn from them. And let me tell you something. The people found God. Glory be, they sure did. They saw the light not through God himself but through the lesser beings, the minions, God's supporting cast put there before their eyes by Jesus himself. See now?

Zach leaned forward and stared between his knees. His face was hot, burning.

The fishermen were to Jesus what the nigger is to us. The nigger is a seedling. After all these years he's still a seedling. If I go and serve every one of em that comes in here how are they going to develop their own? How could I live with myself if I held back their progress? I'm telling you a Christian has to have foresight. Do you know what melanin is?

Zach exhaled in disbelief. I have a decent portion of it myself, he said.

That's right, you do. You do for a fact. But the nigger, look at him. He's made for the sun. The purpose of melanin—

I'm aware of the purpose of melanin.

He doesn't get cancer. Nature's smart. She knew the nigger was designed to work all his life so she made his skin strong, impervious to the sun. You put him inside in an office or a school and he's at a loss. He's a seedling. And I'm not a racist. I'm not. I know what you're thinkin. But it just breaks my heart the hill of his own self the nigger has to climb. Read yourself Booker T. Washington. Read Ives McGee. They'll tell you themselves. Nature herself is against him. She don't even want him to come inside. I would not stand in his way. I would not serve his own so that he might not begin to grow, hard as it is for him to learn. It's my Christian duty.

Zach could taste the bile in his mouth. He sat up straight. We have to go, he said. He stood and looked at the door behind which Jonah perhaps was sleeping. He turned. That means I ought to spend my life under a parasol. Or some lattice that I hold everywhere above my head.

What's that? the doctor said.

I'm a quarter Navajo Indian.

The doctor's eyebrows lifted. His molded balcony of white hair shifted slightly backward on his skull like a loose toupee in a stiff breeze.

If I'm to produce at all in accordance with my epidermal station your god made me to work and think and eat and sleep under a semi-permeable parasol. Or some lattice to filter just so much sun, right? Or only between the hours of six thirty and seven forty five in the morning and what, five thirty and seven at night, right? And for you with your pallor to live and work and eat and sleep in the basement all your life and in the sunless dark of night with your food and drink and defecation pot lowered and raised to and from you on a pulley like Jefferson used for his wine at Monticello so that the infrared rays won't defrock you of your race's translucent robes. That is if we are to further your axiom to its inevitable conclusion, which is the only way to judge an axiom's soundness.

I have no idea what you're talking about young man.

You're an intelligent man, Zach said, aren't you?

Catlin gestured across the room at the line of diplomas and certificates above his desk as if they were oathed witnesses to the faculty of his mind and he tried to look amused though he was galled and coloring, deeply.

Then surely you've heard of Francis Bacon. Surely you've heard of his critique of what he called the anticipation of nature. You mentioned nature, did you not?

I did.

Bacon understood that banal minds formulate principles or laws which one regards as necessarily true—a supremacist's de-

mentia, for instance—and then one goes looking for phenomena to explain it.

I have not had my dinner, Catlin said.

You're an idol of the tribe.

I'm a what?

In the *Novum Organum* Bacon delineated his Idols, ways the
human mind often goes awry. In the Idol of the Tribe he tells us
that our great tendency is to notice phenomena which confirm
our views—

Get your boy and leave.

And to ignore and fail to see phenomena which disconfirm
the theories we hold.

Get the hell out of my office.

Zach looked at the man's perfect, plasticine hair. The body's
degeneration for instance. It would be like concluding that a
man with gray hair albeit in the prime of his life was also impo-
tent.

God dammit to hell! Get your—

You're a textbook exemplar. Sunlight, melanin, labor and
race prejudice. I've heard stronger axioms in grade school.
Thank you for fixing his leg.

He walked through the receiving door and searched the
rooms until he saw Jonah and he picked him up in his arms and
carried him back through the lobby and to the front door and
stopped under the threshold like a man with his bride suddenly
unsure about the enterprise. Again he turned and looked at
Catlin. And that woman, as you call her. I've been out there a
few days now and I haven't seen her eating any grain.

He carried Jonah out into the lot and set him on the back of the
motorcycle and strapped the cast firmly to the seat chrome and
drove toward the exchange. He was livid to the point of nausea.
Jonah was woozy but alert enough to hold on and the cold rushing air finished the process. By the time Zach got to the ex-

change his heart had stopped racing and he began to feel better. Then he began to feel good. The sky was just a wide wintry canvas of darkest purples and orange tints and rose over the western trees. He pictured Anna and The Lake and the boy called Samuel and all the children about the gallery. It would be the dinner hour. He turned the throttle hard and Jonah grabbed him tight for the surging.

Lazar! he yelled out loud. Forgive me one diatribe!

He laughed into the wind which blew his hair and filled his mouth and watered his eyes.

Tree! he shouted, to appease the spirit of the old man.

Grass! Dirt road! Motorcycle! Sky! And for three or four seconds, at sixty miles an hour with the broken boy behind him screaming at the top of his lungs to quit it and steer, he let go of both handlebars and held out his arms.

December 14

A plant on the hallway sill—looks like an anemone, the webs of
Edmund's arms, transparent under the armpits when he was
naked in the bath, the bath! she put him under and he said 'rock
and roll', laughing, I've never heard such laughter, lion's paw
bathtub, dark green towel I ruffled his head with, olive oil soap,
July sleeps with her toothbrush in her hand, my legs—two
anchors hanging off the chair, an old sawdust ant hill on the
baseboard, Patricia slobbering in a pink jumpsuit, Chris banging
his head on the wall when I came in late this morning, offering
him lunch like bait, like bait for what? his mind? a basket of
thirty six pairs of shoes and boots in the hall, beeswax in the
bathroom and the kitchen, candles in the upstairs bathroom,
candles? Anna, Anna, I love her name, this very good wool
blanket, thanks, dandelion herb tincture, Rene chewing my

fingers talking about dolphins, chicken coop, westerly wind, what exactly is a zephyr? yard strewn with light, olives, feta cheese, olive oil, oregano, basil, thyme, garlic crystals on the tines of the fork, Anna in a woven shawl on the swing, July's huge eyes—chestnut, fishing line around the stems of the herbal bouquets, Jonah's oversized veteran's cap, fish soup, melon, icecubes in sunlight, gas lantern, broken glass, red earth, pumice stone, oil lamp, leather chaps, stirrup irons, oatmeal, honey, corn, clay brick, ladle, broken phonograph, oak table, candelabra, wax, neck of the wine bottle, tallow, coffee grinds, woodgrain, tongs, hair, braided hair, loose hair, dark hair, wind-ruined hair, maple syrup, pear preserves, rock chimney, mud chinking, tree stump, woven basket, embers, horseshoe, manger, horseshit, alfalfa, oats, wheelbarrow, trough, elkskin gloves, wheatberries, eyetooth, cantaloupe, orange, sesame seeds, Orion, pine shadow, new moon, new moon, new moon, sable brush, watercolors, wool beret, trowel, spade, yucca root soap, mallard duck, blue grass, elk den, carriage bolt, gate valve, jack rafter, baseball mitt, broken accordion, iron box, ripsaw, rolled sail, dinghy, oars, dock, turpentine, staddle stone, banister, oarlocks, kerosene, calendula, calendula, hashbrowns, old froe, rusty bolt, fireplace mantel, mahogany sideboard, chimney flashings, eaves troughing, licorice seeds, ballast, burnt stump, bread crust, mung beans, copper basin, burlap bag, snaffle bit, egg butt bit, saddle blanket, spider web, bridle, rubber boots, chickpeas, braided rug, armoire, keel,

wood resin, pewter dish, cream sauce, chanterelle mushrooms,
egg noodles, red wine, muddy boots, chin stubble, denim apron,
router, wood plane, jigsaw, chop saw, elbow wrench, lake breeze,
frost, chisel, crowbar, eyelash, wool socks, whiskey crate, frozen
rhubarb, metronome, axle, barley, dust, adze, cotton tick, corn
husk pillow, her jeans, white blouse, blouse, blouse, teakettle,
bare feet, hot coals, sauerkraut, lye, lard, quilt, lug chain, wicker
basket, rake, dried thistle, leather shoestring, mallet, bell clapper,
rusted sprout cans, eggshells, compost, handkerchief, kindling,
sawdust soaked in diesel fuel, shredded wheat, fresh milk, elk,
bananas, July's diapers, spigot, her voice, chicory root tea, this
living hand.

CHAPTER TWENTY TWO

In the early evening of their seventh day of travelling they came upon a dell along a creek near Negreet which came down from the north off the Sabine and ran under the road and forked in the middle of the sunken clearing and diminished on one hand and increased on the other, the strong branch bending to the west and out of sight behind some trees the roots of which shored up a knoll of beachedup tawny dirt like the belly of a small overturned whale. The clearing had been or still was some kind of park. Where the diminished rivulet all but finished into the ground there was a wooden jungle gym of sorts and a tether pole and a square boxframe of railroad ties which must have at one time held sand. Samuel leapt out of the crate and Zach swung his leg over and walked the bicycle down the grade and, stopping to take off his boots and socks and put them in the basket in front, he lifted the bike over his shoulder and walked through the stream and the water took his breath and his feet ached and the sun was not quite gone so that he saw, when he began to step up the other side, his shadow laid out long across the meadow. He stood there and contemplated it while the pain in his feet increased and then decreased and then disappeared altogether, as if the feet themselves were gone, standing there in the freezing alizarin water listening for Samuel's steps behind him on the alluvial shelf, which he didn't hear. He turned around. The boy was still on the other bank. Looking at Zach with that perplexed look which was already becoming benign mocking derision, head cocked to the side, one toe pointing in front of him and just scratching lightly at the ground as if somehow across that spread of grass and gurgling stream the slight sound of his toe in the dirt might get Zach's attention, like the clearing of a throat in a throng. What? Zach said. What have I done?

Samuel looked left, leading with his chin like a grown man indicating, and Zach saw that there was a little bridge not twenty five yards upstream, made of three trees laid crosswise to the creek and glued by moss and worn atop to an almost soapy sheen by years of use. My feet were hot.

He called it across the stream. They were sweaty, he said.

Samuel walked to the bridge, slightly slower than he usually walked, and crossed it walking backwards. When he reached the end of the log he did not turn around but dipped his toe behind him as if he were checking the temperature of water. He stepped on the land gingerly and did a pirouette and took five steps toward the man, looking at him all the while, and stopped and lifted his arms to the sides with the palms up as if he was receiving the great Lord's applause and turned a full circle around finishing in a kind of helix. Then he bowed.

You know what Nate says? You're a piece of work. Samuel you're a piece of work.

Along the banks of the fuller fork there was a small group of army reserves standing about a truck and they were drinking beer from a keg out of the bed. When Zach and Samuel came into view it was apparent that they were a curiosity. The men clustered together and pointed. Zach paid them no mind but Samuel looked back at them. Then one of the men waved and hollered hello. Another did the same. Zach ignored them but Samuel waved back. Zach looked at the boy. He looked across the river. Samuel waved again, vigorously. They all waved back and began to shout together in a chorus to come across. You want a beer? one of the men called.

Zach was about to call out no thanks when he saw Samuel nodding yes. What are you doing? he said, but the boy was already walking toward the group, skipping really, already taking off his shoes and rolling up his pants and running now through the shallow neck of water and jumping up on the bank. Zach followed him. The men were obviously taken with the boy. When he came up they surrounded him and smacked him on the back like an old comrade. Zach stood for a few seconds on the near side of the river in amazement because Samuel was not gregarious; he was a prankster, he was a miniature buddha and a fool and a sage, but he was not a socializer. Zach wheeled the bike up and kicked down the stand and walked up to the group. I'm Zach, he said, shaking hands all around.

Samuel imitated him, shaking hands all around with mock formality, shadowing Zach in a vaudeville fashion and then a man started boxing with him. Samuel began to pull from those vast Samuel stores of god knows how many lifetimes of knowledge some Chinese kung fu that looked for all the world if not practiced at least plausible and even a little dangerous. The men were watching and applauding. Samuel would land a harmless but artful blow and they would roar and taunt their mate and he would pretend to redouble his effort and Samuel would land another blow and they'd roar again. They seemed already to understand somehow that the boy couldn't or didn't speak and it did not matter and Samuel kicked the air in front of the man and in makebelieve defeat the man fell dramatically to the ground and two men carried him off between them on a make-believe stretcher and Samuel came flushed and breathing back to Zach and leaned up against him. Zach put a hand on his head and said, His name's Samuel. He looked down at the boy. When were you in China?

Samuel looked up at him and squinted his eyes.

They were a regiment on leave from a nearby base and this was their first night free and they were camping by the river.

There were sixteen men and they were waiting for their leader, a man named Garth, who had continued on for hot dogs and burger meat and buns when the others had turned down toward the river. Presently they heard the throaty sound of a motorcycle coming down the dirt road. The man was driving with one hand and leaning back saying something into the ear of a girl on the back. He pulled up and cut the engine and she climbed off and shimmied her body shucking the pack off her shoulders and slung it in the bed of the nearest truck. The men just broke into action upon his arrival, pulling hibachi ovens out of their cars and trucks and putting up tents and carrying bags in one hand and beers in the other and cajoling each other and scuffling in little pockets and moving on, making camp. Garth came and stood next to Zach and they shook hands and exchanged names and Garth handed him a beer and fetched another for himself and came back and nodded at the bike. How far you fellows going on that thing?

We're going to Arizona.

He seemed to consider it. That's a long way on that kind of bike. If I can remember right they only have one gear.

That's right, Zach said.

Garth looked at him. You look strong. I'd wager you'll make it. Where'd you come from?

Marjolaine.

I've never been there. Is it pretty?

Zach looked at him. He was probably in his early twenties. In hair and skin color he looked not unlike Zach himself and the two men seemed to acknowledge this without mentioning it. Garth stood with his legs slightly splayed and Zach found that he had assumed something of the posture himself without even knowing it and they appraised the improbable bicycle with their arms crossed at their chests and their beers in hand. He wore a tight black T-shirt and no jacket even though it was below forty degrees not to mention the windchill on the motorcycle and his forearms were dark and stripped with muscle and he wore Levi's jeans with a chain dangling from the belt loops and he wore the army issue boots. The men deferred to him without question as if he had around him a breadth both physically and impalpably sound which could not be entered or challenged or broached in any way and which breadth was measured—had been and would surely again be measured—by exactly the length of swinging fists. But all was calm now as an equine remuda sleepy and digestate in a meadow after a meal. He had a pack of cigarettes in his shirt pocket and he took one out and lit it and offered one to Zach and Zach said no thank you. The girl came up and nodded at Zach and Garth handed her the cigarette and she drew on it and tilted back her head and blew smoke and handed it back.

Yes, Zach said, we're from the Kisatchie. It's beautiful.

I'll have to see it then.

He pulled on the cigarette and handed it back to the girl. This is Jess, he said. Jess, this is Zach. He and that redhaired boy are travelling to Arizona on that bicycle.

She nodded at Zach demurely. Wow, she said quietly, almost in a whisper.

She was young, in her late teens, possibly twenty. She wore a black shirt too only it said Lynyrd Skynyrd on the front and on the back it had a long list of cities where the rock band had toured some year past and she wore very tight jeans faded almost to bareness at the knees and at the rear and beatup holey tennis shoes with the laces undone. She was very pretty with her aquiline nose and delicate cuneiform bones and her pale almost translucent skin and her flat dirty blond hair and her muted green eyes whose lids were painted modestly with blue shadow which was the only makeup she wore unless you counted her nails which were painted red and badly chipped. Zach had already seen how the men did not look at her and Zach did not look at her long either.

Garth told him about the regiment, where they were stationed and what plans they had for their leave and he named the men, pointing to them in turn according to that invisible rank which prevails upon men in groups and all the more so upon those whose very construct and purpose is at least potential combat and who live therefore daily with the knowledge that all the artifice of civilization can drain in a second on the hoarse throat of a single command and so he named them; he told Zach something of the character of each one and of their longevity in the group. Come on and get yourself a dog, he said, and the three of them walked over to the group most of whom were already eating, stuffing the hot dogs into their mouths with one hand, a beer in the other, some of them trying to catch and throw a football at the same time, holding the cup in their teeth with the beer sloshing out over their faces and down their chins or the cup dropping altogether to the ground and them cursing it like a last broken egg. Garth broke off to toss the ball with them and immediately three footballs came sailing his way from the three respective groups and he caught two of them, one in each hand, and dove for the third and missed and rolled and scooped it up and tossed it back before he'd even stood. Samuel was sitting with a group of men who were talking low and seriously and he was sitting among them as if he'd been with them his whole life and was in fact crucial to whatever plan or strategy they were making there squatting or sitting on folded tarpaulins in the dirt. When Zach came up they nodded at him and moved aside to make a space and Samuel nodded at him too gravely as if Zach were the stranger and Zach pushed him over and he fell backward and pretended that he was dead.

When it was dark they all sat around a fire and they told each other stories from their lives and they wanted to know about Zach and he told him the truth, the whole story, abbreviated, from the university to the hospital to the streets of New Orleans and the shelter and The Lake and the search for his real parents on the bicycle. When he was done they all said that he had a lot of balls and that he ought to write a book about it and they wished him luck and told him that he would find his parents because blood is thick and he said that he hoped it was so.

The whole time Garth listened very carefully and when the men spoke of their own lives in the army they often finished the story by looking at him and saying, Aint that right, Garth? and he'd nod slowly and smoke and pass his cigarette to his girl and she would smoke and pass it back and then she sat between his legs and lay her head back against him and Zach felt sick with longing and not for her either.

Suddenly a man sat up. Did you see that? he said. Did you see that motherfucking star? I've never seen a shooting star that long in my whole life. Did anybody see that?

Kurt, you are one blockheaded son of a bitch, another man said. That was a spark, that weren't no star.

There goes Orion, another man said, hefting up his belt and pointing to some rising char above the flames and laughing.

The logs cracked and a slew of sparks flew up and someone said something about the Milky Way.

Fuck you, Kurt said, flipping the whole group off as if he was scanning them around with his middle finger.

I saw it, Jess said, softly. It was a star.

Garth looked down at her. He removed a tiny flake of tobacco or wood ash that had landed on her cheek. He looked into the flames. He looked up at the firmament. Gentlemen, he said. That must have been a star.

CHAPTER TWENTY THREE

The third time Zach went to gas the motorcycle and fill the cans it was just after five o'clock and Nate was sitting in the office reading the paper. When Zach walked in he said, They dug up Elvis and it wasn't him. It's just amazing what people leave on their dashboards. You'd despair of the whole damned thing if all you knew about was what people left on their dashboards.

He helicoptered the tabloid toward the waste basket. Way you talk you might be able to write for one of these. Maybe even own one one day. What can I do you for?

I'd like to work off that hay.

Oh lord.

Pardon?

Oh as in Oh no. Lord as in our father above. He looked Zach up and down, shaking his head.

What? Zach said.

You've gone chivalric. I can feel it.

He looked at him some more, then he picked up his appointment book and flipped through it without looking at it at all and smacked it down on the desk. All right.

When? Zach said.

Pick a day.

Now. Today.

Nate leaned back and looked at the clock on the wall which now said ten minutes after five o'clock and nodded toward it and looked back at Zach with one eyebrow shot up two inches above the other as if he'd proposed something unheard of in the history of the world, like a joyride to the moon on the back of a generator.

Tomorrow, Zach said.

All right.

What day is it?

Today or tomorrow?

Today.

Today's Monday.

Tuesday then.

Tuesdays?

Tuesdays.

Tuesdays at 6:30. Before 6:30.

All right.

Anna doesn't even have a clock out there, does she?

No, I'll be here.

How?

I'll get up. I'm already up, Zach said, smiling.

All right.

All right.

He started changing oil and air filters and cleaning people's cars but soon he was replacing fan belts and adjusting the timing and patching and changing tires with the foot powered hydraulic. He worked mostly with the boy everyone called Joe on account of his shirt. (Only his father called him Bobbie.) The boy worked exactly like his father worked, with slow seriousness and a calm sad face and with an air of almost feminine perfection, picking lint off the car seat after he had vacuumed, writing out a customer receipt with such care it seemed more like he was carving a feature in an ink linoleum block. They walked and stood and even chewed gum identically, moving it around in their mouths when they were weighing a matter and chewing again when they'd come to a decision.

On Zach's second Tuesday they were under the hood of an ancient Buick and Nate was compressing water into the radiator. Bend down there a minute, he said, and see if it's coming out of the overflow or the grid.

Zach knelt under the car. The radiator. In two places.

High or low?

Low.

Oh well, Nate said, and when Zach stood he handed him a screwdriver. Go to, boss.

A half an hour later Zach was still under the car trying to extricate the thing and he was cursing. You seem awful irritated, Nate said. You're scaring my business off. He was bending down and shining the flashlight on Zach's chafed face and he was grinning.

You know they've got two-stepping over at Shall's on Tuesday nights. Or bingo at Liberty Hall. If you like older ladies. It might do you some good.

I'm all right, Zach said. It's just one more screw.

That's the problem with them sons of bitches. There's always one more screw.

In the evening they were at the sink washing up. Nate passed Zach the soap and Zach looked at it in his hand and said, What do you know about Doctor Catlin?

I can tell you he's a bigoted bible thumping fool and that I hit him in the mouth almost twenty five years ago when we were fresh out of school and I've never once regretted it. And that little blind one Patricia out there at The Lake is his daughter's girl though nobody's going to tell you that.

Really?

I said so.

What can you tell me about Anna's dad?

I can tell you that he's dead. There won't be another one like him and he's dead.

He dried his hands on the towel and walked away. A moment later he came back into the washroom. Do you know how to weld?

Zach shook his head no.

I didn't think so.

After lunch the following week Nate pointed to some milk crates full of scrap steel and old mufflers and told Zach to bring one of them over. Put your helmet on, he said, or else you'll go blind and blame me for all your troubles.

He showed Zach how to take the grinder and make a valley between the stock so as to get penetration in the weld and how to set the gas and the voltage for the thickness of the stock. He showed him also how to hold the gun at an angle and to move along the seam steadily in accordance with the heat and speed of the wire feed and how to run a smooth bead thereby. But Zach's beads looked nothing like Nate's, more like bad caulk around the rim of a tub. Nate told him to run beads on the scraps until five o'clock and that the following Tuesday, if they looked decent, he'd let him tack on mufflers.

By the end of the day his work looked less horrible. He was very tired from concentrating without ceasing for four hours and his head hurt and his eyes ached seemingly behind their pupils. His arms were sunburnt and speckled with tiny raised burns and his shirt had about a hundred tiny holes singed in the chest. He had just kickstarted the bike when Nate came out of the office with a large bag. I almost forgot, he said. Miriam set these aside for you.

What is it?

They're cookies.

Cookies?

Christmas cookies.

Christmas? When is Christmas?

Nate looked at him. He took off his hat and wiped his arm across his forehead. Christmas is Wednesday next, son.

I didn't know that. Thank you, he said, stuffing the bag in his pack and sliding his arms through the straps.

He steered the bike home in the dark, over the two corroding bridges toward the bottom and the lake. He saw the lights from the house through the trees and as he pulled up to the shed children came running from the gallery and they called him by his name.

CHAPTER TWENTY FOUR

In the third dream he was in a lecture hall. The dream at first was hardly a dream at all because he was speaking to a large audience on the topic of philosophy which he did every quarter as part of his fellowship requirement. The hall was full and he was speaking with great eloquence and everyone from the firstyears to the deans was nodding with conviction and solemnity at everything he said. And this was no dream at all but simply his life and he was feeling that familiar quality of pride that is not hubris but its cousin whereupon it is the very combination of humility and intelligence that is impressive in the man, and he knew that what he said was true because it was fraught with inconclusion and erudite to the core and he looked up with the resonance of this on his face, so close to smugness, so close, and he saw Anna in the front row in her clothes of The Lake and her hair was mussed and beautiful for it and her face was horrified and she had mulesnot on her tank and mud on her boots and she was looking at him trying to speak and he began to stumble. In his talk he began to stumble which he never did and he began to say antidisestablishmentarianism in the middle of his sentences and he could not avoid the word antidisestablishmentarianism and

he saw rows of heretofore rapt audience begin to stir and mut-
ter and he felt himself begin to blubber and the word took
dominion over his talk and he covered his mouth as if some
pestilence came forth from it and he looked to Anna and saw
that her chair was empty and an impeccably dressed dean came
forward and led him like a convalescent to that very chair and
gave him a glass of water and he could not drink and the dean
shook his head sadly and whispered something into another
man's ear and Zach woke up.

CHAPTER TWENTY FIVE

They built the wall in three days. Anna measuring and cutting the joists and Zach clamping and nailing them to the top and bottom plates. Samuel handing him nails silently in earnest as if he was crucial to the project. Anna wanted the reading room split in two so she could read the children's tales to those who wanted to listen and, through a window, still keep an eye on those who had no constitution for sitting for stories. They put in two windows at Zach's suggestion simply because after she'd shown him how he took a particular liking to curtailing the studs for the structural void just so betwixt the trimmer boards and the headers. On the first window Anna cut the header board too short twice in a row and each time Zach just handed them back to her and made silently an unwavering space between his thumb and forefinger and that was all. On the third day Nate came with the Sheetrock and they measured out the wall again and scored the gypsum with a utility knife and broke it off across the edge of one of the low rectangular tables in the kitchen and nailed it up horizontally, two of them to hold and one to nail and Samuel standing back directing everyone in silence. As if he was crucial to the project. As if without him some flaw in the layout could prove fatal and he alone would be responsible. When the drywall was up Nate showed Zach how to spackle in the joint compound and tape it along the seam and feather it out until the butt ends of the Sheetrock disappeared and the wall was smooth. Then he went to his truck and came back with some paint and brushes and rollers and trays and shook all three of their hands as if he didn't know them at all or knew them so well it didn't matter and clapped Zach hard on the back and left. Anna went out to the yard. Zach turned and looked at Samuel and smiled, inordinately. They spent the rest of the afternoon spackling and taping and painting. Samuel at the corners with the small brush, high on a ladder or low lying prostrate on his stomach on the floor, and Zach with the roller on the main.

Later when they came in to dinner the children had already eaten. They got their plates and sat side by side at the table sitting in identical postures and even identical rhythm of fork to mouth to swallow. At the double sinks Anna and July were washing dishes and Jonah was drying them, sitting on a chair with his dead legs dangling and his braces crossed in his lap and handing the dishes to Chris who was standing on a stool and putting them into the cupboard. The faucet shut off and Jonah strapped on his braces, banging the metal heels into the floor as he stood, and Zach heard him lumber out and he heard the other children leave after and he felt Anna's eyes on his back and he knew she was looking at them. He thought that her look might be saccharine for the figure of camaraderie he and the boy cut but when he turned around it wasn't. It was not even hostile or jealous. But abandoned. And not by him, not by anything he had thought or done, but before even the idea of him. She stared at them and she looked haunted and racked by some invisible force not accountable to this time or this place at all: Euridice somehow come back in addendum to the myth, looking at herself in the glass and simply astonished at what the underworld had done to her.

He spent the weeks in the early winter sun fixing the remaining broken fence and he built a new coop for the chickens. If truth be told it was hardly an improvement over the old one but Anna didn't say anything and Nate, when he came a week later with an array of light fixtures, leaned an elbow on Zach's shoulder and nodded and said that after a lot of imagination and maybe some prayer too it looked pretty much like a chicken coop. He winterized the failing house with plastic over the bedroom windows and linseed oil on the chafed sills and woodcaulk in the gaps of the cracking boards. His skin darkened and his mouth was healing well due to Anna's dexterity and the calendula which she applied twice daily without fail. He rode the mule now bareback at a walk. He had never been on a horse before (or a mule) and he rode her around the lake in the evenings alone and talked to her and told her about the circumstances of his recent life and the fears he had about his life to come. Sometimes Anna walked along beside him and other times she sat the mule and he walked along leading the woman aloft by the halter rope, uselessly because the mule was old and would hardly spook for a shotgun blast, but he felt like a man from another time and place and the feeling nearly overwhelmed him.

In the mornings after breakfast he would take some of the children for walks and he carried on his back by turns those few without functional legs. The others followed in clusters around him and fought each other for the privilege of holding one of his hands. Sometimes he put two or even three of the smaller children on the back of the mule and led them all with a child on his own back as well and some of those he carried spoke nonsensically into his head and drooled on him and he did not mind. The little matronly girl named Rene had taken to him extravagantly and would not leave him alone. She would in fact rub her whole body up and down his leg in unabashed carnal sexuality and Zach would remove her and tell her no kindly in the way one might speak to a good dog. She'd cry and if his back was free he'd lift her and carry her some until she started kissing him all about his neck and the sides of his head and biting his ears at which point he'd feign what anger he could manufacture and yell at her and tell her to go home. She'd sulk and walk alongside him a foot apart slowly decreasing the gap and the process would begin again.

But at night, when the children had gone to sleep, and when he was not in his room making lists or sitting on the dark shores of the lake, he watched Anna. From the upstairs bathroom window on the southeast end of the house he watched her where she sat out there alone. Darkly lit in the low porch light, the light mazy and weak from grime and bugs in the dirty porcelain shade. She sat in the front yard (which was not a yard but a sparse gravel drive the perimeter of which was tamped down, rutted dirt) on the tire swing hung from the thick live oak. She wore a too large leather RAF pilot's helmet with the padded flaps unbuttoned and down about her ears against the chill and she chewed on a smokeless corncob pipe. On the colder nights her breath plumed as if in imitation of smoke but she never lit it, not that Zach saw anyway. He leaned his forearms on the sill with the hair on them often raised and he watched her body's faint swaying, sitting in her barn boots and jeans and the fatigue jacket with the scarf wrapped around her and sometimes one of the tattered wool blankets too, talking. Not loud and not always talking, in fact sometimes just still, the pipe in her hand sometimes as if poised in the act of listening, statuary, thoughtful, and he would even have called it tranquility but for the intensity of her mien, her slightly downtilted and shadowdarkened face, as if a ladle of shadow pooled and decanted from her features at random, as if shadow had a will, a rapacious music of its own. And then a respite, a little peace across the face like a lull in a storm, a little light on the water.

But more often than not he would see her mouth moving in silent or sibilous speech, see her body language change subtly and comment as upon some invisible conversationalist, sitting there fully clothed, wrapped even, and yet somehow with a quality both sophic and dishabille, her hand- and wind-tossed hair, the toe of her boot languid, oblivious, slowly turning the air upon the air, and above it the face, contentious, haunted, the moist fecundity of the generous mouth like some embouchure of spring itself out from the blown vestments of winter. On the whole the scene had about it a judiciary aspect, as if she were her own barrister pleading her case before a supernatural court, as if loneliness and desire were offenses that could be negotiated with the jury of the fates. He'd strain to hear what she said. And if he watched her with trepidation he also watched her with a feeling he himself would not even have been able to call envy.

One night he walked down the stairs and sat on the porch steps. He made sure that she'd heard him on the boards but she did not turn around. Or she did not look at him because she was merely in profile and could have seen him simply by shifting her eyes. And he stood and

I refuse to believe the wind has any idea how long it has to travel before it lifts the hair off the shoulders of a single woman   look at her   the wind is ravenous and forgetful the damp cyclone of a place that is her   whatever is trying not to die cannot be codified   the sound of her teeth on that pipe all the way over here   Mary Lynn down by the creek bed trying to eat those guppies, her and I on our stomachs on the beds of the oak leaves on the sandy shore of the creek, she wearing her father's wool duster, completely lost in it, and naked underneath, both of us eleven years old, me holding the flashlight at midnight for her and she for me while we ate those little fish still alive going down the throat   her father's pipe?   I stood up in front of five hundred people and spoke about Vesuvius   what did I say?   what? what?   her father's hat from the war?   he'd have been too young   her father's father's hat?   he'd be too old   I am no more or less than a thesis, than a sheaf of papers you could hold above any stairwell   she is no more or less than these children?   cripped and crippled she's going to destroy that pipe and then she could eat her fingers, her hands, her whole body   she won't even look at me   fear not pride   look at her anyway   look until you can't turn back from the looking   intelligence is energy that refuses to dissipate?   yes   how far one has thrown the net out not simply what's accrued, god help the self-satisfied schol-

ars   a deer or is it Samuel?   thus become some subject matter
when I was a kid I looked for something in my pockets just to
drop in a stranger's path   don't tell me mirrors give back only
the memory of mirrors and these themselves of further mirrors
last night's dream: the buzzards, half their bodies dipping
ceaselessly into the carcass of the goat, and when Anna came
up to me she was beaming, she was so relieved that I could sit
there and watch that carnage, that I could be still and patient
and horrified at once   maybe the wind driving van Gogh's
paintings into the air was saying Sanity and Sanity   maybe
the wind is sentient   I would like, at least, to straighten that
crazy hat   what book was it that time with the old man, the
traveler in the airport, seeing a young woman in grief and not
even talking to her, not even laying a hand on her shoulder but
something in her accountability to experience, some manner of
fear that was not afraid but participating in a way that re-
deemed him   surely just the deer   he who was so bitter and
incensed by the world's folly   I read him for his bitterness, I
chewed on it like she's chewing on her pipe, but that is the
scene that I remember: the young woman crying over some-
thing important, something private and mythic and worth-
while in its privacy and that redeeming everything   just talk
to her Zachary, just go over and talk to her

Do you mind if I sit with you? he said.

She didn't say anything. She looked at him and took off her
hat and then looked away. She ran her hand through her hair
and started slightly rocking again where she had stopped at his
voice. He sat. He sat for a long time and then he shifted his
weight to rise—he was sitting against the very trunk of the tree
from which she slowly swung—and she turned her chin and
nodded it downward once almost imperceptibly, not looking at
him still, the gesture in it so slight but still enough to keep him
from leaving. So he spoke.

Tell me about Samuel.

What do you want to know?

How long has he been here?

Why?

Because he's special.

Yes he is.

Zach was about to speak again when she said, Have you heard the singing?

Samuel?

No, the shiners.

I haven't, Zach said.

I don't see how you can't have by now. She looked at him now, she swept across him a slow unlidded study.

The men in my family made moonshine out here. For over a hundred years.

She jutted her chin north beyond the house. In the low hills by the creek. When they made a run sometimes there'd be fifteen people bunking in this house. They sing. Sometimes they sound like swine at a slaughter. Sometimes it sounds like a wedding.

What is it tonight? Zach said.

She looked at him and smiled faintly. It's quiet tonight.

I see, Zach said. Ghosts.

Ghosts.

I haven't heard them.

Do you believe me? she said.

Why shouldn't I? Sometimes I think we're all ghosts. Hybrids of plants and ghosts.

Hybrids of plants and ghosts, she said. She looked at him and shook her head. What is your name, your last name?

Brannagan. Zach Brannagan.

What is that?

It's Irish.

She looked at him. Irish?

Yes, he laughed. My name's Irish.

She hunched over a little and drew her knees up to her chest.

Are you cold? he said.

Maybe. Yes.

He got up and went to the rack in the foyer and came back

out and laid the tattered wool blanket around her body and she bent forward to allow him and said thank you.

Samuel's not a boy. And he's not a ghost. Or a plant, she laughed.

He's a man, Zach said.

No. If anything he's a garden. You don't have to tend a man. You don't?

No. You have to tend a garden. He's my garden.

He had the strong desire to adjust her hat. Her features in the weak light looked profoundly female out from the absurd man's garb, her mouth just a darker blossom around the chewedup end of the pipe, her fingers on her thighs, the toe of her right boot in the air. He almost asked about her hat but he didn't. He didn't want to for some reason.

What do you mean?

Anything that touches him grows, heals. He's fertile soil. You'd probably call it loam. Do you know what loam is?

Zach made an openpalmed, resigning gesture with his hands.

He's like a salve. I put him on people. If someone's sick I tell Samuel to go spend time with them, to sit or sleep with them. And they heal.

Is he like that with you?

Who said anything about me?

You live in the middle of the woods with eleven abandoned children and you can't remember when last you left the property. You're out here alone every night talking to yourself and chewing on that pipe. Do you heal?

I'm not talking to myself. You're up there alone every night, do you?

I don't have a choice, Zach said. I have to.

Do I?

What?

Have a choice.

I'm not talking about my mouth, Zach said. Either we both do or we both don't.

What is that supposed to mean?

I don't know.

They were silent. Do you see those trees? she said.

Yes.

Nobody ever planted them.

Is that supposed to be strange? Is that supposed to prove to me that I can't know your mind?

What? that they weren't planted or what I said?

What you said.

You don't have to come out here just to insult me, she said.

Zach laughed, shook his head, expired. Jesus christ, he said.

The late autumn rains were over and the night was completely still and when they were silent the sound of her teeth on the pipe came off the façade of the house. Did you put him on me? Zach said.

Samuel?

Your garden, your salve.

No, that's his own doing.

Has he always been that way?

I don't have nightmares, she said. She said it defiantly, as if it was the phrase that would end some debate they'd been having on the matter, a coup de grace, and then she paused in silence for more than a minute, looking up at the house and at the sky beyond, at the tops of the trees. Zach didn't say anything.

Do you like violets? she said.

I've never really thought about them.

I work out all my problems right here before I go to bed so that when I sleep my mother will lie next to me in that field. So I don't have nightmares. But one night I had a nightmare. Samuel'd been here six months and he'd hardly looked at me. But that night he came into my room, to my bed even, and slept and when I woke up he was gone and I was happier than I'd been since I was a girl. Since before. Now what is that? He's a garden.

What did you dream?

Why would I want to tell you that, or want to remember it?

Zach nodded slowly as if to say he was familiar with that kind of privacy and that kind of amnesia. I talk to myself all the time, he said.

I'm not talking to myself.

Who are you talking to?

My father. She looked at him and her look made him shudder. Because there was more than familial love in the look. Because it felt wrong and impenetrable and had about it the power and exclusivity of fate.

How long has he been dead? Zach said. His throat was thick and he felt cold.

She smiled at him warmly. Cruelly. The pipe clenched in her teeth. She lifted her eyebrows, nearly like a coquette. She took the pipe out of her mouth and with her finger she swept a particle of abraded stem from her lower lip and examined it and blew it into the world. He's not, she said.

CHAPTER TWENTY SIX

Anna had walked to Bayou St. John. Later she would tell him—sitting on the gallery, half the boards of which they had together replaced with the leftover wood from the run-in shed, Zach sitting spraddlelegged against one leaning porchshaft and she juxtaposed on the porch swing, pushing with the sporeblown softness of an exhaling girl the ball of her foot into the boards and rocking, slightly, the other leg tucked under her like a retiring bird, Zach sitting and with a naked razor blade carving the woodresin from the singular hairs of his forearm, one by one, in calm abstraction, trying not to break them off in the process, listening to her voice in tandem with his pointless meditative task (so that he thought for an instant, even as she began to speak, Good, I get to hear that thunk thunk thunk into my body all day tomorrow too), or his body's muscular exhaustion and satiety—all day he'd quartered and hauled portions of a lightningstruck tree, and that without a chainsaw—in similitude to her voice which was speaking with the calm, the impartite retiring continuity that is duskness, her voice a very duskness, so that he looked up at her and out from time to time as she spoke and saw, as if she herself gave them permission to sleep, the tops of the fading trees—that she had no idea that day over fifteen years ago that she was walking to the woman called Kish. She would tell him that she had just been walking without destination through the hills of the Kisatchie with a throbbing and swollen wrist, west, toward North Toledo Bend and the Sabine and beyond, altogether without purpose, or maybe by the scent of her mother's ancestral blood, she who had been born north along the Texas border among the Spanish descendants there, maybe by that aroma alone, she would quietly say.

But she had walked. Fifteen years old. She had not even waited for the funeral. With over her shoulders in a wickiupped burlap bag some crackers and already three day old bread and water and venison jerky and an orange and, dangling by her side or cradled in her good hand, a broken wrist. She had started out in the morning, walking in broad daylight down Jollup Avenue through the heart of Marjolaine, northwest, through even the very town square and on a Saturday to boot, though she didn't even know that, a dozen townsmen and women wishing her with friendly but circumspect distance good morning and their diffident condolences likewise, and she not even turning her head to hear them, to return anything to them, not even her eyes, walking on, churning really, and the town assembling in little adjudicating and already righteous clusters behind her, shaking their heads at her importunate back, muttering to each other that even before what must be the grief and shock of her father's death there was something degenerate about the girl, even beyond the fact that much of the town knew that a fifteen year old girl helped deliver and even helped make the whiskey which was her father's infamy and charm, her self possessed and almost sovereign sweetness (and beauty, let's just say it, the women especially did not brook well her thoughtless precocious beauty) notwithstanding, something degenerate all right; they stood there watching her through the square, thinking it, some even saying it, and then breaking for the shops or the coffee and the idle chatter along the immaculate slow walks and forgetting her before she was even out of sight.

She did not then live at The Lake. She and her father lived in a small house they'd built on the south end of Marjolaine. (The Lake was just a decrepit and uninhabitable house in the bottomland; Lance Beauchamp merely kept both his forty five gallon stills there on the property exactly as his father had done, in the protected wood, and used the cold streams coming down off Salt Peak for the water lines for the flake stands.) She walked through the town and north on the shoulder of state road 78. And even then three townsmen stopped and offered her a ride and she still did not even slow her stride or so much as glance sidelong, the cars rolling alongside her at her pace for a brief time and one, Will Lardner who ran the southend hardware store and dealt thereby with Lance Beauchamp almost daily and was on his way to work when he saw her and made a U turn in the middle of the road, stopping and with genuine concern saying, Anna, it's Will. I don't blame you atall. Get in, it's Will Lardner, putting the car in gear again and rolling slowly alongside, leaning across his front seat, steering with his left hand, offering his right out the window as if he proffered candy or seeds, telling the fifteen year old motherless and siblingless and now fatherless girl (and barely fifteen at that, only three months before) that when his wife died of the cancer he didn't come out of the house for two weeks. But she just walked, all the more tight-fisted (her good hand) against his kindness, and he had finally turned around back toward town.

By late afternoon she was on the old Behemoth logging trail, still walking steadily, her hard thighs pushing up against her hand through the sweatsaturate jeans as she climbed, her breath disproportionately loud and harshseeming in the corridor of woods, though she was only breathing a little louder than usual, or that is what she had been thinking listening to herself until she stopped and heard it for what it actually was: irregular and abrasive as a neophyte saw against the air itself, as if her lungs were foreclosed with a filter of chunky and particulate lint. And she had finally rested. On the west side of the crest of Talla-hash Saddle she took off her boots and removed her socks and looked at her blisters and put her feet in the river and lay down and looked at her blue wrist and the blue sky beyond it that was denseing toward late afternoon, at the tree tops moving in sensuous unconcern, and she had cried until her body was spent and then she had turned over and lay with her face in the creek drinking and looking as in a child's game down as far as she could through the moiling water to the silt bottom and then the surface again, the glintshifting patterns of her unresolvable image and then she had flung the water over her face and hair and donned her socks and boots and begun walking.

By dark the road had become a trail and hardly even that so that she all but bushwhacked until she crossed another logging road and broke free into it and stopped and brushed the broken branches and leaves from her clothes and with not a little effort disengaged some larger twigs that had lodged in her hair. And squatted in the middle of the road and ate, finally, the wet and sweet orange, biting the last vestige of pulp off of the rind and flinging the rind into the woods and licking around her mouth and at her fingers and then flinging the now empty bag itself, just flinging it with a female expiring abdicating grunt and looking to where it lay like a rakish signpost in the foliage. And walked on. Now the road was clear and wide though there was no moon. Some starlight though, some shadows. She was descending steadily. She did not even know that she was exhausted. If someone had stopped her and asked her how long she had been walking she would have been able to tell them but she would have had to carefully consider it. The road meandered its way downward and she flung down it now, not moving so much by muscular effort but by gravity alone, her limbs loose and mindless so that once she tripped on a rain rut the gouge of which was a foot deep and rolled and sat crosslegged there in the middle of the road and held her wrist in her lap where the pain was just shooting now because she'd unconsciously braced herself with both hands in the fall and rolled too her ankle in tentative circles where it had twisted and wiped the back of her good hand across her brow which did nothing but leave a broad swath of grimy sweat like a tribal cicatrice. She sat there and maybe for the first time since she began she considered her situation. The trees above were still. In fact the night was exceptionally calm, exceptionally clear. It was the middle of August. She looked up at the stars. Through the open pergola of trees she could see the Chameleon and the Mensa and at the western skirt of the trees, the eastern stars of the Crux. It was not cold but she began to shiver. She was thirsty. She swept her tongue across her lips and her mouth was only scale, and if she could have seen it, crusted at the edges with dried saliva, vaguely painted out of the dark of night like the faded lip-blanched guise of a crying actress. She got up.

It was not yet light when she came to Bayou St. John. On the porch of the first diminutive shackhouse which she passed three cats were poised on the rail and they watched her, steadily turning their heads against the hinge of their motionless bodies like owls. Her footsteps crunched in the predawn silence and she heard, as in checked intimation of a tentative door opening, a creaking screen frame jar and then jostle into its hasp and then silence. She passed a like house every eighth of a mile now, and then every few hundred feet, and then they lined the road a stone's throw betwixt them, still walking downward, only more slightly so, still on the borrowed vertigo of gravity, only stumbling almost delicately now, as if in absolute obverse of the actual situation, walking as if with great trepidation through a minefield, when the truth was that she was entirely heedless of her body's striding, had forgotten at this point that she was walking at all, completely mindless and incorporeal too, though she was not herself aware of that either, though watching her (as the inhabitants of the houses no doubt were between the sills and the sheets they had tacked up for curtains, a white girl cradling her own hand stumbling down the road toward Bayou St. John at just past four o'clock in the morning) one might have thought that she was drunk. And dawn was a flat impossible sepia on the far side of what she knew were the last trees, the copse in the middle of which the house stood, hub medicinary and hospital and midwifery and secular church and, in ludicrous contrast, liquor store, the mother and son domicile, the very pith and breadth (beyond the facile and conventional utilitarian conception of good and evil which had no currency in the impoverished strife [and beauty too, beauty too] of those people's lives) of Bayou St. John—the bootlegging son everyone called Boom who bought the whiskey wholesale from Lance Beauchamp and hauled it himself from The Lake in a pickup truck covered with hay and peddled it about the Bayou and even from the shed behind the house to the black community come from ninety miles around, and the mother of the selfsame son, old enough herself to be a very young grandmother but who was not and who looked to be in her mid to late thirties rather than her mid to late forties, who tended the sick and delivered the babies and dispensed the casual and sometimes searing psychologic advice to the black folks who came, daily, to this so called leaf doctor, and even, though rarely and never mentioned on the other side of the mountain, some of the whites.

Anna stood looking at the screen door from behind a tree, exhausted, sweatstreaked and mudstained, at once expired and vigilant like a starveling lame animal, and waited until she smelled food. Then she walked softly up. She stood outside the screen. She could see the woman's back where she worked the skillet at the range. And then the woman turned, slowly, her smooth clean brown face the color of chocolate set to cool and reflecting the insides of the copper pan, the turquoise silk-turbaned slope of her Ethiopian head and her almondish eyes which beheld Anna's outline in her own front door. Is you a girl or a ghost? she said.

A girl.

You mighta helloed the house then honey. I guess you wants something to eat.

And then she walked closer, the skillet smoking in hand, the smell of frying hogmeat deliriously good swirling through the meshgrating. I know you child, sho enough.

And coming still closer, opening the door with her free hand, propping it open with her hip now and in one immemorial and comprehensive sweep of her eyes absorbing the travail and the desperation of the girl before her, the gesture of the glance older perhaps than any in all of human physical vernacular, already reaching for Anna's shoulder, beckoning her inside. Child, she said. Child.

Kish already knew her.

Because even late in the latter part of the twentieth century all over the hill country between Marjolaine and Bayou St. John were signs that read: Nigger Don't Get Caught After Sundown. And if Klan lynching was all but obsolete a busted skull and a truck emptied of four hundred dollars of liquor was not. And two years before the Steelhead River had flooded unbeknownst to Boom on his way to The Lake for his monthly supply of whiskey cases. He had had to go all the way south below Telluvue and even as far as Montpelier and cut back up on state road 22 and yet again west on 36 and north on the river road toward the railroad depot of Marjolaine, then back down toward The Lake. It had taken him over five hours when it usually took between two and three and a half, depending on the condition of the road. He was late. When he did finally arrive he leapt out of the pickup truck, putting his thumb and forefinger to his hat and nodding quickly and Lance and Anna leapt up too and began heaving the kegs and cases into the truck, or he and Lance did and Anna arranged them in the bed. But the sun was going down. Boom just stopped and looked up at the light slanting through the trees. We'll follow you, Lance said.

The Steel's flooded.

I know it, you said so. I'll follow you.

We got to go down far as Montpelier.

I know it, Lance said. We'll follow you.

That'd be five hours. One way.

But Lance was already bent to the next case. Give me a hand, he said.

So they did, arriving in the Bayou long past nightfall, close to ten thirty. When they pulled through the narrow drive of the copse and up to the house Kish was sitting motionless in the rocker and when she saw that it was surely her son she leaned forward and put her palm flat down on the porch boards and kept it there for a full half a minute and then looked up as he came lumbering past the steps with the first case in his arms and said, Manchild, don't ever do that again.

So while Lance and Boom hauled the cases around back to the shed Anna stood below the landing and looked up at the woman who had lit her corncob pipe now and begun rocking and breathing and puffing again like a human armature for a plaster cast just cracked from out of its mold into the living world again. Taint no alligators in this moat, that I know of anyways. Come on across girl.

Anna walked up. Ma'am, she said. I'm Anna.

I know that honey. Boom's spoke of you.

He's spoke of you too, Anna said.

And they sat there, Anna beginning to rock slightly without even knowing that she was already imitating the woman, already buoyed up upon the timeless raceless arms, the mothers and daughters and sisters epoch to age to epoch absorbing her as a finite effluvium might osmose into a stratosphere, already lulled into some speakless peace and aching longing too so that she said without even knowing that she was going to say it, I love—from the first time I heard Boom say it—I love your name.

Kish looked over at her and smiled. You want a thimbleful of cognac, girl?

Anna heard the screen door shut behind her. She felt a chair come up under her body and the ice come up under her wrist and the cool metal handle of the fork in her hand and the steaming warmth in her mouth and the flavor of the meat spreading through her whole body like blood to a contusion. And she stayed. She stayed a week and then it was a month and they broke her hand out of the homemade cast and then it was fall moving into winter and then spring again. She stayed with Kish for just under three years. She lived and worked alongside her, worked exactly as a carpenter or blacksmith apprentice works alongside a journeyman, performing the menial tasks and watching carefully and asking only three or four carefully formulated questions a day lest the master grow weary and begin to resent the transmission. She planted and gathered herbs and weeded and tilled the soil and sterilized the surgical supplies in boiling water and iodine and watched with undeviating attention the needling techniques of the acupuncture. She prepared tinctures and teas, liniments and salves and ointments and suppositories and she checked the vitals of the dozens of patients Kish saw for almost spare change during the course of any given day. And, just once, she wrote out the herbal protocol on a note pad as Kish dictated it across the prone body of an old arthritic man who looked at the note Anna handed him as he sat up and then looked at Kish and said, We gots a scholar in the house.

We do? Kish said.

We do indeed. She can read and write in twenty languages at once. Look here.

But more. She cooked and ate and slept and listened under that roof, working and cooking by day and in the evenings sitting on the porch and listening. And she listened in the only way that she could listen, like a privileged guest in the vanguard of a foreign country's tidings. And deep in the night she listened too. Kish had two lovers (and a passel of St. John suitors that didn't interest her in the least), two peripatetic, hardy middleaged men who were not even ignorant of each other and who came from a great distance to stay with her for a few days or sometimes just a night. Anna would lie in her cot those nights in the room adjacent and she would listen to the sounds of their lovemaking and she would clench very tightly her fists and she would not sleep until they were long done and sometimes on those nights she would not sleep at all and she would walk down to the river in the predawn blackness and slip through her clothes and slide into the cold slowly flowing oil and let it run off her backtilted head and down her hair and down her spine and gasp quietly up at the memory of those overheard salacious entreaties and at the cold ignorant stars.

But mostly, as in duplicate of that first evening, she and Kish sat alone on the porch. In silence, among the myriad penetrating nightsounds and the laughter carrying faintly up from the river and then the darkness softly snuffing that out too and everything but the plangent rocking of paired wood on wood like boats moored in a softly swelling bay: the fifteen year old girl and then sixteen and then seventeen and finally the eighteen year old woman sitting in the rocker alongside Kish and drawing herself now languidly from the proffered corncob pipe and passing it back, the two of them distinct and counterpoint, white and young, black and middleaged, and inexpungible from each other's lives as an aunt and a niece might be.

There was an itinerant foster child in the Bayou named Wahkim, a five year old paralyzed from his waist down. His mother at age seventeen had drowned herself in the river and his father was white and unknown and he traveled from house to house and was cared for adequately but not particularly, that is, he was sustained but not loved. When Anna had come to the Bayou he began more and more to gravitate toward her as if by a homing urge to touch against at least the likeness of the white half of his blood, to loiter about Kish's house, lumbering in his braces after Anna around town and through the outdoor market and when Anna left the Bayou it was not even discussed, it was just understood that Anna would take him with her, and Wahkim, who didn't even have a last name, became the first child at The Lake.

She left soon after she turned eighteen. Boom drove them over the mountain, the young woman and the orphan child and a rooster and two chickens in a wire cage in the back, right through the town of Marjolaine to The Lake, Anna looking out the car window at the passing town square and the courthouse and the store façades and the sparse and slow citizens window-shopping and sitting on benches in slow and surreal pantomime like her own avatar come back to visit a life she had lived long ago.

CHAPTER TWENTY SEVEN

She is not spring. She is not. Spring is shadowless. Spring is that brief innocence only clean absolute death can beget, briefly. Even when the blossoms are ripped from the cherry trees they land delicately; they do not make a scar. Summer is. Summer is bursting terrible with shadow, pregnant with it. But not spring. How can she be spring? It had been a week now since he'd sat with her under the oak tree and he'd not gone down to join her again since and nights he tried even to leave the upstairs bathroom window but he could not. It was as if through her layers of clothing and through the night air which had about it that absolute (if windless) stillness which moderate climes have on winter nights, when it is indeed cold but so recently nearly mild in sunlight that the night air seems shocked, bitterly metallicized—through that stillness and through the window and through even the pores of his own heavily clothed body it was as if watching her swinging in the tire he could imbibe spring. That fecundity of breath rising, dampness into air, the slightly protuberant mouth bold on the pipe and the pronouncing breath vaporizing in impassioned silence. But it was winter. *She is not spring,* he thought. *She can't be. Because the face was too ripe with shadow.*

In fact in its endless permutations it seemed in the time it took to fill and expire the lung to register the whole carnal year's transformations—to embody the budding and then the blowing in the wind and the harsh scattering, the molting, and the blooded trampling upon and into the almost unredeeming summer's mud, the pink and yellow petals pummeled by rain and obliterated not into dust but into the succulent depthless quagmire, slowly fading and decomposing like deathtranslucent insects' wings, swallowed-in, and then reemerging, blazing briefly, tragically bronzing, and then quieting to sienna, burnt sienna, and then to freeze, to stun blankly, to winter. And then the budding all over again. And this in a few seconds across the features of her face, the chin turning to or from the light, a glance at nothing from nothing. He could feel it, as if her very breath somehow permeated the upstairs windowglass and raised, in its inexorable passage beyond him and beyond any single temporal thing which the earth could offer her, his forearm's scintillant hair. So he could not leave the window.

And so envy. Because without so much as a sentient conversationalist she compassed the world, and obliviously. So that he—who could read fluently in German and functionally in Latin and who had read (devoured) not only the distillate but the sources, the huge canvas of the history of occidental thought, the tragedies and the exegeses and the schools, the categories (but not the heart's heat, not the blood) of phenomenology, the epistemological and ontological postulations which were the mortmain sum of the civilized western vaults—felt nescient before the writhen experience of her face. That is also to say, for perhaps the first time in his adult life he felt the pure current of masculine eros: the desire to penetrate, to enter in one terrific endless plummeting now the immemorial pulp, the joy and the pathos and the death and the raw dewdappled trembling return which is the inheritance of sex. He watched her and Tell me, he whispered. Tell me.

At which point she looked up at the window. He froze who was already still. Nor did she look away. They could have been counterpoised effigies molded out of a single frozen instant of their lives. Then he did; he came down the stairs and out onto the porch.

I was hoping that you would, she said.

Hello, he said.

CHAPTER TWENTY EIGHT

After supper of a Sunday Zach was sitting at the tiny desk, in the tiny chair, his knees all up about him like an aborigine squatting at a meal. Penning nouns, making lists of what that day he'd seen and heard and felt and smelled and tasted:

January 3

Jenny's coat thickening and darkening day to day, goat smell, do all mules smell like goats? when did you ever smell a goat? the zoo, no, the curtilage, that old lady's curtilage, do horses smell exactly like mules? the morning cold out of her nostrils, the shiver down her whole back when I touched her mane, burnt omelet and swiss cheese, papaya juice smoothie (who ever heard of a papaya juice smoothie?), big pain in my molar at about nine o'clock, mist off the lake and only the tops of the trees visible across it, ducks used to me by now, gold backs and green, one with an all black face, white around one eye, a loner, Neil and Raoul spitting at each other until they laughed, Samuel in a mock swordfight with himself in the clearing we call Bull Clearing (didn't know I was watching), Chris painting

a barn and silo on Jonah's cast, his serious face, Chris's face,
that is, Anna's breasts good god, Anna's breasts under the
beige tank while she stirred the soup, the soup, What is miso?,
her look as if I'd just been born, (fermented barley, rice), a
group of them running across the field, hair flying behind
them, July tripping and Rene coming back to help her, later
July wiping the spit off Rene's own mouth with her sleeve,
wood in my hands, just a handle, my shoulders under a shirt,
the woodsplitting sound like, suddenly leaning up against the
barn door early afternoon, my mother talking about aura re-
treats in the kitchen, fifteen years old, and she not even my
mother?, the light did that? the time of day?, the light on the
fallen leaves in the wind, all that motion, like Prospero, the
leaves called Prospero, the sad roof after my woods walk,
shingles are a perfect square, simple, simple, the children
stomping their feet extra loud for me, Edmund urinating all
over himself during the card game, the faint ammonia smell of
it still on my hand, my hand, my dark, thickening hand, the
sound of Samuel's feet on the boards—

It was very quiet and he heard the birdlike footsteps outside
his door. It had become obvious to Zach, to Anna too, that the
boy followed him everywhere. He'd figured out his habits and
his duties and he joined that schedule with a crafted arbitrariness, nonchalantly, as if he constantly just happened upon the
man and thought that he might need some company or a hand.
Samuel, Zach called. He whispered it.

The boards stopped and he heard the wheezing which was at
once insouciant and rough and which was Samuel's song, his
recitative, part singing, part breath, part conversation with himself or the myriad others that lived in him. It's open. The door's
always open.

He heard the door crack and he kept his back turned and he
kept writing. He felt him come close and stand behind his right
shoulder. He felt the boy's breath on his back and then, in a gesture unfigurable, Samuel spread his hand and put it between
Zach's shoulder blades and let it rise and fall with the breath.

For several minutes. Zach put down his pen. He didn't move. Just that rising, that falling. Samuel walked around him and looked at the pad on the desk and picked it up and tore out a blank sheet and centered it on the desk and picked up the pen and put it in Zach's hand so that he might continue. Then he took the book to the edge of the bed and began reading. He started at the beginning. He moved his lips along the words exactly as Anna did, as if she had taught him to read. It took him over a half an hour. When he was done he looked up at Zach and cleared his throat. For a terrifying instant Zach thought he was going to speak. Can you read it all? he said.

Samuel looked at him for a long time. Finally he stood and walked up to the desk and took the pen from Zach's hand and on the still blank page, all in capital letters, he wrote: EPILEPSY.

Then he walked out of the room.

CHAPTER TWENTY NINE

Zach began to work later and later hours on Tuesdays and Nate paid him time and a half without even discussing it. Late one Tuesday Zach was on his back under a station wagon welding on a muffler when Nate came out of his house with a plate of beans and franks in his hand and squatted down beside the car and when the sparks ceased he reached the plate under and said, Son, why don't you use that thing to heat this up, it's past seven thirty. Zach scooted out from under the car and flipped up his helmet shield and took the plate. I'm done, he said.

Good. Miriam's startin to doubt my ethic.

Your what? Zach said, already laughing.

My ethic, my work ethic. My wife thinks I'm Paul Bunyan and I don't need some accountant or professor or lie detector tester or whatever the hell you were to come out here and make me look bad. Eat that, I grew it in the garden.

Zach took a forkful of frankfurter. You don't even have a garden.

Listen, Nate said. I've got to make a run to the Mounties and I'm gettin a load from Churlesville in two weeks and we need somethin over that hay. Do me a favor and ask Anna if it'd be all right if I brought some boneheads out there and we did it in one day. Not this coming week but the next one, say Saturday.

All right, Zach said.

She's not going to like it, Nate said. She doesn't like anybody out there who's not hurt or brain dead or just plain ugly, like you.

She'll be all right with it.

Nate looked at Zach and raised his brow. Is that right? What, are you her spokesperson now?

I didn't say that. I just said she'd be all right with it.

He stood and leaned against the car. Who knows, maybe I am.

On Saturday morning next he woke early and went to feed Jenny, walking behind the house in the sharp morning cold, the shards of light just now coming cleanly through the trees and their shadows long enough to reach the chicken coop roof and mingle with his shadow on the sideboards as he passed. He called out to the mule before she could see him and he heard her turn in the stall and snort. He told her good morning matter of factly as if she were a sentient man and then he turned around and stood with his back to the paddock gate and his arms around the rail and looked at the morning. He put the sole of his foot up behind him on the low slat and stood on one leg for a time, then the other, then again on both. He breathed in deeply and bent and stretched his legs and rose and he could smell Jenny's breath over his shoulder and he could smell the earth as if it had been turned over entire during the night, as if sleeping was dampness and dampness dispelling in first light was gestation and rebirth was that frosted stillness ascending yet further and aureate on the waking beasts and insects and mineral hills alike, on the needles and boles of the trees and upon the dustless air into atmosphere without fail and without the usury of before and after but on the singular moment alone, ceaselessly, which he could palpate by breathing, by simply extending the palm of his hand. It's a beautiful morning, he said to Jenny.

The mule looked at him and then looked at her grain bucket and back at her manger and pawed the earth. I know, he said. You couldn't care less. I know.

He turned toward the galvanized bins to scoop out the grain and then he stopped. He turned around and looked at her again. But have you even seen it? he said. Have you seen the light on the needles of the pine? Look at it will you, just look at it.

He had just poured the corn oil into the pellets and was sloshing it around the bucket with his hand sopped halfway up his forearm, when he heard the pickups coming down the drive. It startled him, the sound, even though he'd been waiting for it. With his dry hand he held the bucket by the handle behind his back and put his saturated hand to Jenny's nose and she mouthed it clean and then he dumped the grain in her manger and dipped his hands in her water trough to clean them and wiped them on his bibs. When he came around the front of the house they were standing in front of the porch taking in the property and talking. There were four long-bed trucks all loaded down with building materials. Zach walked up. Good morning, he said.

This would be Zach, Nate said.

They shook hands all around. The old man Willard called him Son. His daughter Doris stamped out her cigarette and blew smoke above the gathering and took his extended hand femalelike and loose with the wrist raised and the bracelets around it jangling as if she fairly expected him to kiss it, saying, The pleasure's all mine, my. There was a man named Bankcroft who had a thick pleasant unreliable red face and who wore bright red suspenders and a pinstripe locomotive jersey over his flannels, and a swarthy man they called Canada who didn't shake hands at all but just stood in a pair of darkblue paint- and oil- and resin-marred coveralls with his arms flat down against his sides shifting his weight slightly from foot to foot and just nodded at Zach, neither friendly nor hostile, with an absolutely neutral abstraction that is the face of some men who have little life at all outside of the work they do and seem immortal in the doing of it and lost to the point of obsolescence when they are idle. And a woman named Emily who had been sitting in the car. Ma'am, Zach said, extending his hand as she came up and she took it limply and didn't even look at him, letting him shake once and relinquish her. And the boy Bobbie, standing in his outsized 'Joe' shirt with his hands on his hips in some imitation of his father when he was impatient, stepped forward and extended his hand toward Zach and then took it away just before they touched and slicked back his nevercombed hair and laughed and kicked the dirt. Nate looked down at his son and shook his head.

The men walked around to the rear of the house and the women went to the trucks and began lifting out the coolers and the bags of food and walked up the steps to the house. The men stood beholding the fallen barn in silence, Nate rolling that nonexistent thinking substance around his mouth and Bobbie standing beside him in cut-out paper duplicate. Well, he said, we're going to have a hell of a fire tonight, aren't we. I'm having second thoughts.

Good, Bankcroft said. Some folks in this world still know what a Friday night is for.

What? Nate said, not ever looking at him, still slowly and deliberately taking in the barn.

Not everyone on earth goes to bed at six thirty in the afternoon.

And just what are Friday nights for?

For outlawing Saturday mornings. In my book it's illegal to be up at this hour on a Saturday.

That's why nobody reads your book.

You want the dozer? Canada said, looking at Nate.

That's what I'm thinkin, Nate said. I'm sorry, I underestimated.

It's already hooked up to my gooseneck.

How long will it take you to get back?

Canada spat. Two hours.

We'll put you up a plate, Nate said. A big plate.

But Canada was already making his way toward the drive.

When they came around the house a few of the children were on the porch and in the yard and the sight of them gave the men pause, but for Nate. Bankcroft looked downright afraid and Willard just stopped dead and said, Oh my. Roy came up slobbering and talking incessantly about a holiday and began tugging on Bankcroft's suspenders and Bankcroft looked at Zach and said, Get him off of me, will you.

He's all right, Zach said. If you let him do it now he won't try to do it all day.

Bankcroft tried feebly to joke with him but Roy grabbed him harder and began to pull him around the drive and Bankcroft let him for awhile and then grew exasperated and tried to push him off and Roy said, Hey hey hey, and pushed him to the side forcefully and Bankcroft lost his balance and fell and stood up cursing, brushing himself off. What the hell's wrong with him? he said to Zach.

Roy had retreated, frightened, and he was standing next to Zach, leaning his head into his chest, pointing at the man like the guilty one among a group of suspects. He's twenty eight years old going on nine, that's all.

Neil and Raoul—The Inseparables, Zach called them—came up to the men and just sat down in the dirt and Willard looked down at Raoul and said, Hello there young man.

Raoul looked up with his wandering eyes and began to smack his arm across his own face, hard, and then he took hold of one of the old man's ankles and said, How old are you?

Oh my, Willard said. Oh my. He looked helplessly at Zach. Zach walked over and held the boy's arm still for several seconds and then placed it in his lap and hefted him up and brushed him off on the seat and hefted Neil up too and brushed him likewise and pushed them toward the porch and told them to go and eat. They didn't move. They just looked down at the ground of a piece as if trying to maintain some oath of immobility they had agreed upon.

They want to help, Zach said.

Neil's neck was spasming. His head was jerking to the side as if he had just gone for a swim and was trying to empty his ear of pool water.

Help? Bankcroft said.

Yes.

Bankcroft laughed.

Zach looked at him.

Nate said something about the more hands they had to drag the mess around to the drive the better and Roy went running after some insect in the air saying that there was a fire and that he was the engine and the boys walked slowly toward the porch and then began to run for it in a race and Neil tripped and fell to his knees and scraped his chin and lay wailing and Raoul came back and petted his head like a dog and told him not to cry and Neil ceased and got up on a jump start to beat Raoul to the gallery and Raoul screamed that he hated his guts and ran after him with his fists clenched in a fury and Rene and Patricia came around the east end of the house and Rene saw the strange men and they grabbed each other's hands and Rene screamed and Patricia did too in domino though she could not of course see the cause of her own distress and they ran for cover and then Anna came out onto the porch. With a huge mixing bowl of scrambled eggs, the door banging behind her. Bankcroft sucked in a breath. Don't tell me that's Lance's girl, he said.

She's no girl, Nate said. She's probably thirty. Close to it anyways. Let's eat.

Thirty? Bankcroft said.

Have you looked in the mirror lately? Nate said. You aint what you used to be either.

I haven't been out here in the daylight in twenty years.

You haven't been out here at all in fifteen. You haven't been in the daylight period.

Bankcroft was looking at Anna. Zach was looking at Bankcroft. Willard was looking from one man to the other. Nate began to walk toward the porch. Willard put his hand on Zach's shoulder and spoke to him solicitously. How long have you been out here, young man?

They sat on the gallery and ate. Most of the children ate inside. Eggs piled high and hot sauce and relish and huge malformed buttermilk biscuits and chicken and hog sausage and a quarter of a stick of butter on each plate and juice and fruit in a bowl passed around and sherbet.

Sherbet? Bankcroft said, when Anna slopped a scoop of it in a bowl and said pass it down.

Whoever heard of sherbet in the morning?

Anna looked at him and said, Doris, you want some?

You don't even remember me, do you? Bankcroft said. You sat on Craycroft's porch and read my hand one time when you were just a—

I remember you fine, Anna said.

I would, Doris said.

Willard? Anna said.

No ma'am, I'm full. Thank you.

Anna looked at Zach and Zach nodded and he took the carton from her and scooped out a portion in his bowl and thanked her and handed the carton back. Nate stood up. Jesus christ, he said, it's already seven thirty.

By the time Canada came back trailering the bulldozer most of the loose boards and poles had been dragged up front to the gravel drive and they'd managed to salvage the core of the hay most of which was alfalfa and they were taking a break. It was mild and sunny and they were already shucking off their layers of flannel. Samuel had come from somewhere soon after breakfast and he sat on a bale with Willard. Raoul and Neil sat on a facing bale. The four of them shared a gallon jug of water. Bankcroft stood with Nate surveying the ground for the best site for the run-in shed they would build in the barn's stead. Discussing direction, water table, prevailing wind. Anna and Zach were separating the wood by size for the layering of the fire. Doris and Emily were inside and on the porch, respectively, struggling with the children. Roy was walking about the site telling everyone to take a holiday. Hugging people. Asking if they'd heard about the fire.

Canada rolled out the ramp planks and coasted down in the dozer and came driving up with a tremendous racket that brought everyone out of the house and put the chickens into an all out bedlam. The children were awestruck. They stood on the porch in that uniform silence which they employed when anything extraordinary was happening at The Lake as if any incidence out of the norm might mandate their pooled resources for which they needed a superior sensitivity.

The remaining poles came up easily on the blade of the bucket, rotted as they were to the core. By now everyone at The Lake was standing around watching. Canada did not so much as look at anyone or seem to notice the audience at all. He surged and returned and leveled with flawless economy. Nate was standing next to Zach. He'll be done in a half an hour, he said. You watch.

He was. He stuck his head out the window and called down to Nate. All right?

Yeah, Nate said. I believe. Leave her in the drive though just in case.

Canada turned the machine back toward the drive and nearly everyone began picking up the splintered corroded lumber and carrying it to the piles.

By mid afternoon the site was mostly clear. There were three mammoth piles of wood in the drive, too much for any tractable fire. While everyone else rested Canada shucked a good portion of the wood onto the empty trailer, bending over and hurling the faggots and broad boards and six inch square posts alike behind him with a vicious backhand motion without even wearing gloves. He worked with the steady violence of a good machine. If anger could be stripped of anger, he worked with anger.

His vigor was seamless, so sustained and fluid that watching him from the porch steps Zach was lulled into a kind of abstract reverie as if he were apprehending Nature itself in its blind compulsion to put asunder and to resurrect the forms of things, tirelessly: a cliff into sand into a cliff, a pile of wood into a pile of wood into a pile of wood. Then Canada covered it with a canvas tarp and battened it down with webbing and ratchets and drove away to spread it somewhere evenly in the woods. When he came back a half an hour later Bobbie was chalk marking the holes at center and Nate was driving the stakes into the ground with an eight pound sledge and Samuel was following, uncoiling the string over his arm, tying it around the stakes and slitting it with a knife which between cuts he held between his teeth like a fugitive villain he'd seen in the movies. Bankcroft was leaning on the post hole digger, waiting. Anna had taken Willard into the house. Zach was carefully watching the processes. Then Canada whistled at him and jerked his head toward the trucks. In anyone else to whistle might be to condescend but in Canada it was more that speech might interrupt the efficiency of the task at hand for the task at hand was god and anything in the service of the task therefore was without hierarchy so that to get a man's attention was to get his attention plain and simple and so he whistled at him. They began to haul the rafters out of the flatbed truck, on their shoulders. They came back for the sheet metal roofing and the soffits and the six by six posts and the tongue in groove for the sill girts and finally the rough cut boards for the interior and the plywood siding and the nails and hammers and braces. They laid it all about the site. Anna came out of the house with two extension cords and Zach carried the sawhorses from the shed, one over each shoulder. Canada went to his truck for his worm drive saw which he kept in a separate drawstring bag like a hallowed gemstone. Bankcroft dug the holes along Samuel's string line, working quickly and well and he called out to Canada, mockingly, that he didn't have all day. Get the ballast, Moe, Canada said. From my truck.

Moe? Bankcroft said.

Moe, Canada said, and grinned.

What was that? Bankcroft said. What was that? Nate, he called, we got ourselves a facial expression over here. We do indeed. Everybody just hold on a minute here. We got ourselves a living creature with a bona fide facial expression.

He pointed at Canada. I saw it. I'll go on the record to save my life. Call the Chamber of Commerce. Call his mammy.

Everyone laughed. Canada grinned again. Get the ballast, he said.

With what? Bankcroft said, but Anna had already gone to the garden for the wheelbarrow. She set it in front of Bankcroft and covered her mouth for the laughter but she did not meet his eyes.

Bobbie eyeballed the boards with one eye closed and picked out the best ones and Willard measured and Canada cut. After the aggregate had set Zach and Anna and Nate began hammering in the splashboards along the bottom border. Samuel went around with the level marking the placements with a pencil, watching the first placed nail on every board with a supercilious raised brow as if the adults were blind or habitually fallacious or too careless to see. Then Bankcroft picked him up. The sound the boy made was an almost unheard of sound, a shriek and a scream both, like an animal hit by a car and not killed but hung up on the fender. He swung his elbow viciously around and his body writhed for a moment as if suspended in electrocution and he would have bit the man through if Bankcroft had not himself yelled and flung open his arms the way a man might let go of some hot iron and let the boy go. Samuel ran. Everyone stopped working. They watched him disappear into the woods. Then they looked at Bankcroft. He looked at Anna. What in hell? he said.

He doesn't carry, Anna said. He never has. He'd rather be dead as soon as carry, it doesn't matter who it is. I picked him up once when he got here and he bit through my arm. I don't know why, what happened to him. I should have told you'all. I'm not used to having anyone strange out here.

Let's take a break, Nate said.

They sat on the ground drinking from the passed jug, looking over the foundation, watching Roy dump an empty wheelbarrow into a makebelieve sea, making with his hands the huge gesture of a tidal wave flooding the land and the people and the animals suffering and dying and then being succored and resuscitated by the survivors, then he dumped another wave. Bankcroft looked at the foundation. We're going to need a ladder to nail that first beam.

Canada looked at him. We don't need any ladder.

He got up and went to the sawhorses around which were scattered the saws and hammers and the boxes of nails and he crammed a bunch of nails head-end into his mouth and walked over to the pole and said to Bankcroft in a muffled voice, Hand me that beam when I'm up.

Then he climbed the pole. He just shimmied up it. When he made the top he wrapped his thighs around the wood and perched there like a carved capital atop a colonnade. He looked at Bankcroft. Come on now, he said.

Bankcroft held up the beam. Canada took it in one hand and with the other he took a nail out of his mouth and with the first hand he braced the beam and with the other he hammered a nail. Then he hammered another. Then he switched hands. He'd hammer a nail with his right hand and before it seemed even the last lick was through the handle was flipping in the air and he caught it with his left hand and pulled a nail out of his mouth with his right and banged it in, three strokes, the steady rings rebounding off the chicken coop wall. Nate was sitting next to Zach. That's ridiculous, Nate said. That's just mother fucking beautiful ridiculous.

Yes it is, Zach said.

Late afternoon found Zach and Anna sitting on top of the roof supports, balancing on nothing but the post and two crossbeams at first, nailing. Canada cut the boards to size and handed them to Neil and Raoul who then handed them up to Zach and Anna. On another set of sawhorses Nate and Bankcroft were cutting the exterior siding and Willard was laying it out along the flanks of the site, outfacing the boards' best sides. Samuel had returned and was staining the splashboards with the finish, his low murmuring humtalking rising off his patient concentration like an effluvium. They were beginning to lose good light. That is, the light was a splendid slanting gilt through the western trees. Zach and Anna worked silently, she holding the board while he nailed down his side, and then he steadying it for her while she hammered. At some point they entered a flawless rhythm. Zach would reach down and the board would be there from Neil or Raoul—he no longer looked down to see who it was—and he'd lift and place it and adjust it and nod and Anna would drive the nails and put her hammer in her hip loop and hold the board and Zach would drive his side. Then Anna would reach down for a board and it would be there. They'd nail it on likewise and move down the beam, balancing, and begin the process again. Meanwhile the light faded and the nails became harder to see and the swinging took on a blind quality of feeling and faith and perfection thereby. He began to notice that his hammer blows were uniform. Five. A sixth at the end to smash the head flush. And the sound and the fine reverberation of it through his body was as regular as his heart. Nate made a mock five o'clock whistling sound and said, I'm about to cut my hand off, that's it. Let's eat.

Two more, Canada said.

They finished the cuts and Nate put Bobbie on his shoulders and they walked toward the house in the dark. Willard was already inside. The two boys and Samuel looked up at Anna and she told them to go on and they followed the men to the house. Zach and Anna were still atop the roof scaffold. He looked over at her outline against the indigo dark. Let's finish the frame, he said.

We can't see.

I know. Let's finish it.

I've got to put something up to eat.

Let them.

They wouldn't know where to start.

Let them.

She looked at his form in the dark. You're crazy, she said.

I know. So are you. Let's finish it.

Maybe she was looking at him, he couldn't tell. She was the color of the trees a thousand yards behind her. All right, she said.

They climbed down carefully and gathered the remaining cut boards and leaned them against the standing post and Zach climbed up to the rafter and she handed the boards up to him one at a time and he laid them across the nailed beams and she climbed up after them, one foot on the boardskirt, the other on the pole, one hand overtop the horizontal girt, the other in his downstretched hand. They began nailing again, leaning down over their work now so that their balance was nearly shot but they struck the nails squarely as if in a dream of work and there was just the even sound of their breath and the high sharp solid reports of their hammer blows coming off the back of the coop and the house and the silence in between everything and the darkness. When they were on the last corner Anna lost her balance momentarily and Zach grabbed her arm to stay her and almost lost his balance thereby and she began laughing and he did too saying, What? what?

I'm going to smash my thumb, she said, laughing.

No you're not, we're almost done.

I'm going to.

Let me see it.

No, she said, laughing. I feel drunk.

You are. Let me see your thumb.

I haven't yet, she said. I'm just going to in a minute.

Let me see it.

No.

Let me.

She held it out and looked away: at the sky, the darkness of trees, at anything at all.

He held it, looking down at it in his hand. Look at that, he said.

When they came inside it was as if they'd been called to an interrogation. As if everyone in the room, even the children, had been talking about them. The kitchen was in a squalor. There were overturned plates on the floor and the children were sitting on the tables and the counters and the refrigerator door was wide open and the sink was piled high to spilling with dishes and glasses. But it was as if all motion had stopped just before the two of them came through the door, as if they had been arranged to pose for a portrait of mayhem as soon as Zach and Anna arrived. Then they broke: the children jumped down from the counters and began to shriek and tear about the house as if they'd been caught redhanded at a forbidden act. Jonah and Wahkim were sitting midway up on the steps smirking down at the turmoil like lifeguards at a pool. Samuel wasn't there. Emily looked exhausted to the point of breakdown. She leaned against the counter with her hands on her temples and looked at some pattern in the floorboard five feet in front of her. Doris was sitting at the round table, flicking her ash in a plate, looking at Zach and then at Anna and then back to Zach. The frame's done, Zach said, to no one and everyone.

Nate came in and asked if there was anything to eat besides bologna sandwiches.

Anna looked at Doris. Doris blew smoke and shrugged her shoulders and made an expression of resigned futility as if to say that she was exhausted beyond all responsibility even so much as to remember that human beings needed to eat at all. She smoked slowly, looking at Zach and Anna. Then she looked at Emily. Emily was still looking at the floor.

There's Parker's elk steaks, Anna said. I thawed them out last night for you'all.

What's that? Bankcroft said, coming in from the porch.

So they ate again. Elk steaks in a pan and sweet potatoes and greens fried in onions. After dinner the children just expired. They seemed completely worn out by the novelty of the day. They fell asleep sitting in their chairs. Anna and Emily and Doris took them up to bed, but for Jonah and Wahkim, and Samuel came in from somewhere and looked at the state of the kitchen and looked at Zach with a bemused and bewildered expression and turned around and left.

Chapter Thirty

They should have gone home then. They should have shook hands all around after dinner and politely bowed out and driven home. But they didn't. Nate, that is, didn't. There was only a morning's worth of work left on the run-in which Anna and Zach could handle easily and Doris and Emily were spent and the men with the exception of Canada of course were exhausted and all but a few of the children were already in bed but the truth was Zach. The truth was that somehow and for some reason which Nate could not have articulated or even conjured exactly though he had some wind of it, which, exactly like some aroma on that wind which had been haggling his sense and which he had been unable to get rid of all the working day, which had in fact increased as he watched and sawed and hammered and measured and watched so that he finally turned to it, or rather yielded to it, and decided even to stay deep into the night to prove it, if only to himself, and for good: the truth was that Zach's presence at The Lake made a slit in the lie that was the town's traumatophobia, the town's shadow, the town's antipathy to loss and grief and suffering and human deformity which is all town's antipathy and all people's too to loss and grief and suffering and human deformity simply because it materialized and paraded the fears of every man and woman against which they had built, with the very fabric and systems and even dreams of their lives, their fragile willful walls. And he wanted the town—this assembled little flake of the town—to see: because the town had rated the Beauchamp girl doomed fifteen years ago, and turned their heads from strife as people will, and deposited their own doomed at doom's door as people will. And deposited there also over the years the refuse of their mounting gossip so that The Lake had become as some inner circle of Dante's hell to their minds what with the land's lore of illicit whiskey and the feral companionless woman who practiced the reputedly voodooistic therapies upon the sick and writhing children when it was no such netherworld and when she was no such woman but one whose loneliness and passionate intensity and distrust far over-reached the yardstick of civilian measure. That is, without being able to say it, even to himself, Nate wanted with his ad hoc crew to plant for the town the first tentative seeds of their shame.

So there were seven adults mopping up the kitchen. Nate a foreman in that too, standing at the counter and washing the dishes like a man does, banging them around the sink and shaking the plates out twice each viciously in the air and then handing them to whomever to put away without even looking to see who it was or if indeed they gripped the plate at all before he bent crashing to the next dish. And the children upstairs earlier and more tired than they'd ever been on the whole. And Canada out in the dark putting gasoline on the wood for the fire. And then there was the fire and they sat around at first in jackets and blankets and then plain clothes for the heat and Zach brought Roy out to see and he stood there in his pajamas naked in his joy over the simple brightness. They were passing around a jug of cider.

Anna, you can't tell me there's none of your pappy's ruckus juice left on these premises, Bankcroft said.

Anna was pulling briars out of Patricia's hair, jerking softly at her head, and the softly babbling girl was just letting her, ragdoll and limp, as if her head was a buoy floating on a swash current which couldn't make up its mind whether to uprush to shore or backwash toward the rip. She suffered from strabismus and she was badly crosseyed and already blind in her left eye and the foveal field of her right was clouding so that she had to turn her head to the side to look at what was in front of her if she was to see anything of it at all. She loved light inordinately even as it exacerbated her amblyopia and she was trying with great effort to stare into the flames as if they held a message for her for which she'd waited all her young life. Anna stared into the fire as well and didn't say anything to Bankcroft. She just flicked the briars into the flames and watched them smolder quickly and rise as ash.

Bankcroft was watching her. Read my palm, he said.

Zach looked up at him.

Anna, read my palm.

Bankcroft looked at Zach and then motioned his head at Anna. She can read in the palm. She can tell you things even God hasn't marked in the recipe book. Even as a little girl. Her mother could too and once—

When did you ever see my mother read it? Anna said. My father said she never told anyone when she did it and she never did it in public unless you count him for public.

Fourth of July, 1963. Out on Riley's dock. She picked up Miss Josephine Romear's palm and I'll never forget it because Josephine was eating a tunafish sandwich. And the sun was setting and the boys had cut Billy's boats loose for a prank and everyone was looking to see if the wind would take them out of the harbor and Billy was saying how he was going to take his woodplane and scalp em if he ever caught em and he was saying, Son of bitches, Son of bitches, and you know Billy didn't have all the cards in anybody's deck and I said, Billy, it's sons of bitches, sons, not son, I doubt one kid could wreak havoc on all sixteen of them boats at once, let alone have more than one mother. And he looked at me like he was going to kill me and I think he might well have but then the wind blew. The wind blew easterly, lucky for them boys. For me too I guess. The boats came back in like a line of ducks. And the sunset was a sight. Just a hell of a sight. All up under the clouds like the light was trying to hook them in the mouth and take them back to the horizon for dinner. Your mother just took it out of her hand—

What? The plane? The sun?

God damn but you are difficult, girl. You and she both.

Anna laughed. The sandwich?

I reckon the sandwich, yes. And put it on Josephine's thigh and said that she wanted to have a look at something. Then she just held her hand up and traced her finger around like she was tickling. Then she looked in Josephine's eyes and I thought she was going to cry. Not Josephine, your mom. And Anita said, Josephine, just live. Just do whatever that is to you now but do it, Honey, and now. And if anyone crosses you cross them back. And take that sunflower and shake it out in the yard. Cross em hard, she said. What? Josephine said. Cross em, Anita said. Then she just threw it—the palm, Anna, she threw the lady's hand—back into her chest and Josephine didn't even tighten up the muscles in her arm or nothin and her hand just went phhwap against her chest and fell in her lap. And your mom, good lord help us all, she just picked up that tunafish sandwich and flung her hair out of her face behind her shoulders like she'd do and took a bite and said to Josephine, Honey, why don't you put some relish in this to cut your mustard next time, Jesus. And Josephine she died later that month.

The fire had caught hold of itself while he talked and the flames rose ten feet off the peripheral embers and the heatcracking from the freshly caught logs sounded like bullwhips striking at the air. The heat flushed the faces of all those sitting around and their backs were cold against the night and the fronts of their bodies were hotly aglow from the fire so that they felt like they were of two worlds at once and it was as if they experienced a width of things in a single moment and it made them serene.

I swear it. Read my palm. Read me in the palm Anna and stop making out like you don't know a damn thing about it.

I'm not making out like anything at all. I just see a man fixing to make a fool of himself and I'm trying to head him off at the pass.

Read it in the palm then.

No.

Read in it, daig gone you. I had a dream. I had a dream last night and you can put me at ease. I'm anxious.

You are, Anna said.

You would be too if you seen what I saw.

I see what you saw. Anna looked up and smiled. Almost bashful, Zach thought. Sly and bashful and downright selfbemused, and his heart beat hard in his chest and he looked at her across the flames and cursed his bones because they were squeezing his chest like there was suddenly not enough room in there for anything, not even air.

Nate, who'd begun nodding off as soon as he sat down, woke up. Where is Bobbie? he said, and then he put his hand out and felt the sleeping boy's head.

Doris got up and walked up the steps of the porch and woke her father Willard and brought him sleepwalking back to the fire. Are we going to play strip poker? the old man said.

Jonah looked at Anna without blinking. Samuel sat down next to Zach and rested the back of his hand on Zach's thigh with his palm upward as if he might be preparing to warn the gathering of too much humidity or snow or radioactivity from the beyond should such a phenomenon just happen to occur.

No, Anna said. Bankcroft's going to sing.

Really now, Willard said, looking at him.

And then the remainder of children came filing out of the house and down the steps, as upon a summons from a uniform dream, those in need down the ramp navigated by some child with practicable legs with Emily behind them all like some noviciate shepherdess whispering something about taking care but the children paid her no mind at all.

They sat down. Anna looked at them. She laughed. It's not like we've never had a fire, she said. These are human beings, she said to the children, indicating the strangers there assembled. They have two arms and two legs but they won't eat your bananas.

The children just blinked at her and waited.

What did I see? Bankcroft said.

No.

Are you telling me that there's going to be here a stoning. We've got a hell of a peanut gallery here now and they paid their money and there's going to be a stoning here unless someone gets read in the hand and it's going to be me because I'm the party in need. I'm the one all vulnerable now with all my ill omens and my wishes in my lap for all the world to see.

Get that man a wife, Nate said.

Or an ambulance, Doris said.

I had a wife, Bankcroft said.

I know it, Doris said. And you spit in her pie.

I what?

She blew out a stream of smoke. You spit in her pie. She told me.

Well, Bankcroft said.

Why did you do that? Doris said.

I don't recall. I don't even want to think about her.

I can tell you she's not thinking about you.

You're a sweet old lady, you know that?

Hush, I'm a good piece younger than you.

Stone me then, Anna said.

Good lord, Bankcroft said.

I would like a little peace, Nate said. If there's going to be a telling I wish someone would tell it.

Hold up your palm, Anna said.

What can you do from over there?

Just hold it up.

I can't even smell you from there.

Zach felt something like a taut string break in his body and he looked across the flames at the man Bankcroft who was maybe fifteen years his senior and portly and avuncular and benign for it but the string broke in his body regardless and the feeling took him by surprise and then he liked it. Let it char and smolder there inside. And fray on his own quiet breath. And cool. And mend. And then he looked at Anna.

You don't need to smell me, she said. Hold it up.

Bankcroft did. Anna didn't even look at it. Everyone knows you still owe Smiley money. But what you don't know is that he cut out two of your spark wires to your distributor cap early this morning and tonight on the way home—

I'm on Nate's couch tonight, if he don't mind, late as it is.

Nate just nodded, friendly and grave.

Tomorrow night then. On the way home your plug's going to foul and you'll get out and lift the hood and then Reeb and those boys—

Reeb's got a wife and three kids of his own now, Bankcroft said. They're in Arkansas goin on ten years next month.

Somebody's going to come around Truckee bend in their jacked-up Buick and ram into you and you're going to die and your entrails are going to spill out and be the only thing left of you on the road and the next day Jack and Jill are going to be walking across the street and Jill's going to slip on your inside parts but Jack's going to catch her just in time and hold her up like he was dipping her in the ballroom and kiss her on the mouth and she's going to fall in love with him forever and they're going to name their first born—what's your middle name?

I don't have one.

That's too bad, Anna said.

Rumpelstiltskin, Bankcroft said.

They're going to name it Rumpelstiltskin and pray their thanks to you like a wooden idol all the days of their life.

She picked another briar out of Patricia's head and flicked it into the fire and then turned the girl's whole little body around and told her in her ear to quit looking in the flames. OK, she said to the gathering. You'all can go to bed now.

They did. They got up and filed out exactly as they had come.

Sleep in your own bed, Wahkim, she called over her shoulder.

Why? he said.

Because you're the tin man and you've been sitting by the fire and I don't want any of my kids to be grilled cheese come morning.

All right, he said, laboring across the yard in his clanking braces, pausing again and looking behind him with his body twisted, holding the pose as if he was still considering what she said. Then he laughed.

Bankcroft crossed his hands at the knuckles and looked across at her. You're a sweetheart, he said. Thank you. How on earth did you know?

You're welcome, Anna said. She looked quickly at Zach and Zach thought that he saw something flicker in her eyes that he liked very much but she cast her eyes down and he wasn't sure for the light anyway which flickered indiscriminant on everything and he wasn't sure what the thing he saw in her eye was besides, guttering blazeshadows or no.

Somebody's a piece of work, Nate said, glancing at her sidelong and turning over again on his side.

That's all right, Anna said, quietly.

Yes it is, Nate said. I miss my wife.

Oh lord, Bankcroft said. Go home if you're going to feed at the nipple.

If I what?

I'm tired.

I know you are.

Nate smiled at Zach. He looked across at Bankcroft. What, are you going to be foreman tomorrow then? Like as not I'd come back and find some poles in the ground with a tarp over it and you sittin in the top of it like it was a hammock in Costa Rica, smokin a cigar saying, Aint I a hell of a hand?

But Bankcroft's chin was beginning to tilt toward his chest. I can't even hear what you're saying, he said.

It seemed (always exempting Canada) that Zach alone was not tired. Even Anna's eyes were heavylidded where she looked up at the stars. Patricia was asleep in her arms now. Samuel was dreaming. He had turned his whole face into Zach's leg and he was conversing in his dream and Zach could feel his facial expressions changing violently upon his leg and he put a hand on the boy's head to hold it steady and his hand was sore and tired from the hammering and there was happiness in his hand and he sat there and thanked it silently like it was another man sitting on his haunches at the bottom of his arm. Thank you, hand.

Nate looked over at Canada who hadn't said a word in over two hours. You got your harp?

Canada just stared into the flames as if he hadn't heard him.

Play on that thing, will you, Nate said.

Canada never even looked away from the flames. He just tilted to the side and reached into the pocket of his coveralls and pulled out a harmonica and began to play. He did not sway or express at all; he just sat like a statuefied musician but the sounds that came out of him were mournful almost beyond bearing and Zach thought again about the incommensurate nature of the world and its surfaces and then he felt an immense loneliness like a wave breaking inside his body and then a quiescence, like that selfsame swell sifted down and swallowed by sand. He looked at Anna. At her neck. She'd loosed the top buttons of her wool flannel which itself was cinnabar and like her skin darkly lambent in the light and she looked up at the stars yet and the flames tripped their amber gamboling figures on her open neck which was hot in the flames, even to his eyes. As if his eyes could feel. As if the flames were tonguing her. I have never even looked at a woman before, he thought. He almost said it out loud.

They were all motionless now before the fire, and silent, bequieted by the plangent music, sleeping or almost sleeping. Zach looked at each reposed form and he felt an unspeakable calm. The fire was still strong but it was ebbing, slowly. Then Nate said something about a dinghy. As if he was already dreaming. One dinghy never did come back, he said, mumbling.

He raised up on his elbow. Don't you remember?

He was talking to Bankcroft but Bankcroft was dozing. Nate didn't seem to care.

It was the damnest thing. That whole line of them came back but one just kept going out like it had a mind of its own. A sail even. They never even found it. It was the damnest thing.

Then he got up slowly and walked around kicking everyone gently, telling them to rise, telling them it was time to go. Everyone began to disassemble themselves out of blankets and back into jackets and they walked up to the house for the coolers and the leftover food and the tools still on the wings of the porch and clumped on the steps. But Anna called Bankcroft back. She asked him to sit down in front of her.

I may be foolish but I'm no fool, he said.

I know it, Anna said.

She held his hand and looked down into it in the light of the ebbing flames. Zach asked if she wanted him to leave and she told him no, that she wanted him to stay. Samuel was still asleep only now he was completely prone on his back with his arms flung out over his head and his legs spraddled in complete trust under the dome of the universe. Turn your hand toward the light, Anna said to Bankcroft. I can't see.

The morning's work went quickly. They nailed the already measured and cut plywood siding to the frame and screwed the corrugated roof down to the nailers. All that was left was to stack (carefully now) the healthy hay and they built a ladder from some of the residual wood and tiered the alfalfa inward from four sides and tied it with baling and stood back and looked at it. Then they cleaned up the yard and put the tools back in the shed and washed their hands and faces in the hose holding it each for the other and drank from it after and then they sat on the porch. The birdlike twitterings of a twig against a pane. A child crying in the house.

CHAPTER THIRTY ONE

The following night they were in the kitchen. The small light from the stove. The small light from the table lamp with the burnt yellow shade giving the room a soft glow. She pulled the lamp closer on the table and sat as she always sat, straddled with the chair backwards, and he sat facing her. She dipped the gauze into the calendula succus and dabbed at his mouth. She had taken the stitches out over a month ago and she had applied the succus twice daily ever since. She rested her chin on the back of her own hand atop the chairback and looked at him and said very softly, very seriously, You've healed. This is the last time.

Zach put a hand to his mouth, a finger. She didn't keep any mirrors in the house for why, she said, look at what cannot be altered but by time, but she hadn't said it in those words. When Zach asked about it she had said, We are always the same and we change and there's nothing to do about it. So she applied the succus herself that it might be done accurately and that she might check the progress meanwhile and, lately, that she might touch his mouth. More than sixty times they had sat in this silent ritual. He looked at her eyes and they blinked slowly and they were wet in the light. She held the gauze and looked at him and dipped it in the succus. A hoot owl. No sound save their breathing. No sound, no sound, no sound. She touched the corner of his mouth very gently and she put down the gauze by the lamp and covered the lid. She reached forward with her bare finger which she had never yet done and wiped some excess succus off the corner of his lower lip. Kiss me, she said.

He inhaled the breath from her own mouth. He felt his heart beating against the bones of his chest. He could not look at her eyes so he looked at her hair: some wild waxen lacquer in that light and he looked at her neck which was long and already tilted slightly and exposed as if in anticipation and he wanted to bend down into it and put his mouth to it and speak into that softness the whole history of his life. I have been sick, he said.

We are all sick. Kiss me.

No, you don't understand. I have been sick. I have been hospitalized. I tried to die. She stood up and turned the chair around and sat back down and leaned back and let out a long volume of air and then she turned out the lamp. Starlight came in from the huge northern window and the shadows of the hanging herbs lay about the kitchen. They sat. The owl again and then nothing. Not even wind to rattle the wonky siding of the house. After a long time he heard her blow at her hair and then she cleared her throat and said, My mother died having me. From the very beginning it was just him and me.

He couldn't tell if she was looking at him. Her face was as dark as her hair and she spoke quietly in a tone and of an annunciation he'd never heard in her before.

She hemorrhaged. She hated doctors and hospitals so she did it at home and she died. It was winter, December. Do you know how many thousands of times in my life I have seen my father holding me all bloody in his arms in our kitchen, looking down at my mother, telling her to breathe? Telling her Look, look at your baby girl and calling her name and telling her to breathe. They put the mattress in there so they'd be near the wood stove. Near the hot water. Standing there holding me while my mother died and then kneeling I guess beside her calling her name and holding me, I see that in my head and I—do you know how many times? So it was always just him and me. He was an electrician. We lived in Marjolaine. I rode with him in the truck. There's pictures. I'm wrapped up in blankets in the front seat. And when I was older I rode with him all summer. My whole life I had a three or four day school week. I always missed some. I hated school. I hated it so much that I'd cry like a fool not to go. He'd put me on his lap and tell me that if I made it through high school I could be an electrician and then I could work with him all the time. His name was Lance. Isn't that a beautiful name?

Zach didn't say anything. She played with her shirt and pulled a little of it out of the waist of her jeans and shifted her weight. He thought for a moment she was going to cross her legs. She had a formality about her that he'd never seen. As if she was speaking to a complete stranger (or an audience even) something which had to be recorded for posterity.

We were going to go into business. We had all kinds of names for the company, you know, stupid funny names about a father and a daughter. I was fifteen. We built our house that summer. He wanted to move out of the old one because he couldn't get shut of my mother. I had dropped out of school by then. I didn't ever once get to look at her or even hear her voice. Can you believe that? I didn't even know my own mother except for the smell of her clothes and that faded too every year even though I never washed them.

She paused.

Zach didn't say anything. He just leaned forward on his elbows and looked at the floor.

The only thing I didn't do was climb because it was illegal and dad could lose his job. Everything else I did. He paid me like an employee. On climbing calls I held the ladder until he got to the pegs. I was watching some sparrows down the wire when his body froze. She clucked her teeth.

You would think that it would've jerked, jolted, but it didn't. It just froze. She held her arms out in front of her like she was embracing the trunk of a tree. Like she was demonstrating what stillness was.

I wasn't even looking at him, but I saw it. You know how it is with your jaw when you're chewing something that's supposed to be soft and you come across a bone or a stone in it? His body did that. And he fell. Right at my feet. Stiff as a two by twelve. With a crazy smile on his face. I broke my wrist trying to catch him. And you could smell it in him. Like what it was, you could smell it in him. So I know about dying.

By now his eyes had adjusted to the darkness. When she looked up at him he could see her own eyes deep in their sockets and they looked endless and removed as if the room and even the night entire pooled in her skull and it gave Zach pause. I came out of a dying woman and the only world I had died at my feet. Smoking. And he was the best man there ever was. Kiss me.

Did he touch you? Zach said, under his breath.

Kiss me.

He leaned forward, and then he felt a rage in him from he knew not where and he suddenly stood and turned and kicked the chair across the room and shouted, I have been sick! And you want me to join the rabble? you want me to join the rabble?

What? she said, what are you talking about? but he didn't even hear her.

He went to the stove and turned his back to her and lifted it off its moorings and it came crashing down and the pilot went out and now a firmer darkness in the room.

When Zarathustra came down, when he came down from the mountain he said all the wells were poisoned. He said that their repulsive smiles glittered up to him out of every well. You don't even know me, Zach said. He was beside himself, blurting.

I am still like the madman in the market. I am still like the one in the marketplace who lit the lantern and went to all the people looking for God, asking for Him, and they laughed at him, and he said, 'Don't you hear the sound of the shovels digging God's grave?' and they laughed at him, and he said, 'Whither are we moving now? away from all suns?' and they laughed at him, and now you're laughing at me—

What? she said, you think that talk scares me? and she was crying and he heard her and he ceased and he clasped his hands behind his head and made himself look at her.

Goddamn you, she said, I am a woman.

I know. Good god you are beautiful. I don't even know what's wrong with me. He turned and crossed the kitchen and went out the door and down the porch steps and stood in the drive, the gargantuan night cold on his head.

February 28

*Three Dalmatians across the lot, a spice factory nearby, cinnamon
for sure, allspice, cumin, something, something, and something
else too, a demolition in Drydesdale (we stayed and watched—an
old elementary school), one cow and one horse in a huge field
standing together, rain at about noon, bologna sandwiches under
the awning of a funeral parlor, the bell tower in Wyeth, Wyeth,
population 1003, Samuel humming up into the vaulted ceiling of
the church, a man named Lancey in the park, good face, about
sixty, picked up the whole bike to see how heavy it was, "the
secret is to rotate and not to push," big laugh, two blue barns
(never seen a blue barn before, and two in one field), a mother
and daughter arm in arm in Flint, beeswax under my nails from
the preserve the man Lancey gave us, cold wind on last year's
dead crops, a donkey riding in a huge cattle trailer, alone, Samuel*

waving his hands up and down like a bird and suddenly the smell of eucalyptus, a beat-up VW bus with "Fortunetelling" written in bold yellow letters on the side, a cracked clay pot with a single geranium flower in the shoulder of the road, the memory of honeysuckle, a busload of children waving, I waved, Samuel didn't, tomato and basil sandwiches in the afternoon at the general store, the storm breaking, sunbeams down through a crack in the clouds, a small bridge (Samuel loves bridges), the ruins of a toppled silo, a rope swing over a creek, a sign that said "Imported Quince," what is quince? imported from where? the Pleiades out early, Orion too? cold wind out of the north, Samuel nearly sitting in the fire, millet and canned tuna for dinner, light-shadowed school yard, blowing my nose in my dirty shirt, strawberry preserve for dessert, Samuel cleaning the jar with his fingers, licking them, his wrist actually small enough to fit down in there, this Indian fig in my hand, the man in Flint who just handed it to me, Indian fig.

CHAPTER THIRTY TWO

There were two books at The Lake from which Anna read to the children, *The Adventures of Huckleberry Finn* and a dogeared volume of children's fairy tales. When she read she traced her finger along the page and read slowly enunciating clearly and Zach did not watch her read because he saw that it made her uneasy. But two nights after his paroxysm in the kitchen he heard an uproar from the reading room and he came down the stairs and leaned in the doorway. Patricia was in Anna's lap as she always was when she read; in fact she was the very gauge and temper of the story so that if the nearly blind girl registered boredom the children were bored and if she was vigilant so were they. They were all there except for Roy who was in the newly adjacent room banging two plastic hulking men together as if they were wrestling. She was reading the tale about the donkey and the hound and the cat and the cock who, to avoid imminent death from age and decrepitude at the hand of their human masters, are walking to a city far away where they dream of becoming musicians. She had read the story before and the children loved the story mostly for its denouement where the animals are seen playing in the square, according to their natures, and the people are coming from far and wide to behold the quartet and marvel upon them. But as with many of the stories there were pages missing from the battered book and so the version never told how the travelers crossed a river they reached midway on the trip. It only said that they stood on the banks and were dejected at their prospects. On this night Patricia had stopped the story. She spoke into her own shoulder even as her rheumy eyes rolled toward the ceiling. How did they cross the river?

They walked, dopey, it was a creek, Neil said.

Creek, creek, creek, creek! Edmund said, moving his head around in the air.

Anna said it was vast, Wahkim said.

I did? Anna said.

You did Anna, Raoul said.

Samuel was in the corner as he always was when she read. Sitting with immovable attention with his hands cradling his knees, watching her mouth make the words. Anna looked at him. He nodded solemnly at her that she had indeed said that it was vast. She flipped back a few pages and bent to the book and traced her finger and stopped and looked up and said, with an air of mock formality, 'It was a vast and swift river.'

Swift, swift, swift, swift, swift! Edmund said.

Patricia turned her mouth into Anna's neck. How? she said. How?

Hold on, Wahkim said. How swift?

Jonah rolled his eyes. Swift, Wahkim, swift.

Can you wash your hands in it? Wahkim said. Is it swift enough to get the dirt off your hands?

They all looked at Anna.

Roy stuck his head through the yet glassless window and said, I'm in jail.

Anna posed in thought. She looked around at them. She held out her hand as if it were dirty and she dipped it down in front of her in the imagined stream. They watched her hand as if they could see the very dirt particles dislodging from her fingers in the current. Yes, Anna said. It is.

Then the story lies, Wahkim said.

Patricia began to cry. Jonah hit Wahkim. Wahkim hit Jonah back and they stood up desperately in their mutual braces as if they would fight looking for all the world like the caricatures of two stunted medieval knights unhorsed at a jousting. July began opening and closing her mouth as if to swallow a fly that was circumnavigating her head. Chris yelled at Jonah to hit Wahkim again. Edmund hunkered his chin down into his chest and lifted his shoulders and rolled his neck left and right as if to cover his ears by turns with the raised stubs of his arms and started screaming No no no no. At this point Zach came down the stairs and leaned in the doorway. Rene went up to him and took his dangling hand and put it in her mouth. He took it out. For a moment the room quieted. We can't cross the stream, Raoul said to Zach, seriously.

Jonah and Wahkim sat down. Zach looked at Anna. She bent her forehead into Patricia's head and tried not to laugh. It's not funny, Patricia said, slobbering, starting again to cry.

Funny, Edmund said, laughing hysterically now. Funny, funny, funny!

Zach, Wahkim said, can donkeys swim?

What stream? Zach said.

The stream they have to cross to get to the city! they all screamed at him.

July softly threw up on herself. She did so often and it was no surprise and Anna set Patricia down and went to the kitchen for the rags and everyone got up to leave but Zach put his hand across the frame to bar the door. What kind of stream is it?

Swift, they all said.

Vast, Jonah said.

A troll's hair can float, Zach said. Everyone knows that.

They looked at him. What's a troll? Chris said.

A tiny person who lives in the woods and eats kids like you at night, Wahkim said.

They all screamed. He's right, Zach said. Not all of them are like that but these trolls are definitely the kid eating kind. The troll I'm thinking of in particular has eaten ten million children.

The children gasped.

How about a log raft like Huck's? Neil said.

Zach put an index finger to his temple, considering. There's no logs in troll country. Just some light branches and sticks. But a troll's hair can float, even with an elephant on a single strand of it.

They sat down, staring at him. Anna came back with a change of shirt for July and she turned her around toward the wall and lifted the soiled shirt over her head and wiped her neck and chest.

Titties, Chris said.

Shut up, Anna said.

Neil and Raoul laughed.

Shut up, Jonah said.

Everyone, for a moment, looked at Samuel until the laughing stopped. Samuel was looking at Zach: wise, bemused, serious, alone.

But, Zach said, you have to find one and cut its head off.

They all screamed again. Anna looked over her shoulder at Zach. She sat down and set the girl on her lap as before, Patricia's head lolling loosely about her chest.

Raoul looked evenly at Zach. There's a donkey and a hound and a cat and a cock. The donkey plays the piano, the hound plays the drums, the cat plays the violin, the cock plays the flute.

That's very difficult, Zach said.

Yes, Wahkim said. It's swift enough to wash your hands.

What? Zach said.

Shhh, Chris said. Tell about trolls. I'm scared.

Walkin Wahkim! Edmund blurted.

The trolls are great horsemen, but their eyesight isn't sharp in the day. So the donkey could be a decoy, Zach said.

He squatted in the doorway and ran his finger in designs on the floorboard as if he was figuring a plan. Is it daylight?

They looked at Anna. She opened the book arbitrarily and

arbitrarily put her finger down on a line and said, When they got to the river it was daylight.

It's daylight, Raoul said.

All right, Zach said. Here's what happens: The donkey knocks on the troll's door and says, Open up, I'm a horse. The troll who can't see well in the daylight says, I've been looking for you. Hop on, the donkey says, are you hungry? Yes, the troll says. Get your gun, says the donkey, and we can use my hound to hunt the rabbit. All right, the troll says. The donkey gallops—

Donkeys don't gallop, Wahkim said.

They don't? Zach said.

Nope, Wahkim said.

Zach looked at Anna. Is that true? he said.

Anna shrugged. Galloping just means a four-beat gait.

Good, Zach said, then this donkey gallops.

Then that's a world record, Wahkim said.

It's a famous donkey, Zach said.

Famous! Edmund yelled.

The donkey gallops behind the trees where his friends are waiting. He points to a pair of trees not far away and tells the cock and the cat—who plays the violin?

The cat.

Can we borrow it?

I'm scared, Chris said.

Neil and Raoul looked at Jonah and Jonah looked at Wahkim and then all four of them looked at Patricia. It was as if in the silence she could sense them. She nodded.

Whew, Zach said. All right, the donkey tells the cock to snip the strings off of the violin with his beak and tie them together to make one long string. Climb that tree over there, he says to the cock, with your end of the string, and climb that one over there, he says to the cat, with your end, and don't let go. Now I'm going to have the troll on my back, he says, and we're going to be galloping, moving fast. When we come running through the two trees each of you grab hold tightly to your end of the string and stretch it between you and it will cut the troll's head right off. Come with me, he says to the hound. Then he gallops back to the troll.

Where does the troll live? said July, in a whisper.

Everyone stared at her because she hardly spoke at all, sometimes no more than a few sentences in an entire day.

In a tree. In the roots of a great tree older than the world.

If it's in the world it can't be older than the world, Wahkim said.

Shut up Wahkim, Jonah said.

He's right, Zach said. This tree was the first tree. In fact the world was just a fruit hanging on this tree.

That's stupid, Chris said, and got up and stood with his forehead against the wall, pushing back on the balls of his feet and letting his head bang back into it, repeatedly.

Roy came back to the window. Somebody help me, I'm in jail.

So the tree where the troll lives is older than the world. The donkey gallops back and lifts up a root and calls in, The horse is here. I've got the hound. Are you hungry? How about some rabbit? The troll comes out with his gun and his rabbit hat for good luck. He climbs on the back of the donkey, the donkey gallops between the trees, the troll's head is cut off by the string, the cock plucks out his hair and they tie it around some sticks and bundles of grass and make a raft and float across the river.

Holiday, Roy said through the window, sadly. I want a holiday.

Zach stood up. The end, he said. He bent down and picked up July and lifted her over his head onto his shoulders.

Oh, Patricia said.

Everyone was silent for a moment and then July spoke again. What happened to the troll? she said, softly.

Zach mulled. He looked out the window through the crack in the curtain. The moon was waxing. He squatted and lifted the girl down and stood again.

Of course the troll was bald now, he said.

The children looked at him.

He was bald. The troll got up and brushed himself off and bent down and picked up his own head.

The children screamed.

He picked his head up by his nose and threw it, with all his might, up in the air and you can see it even now—Zach whipped open the curtain—hanging in the sky!

They broke into a pandemonium, screaming and laughing and scrabbling toward the window and looking at the moon and pushing each other aside the better to see it and hiding under each other's bodies in melodramatic terror.

Zach looked at Anna. She looked at him and shook her head. Bed, she said, and the children filed out and when the last one was gone she sat in stillness studying him.

Goddamn you, she said.

CHAPTER THIRTY THREE

Late that night he was hungry and he could not sleep. He rose from the bed in which he'd been lying propped up under two blankets and by the dim light of that same storied moon making lists. He put on his jeans and a shirt and took his notebook and pen downstairs and chunked wood into the fire and went to the kitchen and turned on the light and she was sitting at the round table in the dark, fully clothed, unchanged from the day's attire, an untouched hunk of dark bread in front of her on a plate. She was sipping tea. There was another mug at the table, an empty mug. She turned on the low table lamp. Turn that off, will you, she said, squinting.

He came to the table and sat down and she poured into his mug without even asking if he wanted any tea and he said thank you and she looked at his notebook and said, What do you write in that thing?

I make lists.

Lists?

Lists of things, lists of the things I see and smell and taste.

She looked at him. Read me some.

He looked down at the notebook and looked at her. It's just a list.

Read it to me.

It's just like you looking around this room right now: stove, tea, mug, lamp. It's nothing.

Read.

He cleared his throat. He felt his face flush and he laughed at himself who not long ago had stood in front of hundreds of students and faculty members and scholarship donors and lay Charlottesville citizenry in an auditorium and intoned flawlessly, bloodlessly, about various subjects of philosophy:

February 6

Three new creases in Nate's boots, pumpernickel, Anna's pumpernickel bread, a little blood clotting under my fingernail, a sunset of blood, a fire on the end of my hand, god, Michelangelo touching god, he would bleed, he bled, a fountain of sunlight on my headboard knob at noon today just before lunch, mango, raspberries, cherries, Raoul and Neil swallowing seeds, Neil's laughter like, like, like, the stars hung up in the branches, a little silt at the bottom of my bed, naked now, high three-quarter moon sifting through the trees, endless window, no curtains, I'm glad, no shades, naked under a naked window, three new creases in Nate's boots, my heart pounding strong, sleepless and strong, the sand on my toes now, where is it from? sand, that's loneliness, not sand, loneliness?
the sleeping stars, two hemispheres of light on the ceiling when I turn my head—

He paused.

—the plum of Anna's mouth, a look is nothing but a dagger, a dagger dipped in syrup, dipped in wine, Wahkim's laughter drifting up, her feet are always bare, like grapes, scarred grapes on the wood, this afternoon a sudden cavity in my chest and then the sun through a window of cloud, fabulous, I had to run, I ran, my feet under me like drums, the taste around my mouth, didn't shower, like dusk, I taste like dusk, later Patricia and I sitting on the couch, Where are you? Zach, she said, I'm

here, I said, Where? she said, Here, I said, Make a noise, she
said, Noise, I said, she giggled like,
like sourceless water, Your eyes, I said, are beautiful, I'm blind,
she said, the warped smoothed floorboard in the moonlight, I
leaned close to her and looked as hard as I could into her eyes,
I'm blind, she said, Yes, I said, your eyes are paintings, Paint-
ings? she said, Yes, paintings. They're landscapes of snow,
Snow? she said, Yes, I said, with mountains in the wind and big
white drifts at the bottom and sunlight on the peaks of your left
one and a few trees too, Trees? she said, Yes, trees, and there's a
stream coming down from one of the mountains in your right
eye and it's cold and clear and you can see the sky reflected in
it, My eyes? she said, Yes, I said, quiet now Zachary, hum if
you have to, quiet, night on top of the night, two nights, black
almost blue, thankful, I'm hungry for aged cheese, for wine, for
mushrooms soaked in brandy and barbecued with the edges
burnt, blue almost black, for wine, for very winey wine,
black almost blue . . .

He shut the book. He blew across the surface of his tea and
gulped once, loudly, and looked at her. It's just a list.

She was holding her mug very tightly. She was holding it so
tightly that her fingertips blanched where the blood shunted
back from the nails. Then she let go. I have to sleep, she said.

Me too. He started to rise.

Don't go, she said.

The room seemed like some portrait of a room. The woman
stroking maybe a dozen entwined strands of hair downward between the thumb and forefinger of one hand, the fingers of the
other curled lightly to her navel, the copper teakettle on the iron
trivet, the antiquated rangetop, the iron pots hanging and their
shadows on the wall. He seemed to himself like some portrait of
a man, checked at rising, one hand still on the table, already
turning away, looking back at the woman. He sat back down.
And now the shadows played about her face, the shadows from
the lamplit room and the shadows from within and he could not

tell the difference between them and her face traversed what depths what haunts of time converging and she put a finger to her mouth as if to hold the kissless flesh at bay, as if to anchor herself.

I think some deer got to the hay, he said. There were tracks out by the shed tonight when I went to feed.

What could anyone put between the pages of a school book that would make you want to die?

Do you believe in god? he said.

I had all I needed to know about god in the lap of childhood.

Are you going to live in terms of that man for the rest of your life?

Life, she said. She tossed her head and looked at him.

He was larger than life. He was storms and whiskey and the piano. He played the piano. Crazier than a carnival. And when he was drunk he played it so loud it would get so he was just trying to break the keys with his fists and he wept for her and the whole house shook and I lay up there in my bed listening to that waltz get worse and worse until it was just the keys banging without no mind to the song anymore at all and his weeping. He sounded like three men. I could put my hand up behind me and feel him in the wall. And the keys they never broke. He yelled out her name until he was hoarse and then he'd come upstairs and sit on my bed and tell me stories about her. All he could think of down to the paint color of her toenails in the sand down at the beach in Mexico where they went to fish. The way she chewed her hair when she was sleeping. The color of her skin on the white sheets. He'd just fall asleep on my bed, right there sitting. And in the mornings I'd make breakfast. Ham and potatoes and juice from two dozen oranges in a single glass. The sun came in that kitchen, good god, and the sound of birds and all. He smelled like wood, like wood after a rain in the sun. And I was his girl. Life. This is life: she indicated the low tables about the kitchen, the house, the children upstairs.

Zach stood up. You'll have to excuse me.

He walked across the kitchen but just before he got to the stair he stopped and turned and walked back and leaned on the table. What am I then?

I don't know. A ghost.

A ghost.

You said yourself you don't even know whether you want to live or die. How do I even know you're here? For over two months you've been living under one roof with a woman you call a plum and you won't even—fool, you fool, you—

I am here. Your father's the only ghost in this house.

He reached down and from the hunk of bread on the plate he tore off a small piece. He stood before her and held it in front of her mouth.

What is that? she said.

I am a fool. An idiot.

Yes, she said.

So are you, he said, moving his hand toward her mouth.

Now we are Jesus?

Shhh, he said, moving closer to her. Shut up.

She raised her brow in surprise. He pushed the bread and his fingers into her mouth. Her lips quivered. She took it. He looked at the bread until it was gone and then he looked at his hand.

Chapter Thirty four

The Texas and Pacific Railroad still made a single monthly run at night through what was called Eve's bend on the southwestern tip of the Kisatchie forest. Several minutes after the train passed and for up to forty minutes ensuing depending on the humidity of the air and the barometric pressure and the speed of the train, the tracks would sough. They reverberated a high desultory moan. Zach had heard it in December and he had asked Samuel about it and the boy had taken him to the tracks and made with his hands the gesture of vibration over them and Zach had understood that the moan issued from the rails though he thought Samuel meant that they were warped. He had nodded and thanked the boy and then Samuel had lain down on his side on the three inch rail with his cheek in his palm and his elbow propping him up and feigned to sleep, vaunting his effortless balance as if it were routine for him to come to the place and nap in a death defying act. Zach fished in his pockets. Have you seen what happens to Abe Lincoln's head?

Samuel opened one eye at him as if the man was bothering him at an inopportune moment. Then he rolled backwards off the rail and down the ballast rise and sprung up and landed already in stride and began walking the mile and a half trail back to the house, Zach falling in behind him.

But when the sound came the following night Zach was not prepared for it, the sadness of it. His pen froze and he turned out the light and went to the window and cupped his hands to the glass that he might render in nature some visible correlative to that pathos which was already pitching in incipience this month louder than it had peaked in the last, but the trees just blew and the sky just was with the moon pushing to fullness and the stars fading around it.

He heard the boy's steps before he even registered that he heard them. Heard them it seemed as surfaces hear the shadows which play upon them. As the western wall nightly heard the shadows of the leaves he had taped again to his east window— as he had taped like leaves in the hospital ward, in the eastern window of his flat on Grady Avenue, and before, and further before, starting with one leaf he'd watched in childhood actually in its instant of loosing from the topmost branch of the oak in their backyard to its instant of landing on the speared stilts of three (he, as a boy, counted them, lying down cheek to earth alongside it but not yet touching this miniature dolmen) blades of grass, and had taken it in hand thinking even then something unformed about death and fragility and perhaps even patience, watching the leaf taking all that time, the sudden carcass of it supernatant on only air to earth, and standing on the over-turned galvanized bucket he'd taped it to his eastern window so that the morning sun filtered honey through that made timeless place, monthly—just as now, the moon's light played its shadow upon the western wall which shadows of late had lanced earlier and earlier upon the bonecolored stucco of his room as it waxed and rose. He heard the steps as if he had been waiting for the sound without waiting for it.

And turned as the door opened and the light flicked on. But the boy's face was not clement and washed of any need as was its way but grimaced instead as if it simply withstood a driving rain; the eyes were not patient, but wild, desperate. As Zach had never seen them. It was the first time Samuel had not knocked or at least shuffled his feet obviously so that Zach might call him in. He turned back toward the top of the stairs and did not even turn around or so much as glance behind or even peripherally and Zach got up and followed him down the stairs.

They donned their boots in the hall. In silence, not even looking at each other, Zach not even saying What? What? in silence to the boy. Not even needing to. Not even needing to know the nature of the child's driven desperation. And in the not knowing, calm. And in the calm, wide. I feel wide, he thought. Why do I feel wide. I am not, I know it, so why do I feel it?

Outside the moan bent. Curved. Was a kind of time. A warping of time. They stood under the sound as if hesitant to go forward, to enter it. And then Samuel walked down the steps.

They crossed the drive and passed behind the shed and into the denser wood, into the wind coming light and from the south. They crossed over the creek on the laid stones. The air was cold but thick like summer. He had never seen Samuel walk so quickly and just as he remarked it to himself the boy began to run. In the woods it was nearly pitch black. Samuel wore a dyed sweatshirt, faded indigo, with on it not a single blanched circle or design to configure him out of the darkness, and the ridiculously oversized denim pants and those in imitation of Anna, bunched and caught up with nothing but a cotton rope, and the black rubber barn boots which curled his toes so that on rainy days or in the hothouse mud he had to periodically pull them off and sit and massage the blood back into his toes which he did like a man in the comfortable abstraction of a daily task, like cleaning a pipe. And then he would stand and brush his palms brusquely down his thighs as if they were dirty which they invariably were not, and go back to work. Now he ran beyond all thought of discomfort, becoming invisible and visible by turns and stretches in the trail, so that Zach was no longer calm, keeping his eyes on the slightly pale slit of the back of the boy's neck, the space between the dark shirt and his hypothesized hair which slit in the dark looked like a receding grin,

Cheshire, floating on a dark water through a dark harbor out into a dark sea, yawing erratically. Zach kept his eyes on it, his heart beating more now from fear than from the running.

And now he said it: What? What? but the boy did not hear him, or maybe he didn't even say it outloud, or said it so loudly into himself that he swallowed it.

The branches cut him. He tripped twice on a root or a stone and fell in the mud and scrabbled up but the boy did not even stop and churned on, relentless, again disappearing in the myriad thickness of the woods. A branch struck him across the face and seconds later he felt the sweat stinging where it cut him and he said the boy's name and put his finger to his cheek and then to his tongue and he could taste nothing but the running itself and the faith in the boy, could taste the blind pure faith in the strenuousness ahead of him which was too small to part the wood for him but broke the trail all the same, snapping and plunging. In fact Samuel was all but fading out of sight, ahead of him. Samuel, he called, and this time he knew he'd said it because he felt the cool air bristle on the back of his throat. Samuel.

It seemed that the woods themselves made a corridor for the boy's form alone. That the trail (and it was a trail, Zach could tell that it was or had once been a trail though one he'd never been on; even in the panicked rush he thought to himself that Samuel must have known it well to be disappearing through it deerlike as he was in the dark) made a five foot hollow, almost too low to duck through but a clearing enough to make him believe he ought to be able to walk, to keep pace with the boy. He is like a pair of knees, Zach thought. He is like a pair of knees with eyes in them, and the dark loves him, the night loves him.

And then he hit him, ran into him. His teeth actually slammed into themselves on impact, top to bottom row, audibly. Jesus, Zach said. And then he said it again: What? What?

Samuel stood breathing, holding his arms out to the sides that Zach not pass him. And then he pointed.

There was a white shirt in the clearing and it was chopping.

They looked at it. Without astonishment or even fear now, just with a kind of sated apprehension of the uncanny and inscrutable forces of nature, as two brothers or a son and a father might behold from an unscathed hillside the gaping orifice of their roofless house after a hurricane, even heaving as they were their breath becoming so quickly of a piece. Out beyond the opening where they stood and beyond still the shirt which seemed suspended in air, poised and sentenced to its own ardor by the very air itself, there was a listing, broken shack, or not even a shack but a sagging roof suspended between sagging walls. A yet denser darkness cut-out inside visible through the facing door whose lintel hung down in a diagonal in exact and almost artistic juxtaposition to the leaning of the roof. And scabrous vines crosswise about the mouth of the door and encompassing the structure entire so that the building looked inhumed in the air itself, caught in a net of dead vines as if it had been poised at one time to be lifted out on the hook of a crane which had given up the notion, or just broke, the cancer of the distillery left there to rot in the body of the woods. It smelled bad. It was not the wind that smelled. He couldn't say of what exactly: sulphur perhaps, burnt lime. He stood in the wind licking at him, sour, seductive, with a scent he thought if not of evil then at least of unredemption, like the scent of failure, of old dusty and useless rooms in abandoned houses, rooms in which nothing of consequence had been thought of or dreamt. But it was not, as he had thought, the wind. All that time over here I thought I was just sad, he thought. I thought it was the wind on this side of the house making me sad. Walking over here, he thought, I thought there was just something wrong with me.

There was a tree and a tire hung in it not unlike the one directly off the gallery steps of the main house. The earth of the knoll mounded, planetary. A white nylon lawn chair just blazing out in the darkness placed at the crest, or more truly the apogee of the hillock, because the clearing did seem to float and stretch away from that rank structure and all that density of wood as upon a select and reverse gravity, the chair broken, crippled and leaning, ludicrous, and beyond its plastic aberration the shirt not just chopping now but swinging and now prodding at the earth almost carefully and then swinging again, wildly, as if it was killing something already dead, and then again tamping delicately, as if apologizing for that very same act.

Her back was to them, her breath harsh. He would have said her name, was in fact about to call out Anna, but Samuel backed him further into the shadows. And squatted. And so he knew that this was not something that the boy wanted him to stop but rather to see. To witness. Zach whispered her name.

She held a shovel. She was looking for something. And now he squatted too, his chin above the boy's head only by an inch so that he could have leaned forward and rested upon him, easily. He didn't. And then the light metallic tink. She fell on her knees and began scraping with her hands at the place. And then she stood and began frantically shovelling, hurling the wet earth behind her, until the thing whatever it was emerged and she knelt down again almost in consecration of it or supplication to it and pawed the mud off it and began shovelling again and then bent and lifted the glass jug out of the ground which made a sucking sound of resignation the boy and the man could hear twenty yards away. She held it up like a newborn, like a child. Like a child swung upward to kick its legs in joy in some dusk, Zach thought.

She set it down and looked at it. She laughed. And then coiling her body one hundred and eighty degrees as if she might simply walk away from the scene she swung the spade back around and smashed the glass and stood over it and watched the liquid absorb into the earth and seconds later the wind brought the heavy smell of whiskey on the air to the boy and the man squatting in the harbor of the woods. She stood looking down at the smashed bottle and the earth. Then she commenced to digging about the whole hill. She brought jug after jug out of the wet ground and smashed them. She's barefoot, Zach whispered into Samuel's ear, and Samuel without taking his eyes off the woman turned and gripped Zach's arm that he not rise.

She doesn't have any shoes on, Zach said. She's going to cut herself.

It was true. At first it seemed she tired. She looked, for a moment, like a golfer at a tee: paused, gauging, the shovel upon her shoulder. And then she tired further and lowered it and rested the spadepoint in the dirt and rested both hands on the handle like a farmer at his plot and lifted one of her feet and looked down at it and cursed.

In the silence they could hear the last expiring warble of the tracks, and then nothing. She stood under that vast quiet and lifted once more the shovel and swung once more with a kind of spent female finality at the neck of the last righted bottle. Just the spout broke off on the blade. She knelt and picked it out of the mud and wiped it on her shirt. She sat, fell in the chair and bent over, facing away from them. At first he thought she was crying. And then he knew she was not. It seemed from their vantage that she began working at something in front of her. She seemed to be drawing in the mud, to be concentrating, her body at once obdurate and spent. Shit, she said.

Samuel rose and turned back down the path quietly walking and Zach turned and watched him as he hunched slightly around his own body as if it were a thing he was protecting from itself, himself, until he disappeared. He turned back to Anna. She was still hunched over working at the earth in front of her with the decapitated spout. He looked again down the path but Samuel was gone. He turned and looked at Anna. I have seen those scars, he thought, I have seen my god those scars and he knew she was digging in no dirt and the aloneness he felt was like nothing he ever knew he would have to or was supposed to feel or bear because he'd never cared for anyone before. It's not even my loneliness he thought, and that's why I almost can't bear it.

He saw himself rise and walk out from the woods and across

the clearing and stand in front of her. He saw himself bend and take from her hand, or try to, wringing her wrist back and forth as if she had drunk rather than squandered the liquor and sat inebriated brandishing a knife at him which she might as well have been, the jagged glass with the waxed cork still sunk in the lip with which bladed edge she was making a fine and careful cut in the bottom of her foot, holding for steady purchase the fingerlooped handle of the spout against her flexed sole. Wounding herself along scars, Zach thought, along scars healed from time past and before, maybe as in some terrible self-inflicting rite, before and before. I have seen those scars, he said to her.

Go away, she said. You're not even here.

I am.

She looked up at him: calm, almost radiant, sated. No you're not.

With a jerk he wrenched free the brokenoff spout and hurled it into the trees. I am, he said again.

She looked to where the spout had disappeared into the woods. Then she attended calmly to her foot, peeling back a section of skin and sawing the last of it against her thumbnail. She turned the protruding glass slightly and very carefully removed the lodged shard from her foot and put a thumb to the gushing place and looked up at him. Why did you do that? she said.

Why are you cutting yourself with it?

Because I already cut myself.

What?

I stepped on some glass. She held up her foot, proffered it up to him academically and showed him the gaping wound behind the arch at center, toward the heel. He bent and peered closely at it where the blood flushed out freely until she closed it again with her thumb. I was trying to cut it out before it went deeper. It hooked. I was trying to cut it out so I wouldn't pull half my foot out on the snag. Then at least I could have walked to the house to wrap it.

Zach just looked down at her. He didn't know what to say. You're not cutting yourself?

I am cutting myself.

I mean cutting yourself.

Why on earth would I be cutting myself?

He felt his face color and he was glad for the dark. Oh, he said. He felt suddenly tired. He turned around and was about to set the jar down and leave. Go, she said. You're not even here.

He turned back around. I am, he said, goddammit. He picked up the jug and began to pour the whiskey over her foot. She winced but she did not move. Keep going, she said, it'll clean it.

Do you see? he said.

I see, she said. Keep going.

When the jar was empty he flung it down and looked about and found another one half full and sloshed it too over her foot, shaking it out roughly, regardless. He looked for other jugs. He poured over her foot the remains of every jug on the hill which she had dug up and still held liquid. She sat and watched him harvest the jugs and return, sat with a quiet patient air, an air almost of spiritualized tolerance. He knelt. He put his hands on the leaning and cracked and useless armrests and shook the chair. He himself was shaking. What the hell are you doing? he said.

She looked around her at the broken shards of glass, the spadewrenched upheave of wet protruding earth; she looked at the ramshackle listing crib. She looked at him with an infinite calm. I am smashing jugs.

Zach knelt motionless in front of her. He looked at her bleeding foot which she cradled now in her hand. He looked around at the knoll, at the dizziness of the nothing and the everything, the uprush of the trees and the flat disc of the night lidding the alcove they made and then he looked at her again. I thought that you were—I have seen those scars—I thought that—

What, these? she said, pointing to the curve of her right instep (and there was a hint of triumph in her eyes, if it were light enough he would have seen a quiet placidity the aroma of gentle vanquishment, second dark cousin to joy) where across the bone a line of raised welts like swollen veins or even calculated brands traversed the high arching length of her foot. Shane ran over me with the rototill. I can't even remember how many years ago. He doesn't even live with us anymore.

Zach started to rise. Go, she said, you're not even—

Goddammit! he yelled, sinking back to his knees as if the uprise had been just a coiling, just a marshalling of muscle and rage and he struck his fist with tremendous force into the earth.

Goddammit! He struck the earth again, and then again, and then he ceased. He waited until he could breathe and then he whispered, his fist all but disappeared into the mud: I am here.

For a moment they were completely still. Then she breathed. She moved the back of her hand toward his throat and it rose as upon an invisible slipstream and touched, lightly, like a helium balloon to a ceiling, his chin. She left it there. I'm sorry, she whispered.

He looked at her foot. Do you want me to carry you back?

What do you think? she said.

I didn't think so.

He stood and turned and began to walk toward the branches that bowed over the entrance to the trail.

Zach, she said. Of course I do.

He stopped. He walked back toward her. He turned and squatted in front of her and she climbed up on his back and she wrapped her legs around his waist and wrapped her arms around his neck. He bowed through the limb rondure to the path and the branches scratched at him and he did not care.

He had to set her down several times for the low traversing boles. She knelt underneath them and hopped on one foot while he balanced her by her hand and she held on to the trunk with her other and said curses against herself for the foolery of walking barefoot on shards of broken glass she'd smashed by her own hand. All the while he carried her he stepped very carefully, his back bent low, her chin on his shoulder, the branches clawing at his hair and face and she dipping her face behind him, the foliage scraping along his shoulders, walking circumspect, almost dainty down the low trail that the branches not snap back upon her.

When they got to the porch he squatted down and she slid off his back onto her good foot and sat down on the steps. She tossed her head and looked up at him. He backed away from her as if she were an animal that had been tranquilized and was coming to. She looked down the length of her body and then she was laughing. A fullthroated limitless laughter, holding her shirt out in front of her, laughing and laughing. What? Zach said.

She tried to tell him but she couldn't stop laughing and she pointed at her shirt where it had ripped on a branch and revealed beneath the tear her undershirt and the ropetied waist of her jeans and she could not speak for her laughter. What? Zach said again. What?

I've waited thirty—she broke, laughing—I've waited thirty one years for a man to pick me up and rip my dress. I thought I'd have to—but then she was just laughing and so was Zach now and he walked toward her and he grabbed the two frayed pieces of her shirt one in each hand and ripped it all the way to the collar and neither of them could speak now for their laughter and he leaned his forehead into hers and when at last he could get a breath he said, You terrify me.

She put a finger to his mouth and said, Thank you.

It's nothin but my Christian duty, he said, and they laughed some more and Wahkim cracked the bathroom window and called down to be quiet please and they doubled over themselves and quaked there in mutual fits of silence.

CHAPTER THIRTY FIVE

By the time Zach and Samuel got to Bayou Chicot it was getting dark. At a filling station attached to a restaurant Zach coasted the bicycle past the pumps and looked down the road. Then he kicked down the stand and Samuel ducked and Zach swung his leg over his head and stood and looked again at the road. The sign pointed in three directions: Lorraine, Lone Star, Pine Clearing. Zach looked at Samuel. Samuel looked up at the sky arcing his head from east to west and then, from where he sat in the dairy crate, he let his head come forward and bang dramatically on the back of Zach's seat. He kept it there and began to feign to snore. All right, Zach said. I need to piss.

He started to walk toward the store but then he saw the air and water pumps alongside the building and he took the waterhose off its spool and unraveled it walking all the way across the lot back to Samuel who when he saw him coming tilted back his head. Open up, Maestro, Zach said, and aimed the stream into Samuel's upturned mouth.

The restroom was off the anteroom to the restaurant and Zach was a long time coming out. The place was full. When he did come out what he saw was a busload of elderly tourists from the east coast transfixed on something performative and gesticulant among them and that something was Samuel. He was holding silent court. The travelers were spellbound. Samuel was pulling various tools and utensils out of the basket in front and he was squatting right there in the lot and one by one demonstrating their uses. He lit the stove and turned it high and low and finally spat on it so that all assembled heard the sizzle and held their mouths and gasped and took a step back. Then he blew up the diminutive air pad and lay down on it and for a few seconds pretended to sleep. He got up and looked about the crowd and found the most able bodied victim he could and took his hands and placed them firmly on the bars and had him straddle the front wheel and indicated with much animation that he must needs hold the bike very steady and then Samuel, in a feat Zach himself hadn't even seen, took seven steps back as if he was an Olympic jumper with a practiced routine and ran in a curve and landed squarely in the crate. And bowed from where he sat to the applause. He got out and put a finger to his lips and pointed to Zach who was walking toward the crowd.

They took a table by the window. The table had only one menu on it and Zach handed it to Samuel who glanced at it a moment and then Zach took it back. It was the first time they'd actually sat in a restaurant. Zach had some money from working with Nate but not much and they had to make it last as long as they could so they ate primarily out of cans on the curbs of filling stations or in the evenings by the fire once they'd found a place to camp. But they'd been riding for more than eight hours and they were tired and hungry and it was getting cold and it wasn't often besides that a bustling restaurant just blazed upon them at six o'clock in the evening. After a few moments the waitress came up and asked if they were ready to order. She was pretty in a girlish way. Zach looked at Samuel. Go ahead, Maestro, he said. Order.

The waitress turned to Samuel. What'll you have, sweetie?

Zach still held the menu. Samuel looked at Zach. Go ahead and tell her what you want, he said.

Samuel stared at him.

The waitress flipped her hair with the back of her free hand. I got a heap a tables y'all, if you don't mind.

Tell her what you want.

Samuel looked at the waitress then back to Zach then at the waitress then back to Zach, glowering.

Does he speak? she said.

Zach looked at the boy, the corners of his mouth lifting slightly. He does. He speaks Egyptian.

Egyptian?

He's from Egypt. He's royalty. He speaks Egyptian. He speaks Egyptian and then I translate. We're on a tour of the local ruins. You may have some Egyptians buried in these hills.

The waitress looked at him. You're full of it.

No I'm not, I'm serious. He's Egyptian. Have you ever seen an Egyptian?

I've seen King Tut on the *National Geographic* in the school library.

Well look at him, doesn't he look like King Tut?

She looked at Samuel. Despite himself the boy did seem to compose into a sovereign mien. Or already was.

You're full of it. Come on y'all, I got tables.

Say something in Egyptian.

Samuel was stewing. His arms were crossed against his chest now and he was fairly snorting.

Y'all, the waitress said, tapping her pencil to her pad, I don't got time for this.

Tell the lady what you want.

Samuel turned his head to the side and leaned forward like he would come across the table and bore a hole in Zach's head.

Y'all!

Suddenly Samuel snatched the menu out of Zach's hand and scanned the price column quickly and pointed. She leaned over. The filet mignon? she said.

Samuel nodded and held up two fingers. He sat back and beamed across at Zach. For a moment Zach's face lost all color.

He looked at the menu. The filet mignon was $21.95. Each. Samuel was just beside himself. He fell down sideways in the booth and held himself, laughing, wheezing. Zach called out to the waitress but she didn't hear or she didn't dare turn back around.

That night they camped in a playground on a knoll beside what looked like an abandoned two room schoolhouse overlooking a range of ghostlylooking cattle silently shifting in the night. Samuel would not sleep. With the pen flashlight he was bent over studying the pocket atlas. Twice Zach woke up and watched him for a time and went back to sleep. Almost surreptitiously Samuel had become the chief navigator of their group and Zach thought that he was plotting a route. When he woke up a third time two and a half hours had gone by and suddenly he realized what the boy was doing. Oh lord, he said, out loud. He's looking for Egypt. Samuel, go to sleep. Egypt's in Egypt.

Chapter Thirty six

He lay awake in his room with the smell of whiskey and mud on his hands and very late that night he heard the motorcycle start. He thought perhaps he'd fallen asleep after all and he was dreaming but he heard clearly the throttle gun and the click-lull-rev click-lull-rev of the up-gearing and then the sound died away. He sat up. Silence. He got out of bed and put on his bibs and walked downstairs and out to the porch and shut the door behind him. He turned his body into a humid cool, the air almost sweet as from the aroma of drenched buds but it was January and it was just a southerly wind off the sedge skirting the lake. He watched his breath cloud out and vanish and then he inhaled deeply the aroma and held it and let it go long and even through the downshaft of the porch light and into the world. It's not even spring, he thought. Not nearly. How can it smell like this?

He walked to the shed to see if the bike was surely gone and it was. He stood. He looked back at the house where eleven children were sleeping under the roof. He looked back down the road. He looked back at the house all dark above the porch. And then the hairs on his neck began to lift and his skin began to tingle. He did not know if she was gone for ten minutes or ten years.

It must have been close to midnight. He went back inside and climbed the stairs and crept very quietly into the rooms and looked at the sleeping children. He watched them for a long time. He went from room to room and watched the diminutive chests rising into the air and the unconscious limbs hanging off the beds and the troubled little vowels of their mouths as they slept and he watched their dreams. He squatted beside them and in the cast light from the hall he studied their faces. The translucent, flickering eyelids. The disheveled hair and the random arrangement of the limbs as if a mistral wind had come through their separate dreams and blown them of a piece. He smelled the clean musky innocence of their breath. He sat motionless before every child and studied them and tried to see their dreams and he did so with great concentration and then he sat in the middle of the floor and listened to the room on the whole, the orchestra of their fraught air. He thought that he must not sleep. That he must not lose thought of their dreams even for a second or they would wake into the contortions of their lives. And he wondered if they did in fact dream of health. He wondered if by the grace of the same god that had struck them down they came to fruition in their dreams. If their bodies moved like athletes upon a field, muscle and skin and bone sensate married to the world by only gravity and time and light which they could evade and postpone in their dreams like dolphins poised and turning in flight above their element of sea. Or if unbraced and manumitted they strided vigorously over some country course of dew and strongrooted trees; or if some sea air licked them well, some sun bronzed them well so that they licked their own arms and tasted their salt. If they dreamed of their selves— if they saw themselves five-ten-fifteen years hence somehow profounder, more compelling, wiser, truer, fairer, more virile or graceful, more humble or plainly proud, more patient or still, if they kissed lovers lifting them against stone walls or hoisted children of their own above their heads or wept for strangers' lives or saw themselves standing out upon stone outcrops in electric storms to crack the terrifying monotony of their lives. He did not sleep.

He took the blanket from his bed and two blankets from the hall and went out to the porch. He couldn't have said why but he went because he was sure the day was pressing upon the house. He went to stave off the day. In truth he felt like a guard. In truth he wanted to kill something. He wanted anything, a demon or a man or just a shadow to so much as try to wake the children. It was as if he was sitting there with a gun held to the head of conscious life itself so that they might rest unharmed and perfected in their dreams.

By morning he was very cold. He was wrapped like a monk, like a monk exiled from his bunker. But he was awake. At first light Anna drove up on the bike with Doris behind her in a pickup truck. She circled and cut the engine and kicked down the stand and walked quickly up the steps, looking at him, beaming, from the cold her face glowing above the scarf and the fatigue jacket collar buttoned up to her chin, and her eyes glowing brightly from something else. We're going, she said to him.

We are? he said.

I'm taking you up to Salt Peak. With Jenny.

Good, he said. Wake me in three hours. I need to get some sleep.

Two, she said.

Three, I haven't slept a wink, he said, over his shoulder, all but stumbling on the blankets, turning to see her and simply astonished at her beauty. Her face glowed so hotly it looked like she had a fever.

Hurry, she said.

They started out on a trail which met the property's west flank in an alluvial stand of beach pines whose needles looked almost sky blue in the midmorning light, a trail which in all his coursings Zach had not seen. The cut on her foot was not nearly as bad as it had seemed the night before and she'd just bound it under her sock and they travelled afoot at first, taking turns leading the mule. Jenny was trembling with excitement, just beside herself at the prospect of anything in the world other than a paddock fence and a lean-to. She was leaning down and sniffing, looking about her from side to side, snorting.

They walked along a creek and then crossed it upon the stones and Jenny wouldn't have anything of it and she stood pulling back on the lead rope and Anna took the rope from Zach and crossed back over herself and stood at the mule's near shoulder and clucked and walked forward but she still wouldn't cross. Give me a leg up, she said.

Zach crossed back over the stones and interlocked his hands and she stepped into them with her muddy boot and swung her other leg over the mule's back and said thank you and Zach bent down and in the cold creekwater he rinsed his hands. Anna tied the loose end of the lead up under the halter and lifted Jenny's head and made a clucking sound again and touched her sides with her heels and she crossed over easily, looking down into the water as if at her own reflection.

They began to ascend now and the hills made a fold which cradled the creek all the way to Mora Bluff and they walked along it, Anna up on the mule, Zach walking alongside, and she told him about the land. She told him that her blood went back to the pre-Purchase French colonists and she told him about her thrice distanced grandfather and the railroad and the mill and the house he had built and his dreams for his family and America and in a clearing she pointed to the huge slightly greener shadow east of Ducasse Culvert where the pine had been cleared to baldness over a hundred years ago and she pointed to the old mill. She told him about Moses and Swell and the first petty distillery the jujus of which were still hanging in Barely Knee and he asked if she could take him there and she said that she would. She spoke of the long line of Beauchamps and she told him stories handed down of their exploits and mishaps and arrests and night flights in these hills from local sheriffs who packed guns but would never use them on their own veritable brethren and in fact enjoyed the chase as much as the games they had played as children with some of these very same Beauchamps now grown to men in these very same hills and she spoke also of their skills: Jacques' father who was a wheelwright in America and Jacques' father's father who was a wheelwright before him in France and the long line of mule men since time immemorial and carpenters and then electricians that was not only their family legacy but the faultless side of the scale against which they measured their failings and even both their notorious and closeted ills.

In the clearings and along the way she named the trees and the mostly fallow foliage and he beheld the swaths of aberrant oak and sumac which she pointed out and the pine, the dense undulating thick darkness of the pine, and she talked with a quality tranquil and animate both as she sat the mule and pointed out over the land and he listened carefully and he remembered the names of all the plants and trees she mentioned and he vowed to himself to return in privacy and look at them long and sit with them and try to know them in what way and manner of knowledge he could not say.

They made the peak by late afternoon. Anna tied Jenny's lead to a stubtree and they scrabbled up the thumb shaped arête and stood in the wind looking south the way they had come and they could see far beyond the forest to the plains out past Anacoco and Slagie and the flat ochre land beyond the Sabine. He looked north where the forest rolled out endlessly before them and then east and west and once for an eternal moment she leaned up against him very lightly and tilted back her head and he felt almost sick with what he didn't even know was his happiness and then they scrabbled down and sat looking south with the sacks of food they had brought in their laps and the wind in their faces. They passed the water jug between them and ate the sandwiches in silence for a time and then she told him about Kish and her life in Bayou St. John, about the learning, the medicine at the hands of the graceful and sagacious woman the

Bayou called the leaf doctor. She spoke about Wahkim and then she spoke in detail of all the succeeding children at The Lake, their origins and their ailments. She started to speak about Samuel.

He has epilepsy, Zach said.

She stood up. Did he seizure?

No, he told me.

She looked down at him incredulously.

He wrote it down.

She sat back down. She sighed. Zach had never heard her sigh but once before and that in sarcasm in the midst of her mock lecture on carpentry and it was strange to hear it in earnest. He has more than epilepsy, she said. It's some disease that takes his breath. It makes his heart beat wrong, more and more all the time. It's what they call a degenerative disease. I think his chest is getting smaller. Sometimes I think I can even see the change in it from the outside. I think his organs are being crushed.

Does it have to do with the epilepsy?

I don't know.

Now the afternoon was a slanting auburn light, the sun not yet level with the darkening waves of the westernmost trees but lowering, and it was cooler and they hunkered down for the wind and they pushed their jackets up against their chins.

What do you do?

There's herbs to quiet the heart. To thin the blood. To clear the lungs. Have you heard that his breathing's worse?

Yes. He can't sneak up on me anymore. I have to pretend. Tell me about the seizures. What are they? What happens to him?

She said that they were infrequent but that they were very bad, that at times they seemed related to some stress and at other times they seemed to have no cause at all. She thought that perhaps he had stopped speaking for the shame of it or perhaps it was something of the other problem and his vocal cords had just stopped working.

They're serious, she said. Sometimes he has partial ones, but he's something.

She smiled now and shook her head and picked up a pebble and threw it at nothing and leaned her head back on the rock. He can stop those from coming on almost always just by humming. That's why he hums all the time. Because he thinks he'll keep them away by humming.

She laughed softly. The big ones he can't stop. The tonic-clonic. The grand mal. I give him herbs. Passionflower and valerian. Breathing exercises. I try to keep him calm. One time he hit his head on the banister and knocked himself out. Another time he spun out right at breakfast. He spun on the kitchen floor and every kid in the house was standing around watching him. When he came to I bent down and held him to keep him steady. He had puke all over his chin and he'd bit his tongue and he was bleeding and you could smell the shit in his pants. He looked up at me like a wild animal and then he looked at all the kids staring at him and he elbowed me though I tried to hold him steady. He elbowed me hard.

She felt her left pectoral through her layers as if she still smarted from the bruise.

It was summertime. He ran out into the woods. He slept in the woods for five days. And from that time on he gave up his bed. He wouldn't sleep in one place anymore. He sleeps outside, or with me. Or somewhere. Does he sleep with you?

Zach shook his head no.

I've taught him to breathe, she said. I read about a study on epilepsy. There's a way to breathe from your stomach that gives you more oxygen and relaxes the organs in your chest at the same time. Opera singers do it too. Lie down.

What?

Lie down on your back.

I am, he said.

All the way.

She smirked. I'm not going to hurt you. Lift up your jacket.

He did. She put her hand low down on his stomach and told him to breathe. A cold hand that was not cold, that burned. She spoke quietly. She told him to imagine that her hand was a feather which he was lifting with his inhalations and collapsing with his exhalations. She said that it was good for everyone to breathe like this because one took in three times the amount of oxygen per breath and that the diaphragm was lower than people imagined and that the chest was useless.

But Zach wasn't listening. He had closed his eyes. She stopped speaking. He had seen her in treatment burning some herb a few inches from the skin of some of the children and her hand was so hot, or his belly under it was, that for a moment he thought she might somehow be performing the same cure on him and he opened his eyes. She was looking at him. Her hand wasn't even on his stomach anymore. He felt naked; he didn't know when she had taken it away.

He sat up and leaned back against the rock. Does he breathe like this all the time?

Yes. I read about it in a book.

Where is he from? How did he get here?

He just came.

She told Zach that Samuel had been very clean when he arrived and that his hair was combed in a style of antiquity, greased, parted to the side. She said that his clothes were expensive and also outdated: a bright red vest, corduroy, with a tiny gold trumpet pinned to his chest. She said that she'd saved it and that she would show it to him. He wore plaid pants and shiny diminutive loafers with pennies in the tongues and he carried a red duffel bag which had been packed very carefully and she laughed and said that he even had a kit for his toiletries. She said that he must have been dropped just up the road because he had come in walking but his shoes hadn't been muddy. Then she turned and looked at Zach, her head flat back against the rock with her hair splayed upon it in the wind. He didn't just come. He walked into the kitchen. I was washing dishes. He just walked in and dropped his bag and went through the entire house, both floors, opening up every door and closing it again. And when he'd done with that he came back down to the kitchen. I was sitting in a chair then over at Neil and Raoul's table in the corner and it was the middle of the afternoon and I was alone in the kitchen and I don't even know why I sat down but I did and he came up to me and stood looking at me, you know the way Samuel can look, and—

What way?

What?

How did he look at you?

She looked up at the sky as if sky itself could dispense such a description. Like I was a forest on fire and he was standing there watching me burn with a hose in his hand as if he wasn't sure whether it would be better in the long run for the earth to just let me burn or to put me out—like that.

Good god, Zach said.

What?

That's just exactly how he looks.

I know. And he stood there looking at me like that for a long time, I don't know, five minutes, and then he took that gold pin out of his lapel and opened it and pricked his finger on the tip so that it bled a little and then he rubbed it into the palm of my hand.

Really?

Yes.

Why?

She looked at him. Do you think when someone does something like that there is a why? Is there always a why?

She looked at the setting sun. Why is the sun? Why is a mule?

What did you do? Zach said.

I held out my other hand.

Zach looked at her. He looked at her hands which were sun-dark and thinnish and strong and relaxed on her thighs. She laughed. And then I barely saw him, he barely looked at me again for six months. And now—

She broke off. She threw another pebble at nothing. She threw a tiny pebble at Jenny's croup and Jenny turned and looked at her and Anna said, Hello mule.

I still don't know anything about him, she said. He is the only one I have no history of. And you.

Me? Am I one of your charges? he said, remembering the first day.

No, she said. No. She tossed her head as if the very idea was some dead leaf that had fallen in her hair.

No. All I know is that you have a lot of school in you and that you tried to kill yourself.

That's about it, Zach said. Is it so obvious?

What?

That I have all that school in me.

Yes.

So he sat there against the rock with the wind picking up and the sun falling almost tangibly now through the last margin of blue on the rim of the western sky and he told her that he had more school in him than she could possibly imagine and that it had done him no good. That he was a philosopher of great promise and that it had almost killed him. He told her that he knew that everything had its proper use and place but that philosophy now seemed to him the enemy of the world. That he had for so long been thinking about thinking that he had no single thought to keep him here, and he told her about Nietzsche and about lying in the road and about the hospital. He told her about Lazar and their long evenings and the smuggled exotic food and the nurse and the pomegranate seeds. He said that Lazar cooked as well as she did, or better, and that she would love the old man because he stood next to trees.

She laughed. Why does he do that?

To see if they'll lean toward him, Zach said, and she laughed again.

I do, she said.

What?

I like the man.

He said that he hadn't seen his parents since he was seventeen and that he'd found out anyway that they weren't his blood parents after all. That he had gone to visit them in turn—they'd been divorced five years at that time—that first break of college to tell them of his studies and his plans to become a philosopher. And he found his mother at home where she lived atop a high hill in Potomac Maryland in a house with seventeen rooms, the five bathrooms not included, and windows all around, found her standing in the center of what she called her Chakra Room holding in one hand a phallic crystal and in the other pictures of men, one at a time, from various countries around the world. A psychic she'd met at some aura retreat had stood in front of her ceremoniously handing her the pictures one at a time. And the idea was that with her eyes closed and the crystal in her hand and the powerful medium of the psychic she would know what country to travel to next to take a lover. And he had stood and watched this pathetic ceremony and turned around and gone out the door with not so much as a hello or goodbye Zachary from this woman, this mother who had been a hippie in the sixties because everyone else was, and had adopted him off the reservation probably because it was in vogue to have a darling and abject Indian child whose identity she then concealed from him as if, out of the magnanimity of her own heart, to buffer his own imminent shame.

Indian? Anna said.

Indian. Navajo. Navajo Indian.

And he told her then of how he'd driven straight to his father's and had stood in the dark study across the huge custom granite-top desk and relinquished the money that came from the man and paid for his food and board and education because he had won a fellowship from the philosophy department but more because he could not brook anymore receiving money from a man with no scruples whatsoever whose singular god and world was that very money he hoarded and grudgingly gave, and Zach had stood there abdicating, and said so.

All right, his father had said. All right. If you aren't a son of a bitch, if you aren't a kept man. That's easy enough to say when I've put the clothes on your back and the food in your stomach.

You've been a kept man. All right. Get out of here. You've been a kept man all your life. And it was your mother I married not—

And he had stopped. And the two men had stared at each other, the trader of commodities and the undergraduate, as if the truth might suddenly materialize and even mollify them both, if they stood still enough, stony enough. But there would be no continuation of that sentence, no word reference to the inexorable forbidden knowing that filled the room like steam searing upward from a quenching, not, at least, until Lazar found the records. And had continued:

You want to know what the world's like? You want to know what it's like? Get the fuck out of my office and don't come back unless it's to beg for money. And then it better be to beg.

He described then how he'd left and driven the rental car (his roommate had had to fill the paperwork out for him because he was still too young to rent a car) down to Virginia and back to the university and the books, the philosophers, Aristotle and Plato and Luxemburg and Gramsci, Kristeva and Arendt, Kierkegaard, Habermas and Benjamin, above all Heidegger and Nietzsche, who were to be his daily bread for the next ten years.

He had been told all his life that he was half Italian on his mother's side and half Irish on his father's, a consanguinity that conveniently matched his looks, but in truth, he told her, he had been adopted. He described how Lazar had discovered this and how he had tried to find out the whereabouts of his real parents and that he could not. The old man knew only that he was born on the reservation and that his father was Dutch and had at one time traded Zuni jewelry and that his mother had come from a community called Window Rock. The records showed she was only half Navajo. That was all the information he could get.

He explained about the rucksack and the money and the shelter and the men called Mull and Willy and the razor and his mouth and how he'd gotten off the bus for no reason at all in Marjolaine and about Bobbie and Nate, which story she already knew. He said that he was going to Arizona to try and find his blood parents and to introduce himself to them, whoever they might be, so that he might begin to live.

When he finished she sat forward and looked at him very seriously. She picked up a pine needle that had blown on her thigh and put it between her teeth. Her face looked rinsed and smooth and her eyes were wet. From the wind, he told himself, from the wind.

She studied him for a long time. Be careful, she said, finally.

Of what?

You may not like them.

I've thought about that.

Maybe, she said.

Maybe, he repeated. She was forever saying maybe.

What do you mean maybe?

Your voice. You're expecting them to be what the other ones weren't. You have no idea what you're going to find. They gave you up in the first place. They might not even be alive.

He looked at her a long time and then he nodded his head.

Now the west was bright orange and the clouds burned at their edges where the sun had plunged. Distanced north and south along the horizon little crescents of silver backdropped by the matting blue lined the earth like spume crashing against the cliffs of another antipodean world. Look at that, he said.

The truth is, she said, I really don't know what philosophy is.

He was still looking at the sky. You don't need to know.

You don't need to tell me that. I think about everything all the time. Is that philosophy?

No.

What is it then?

I don't know.

For ten years they paid you to read all those books and you don't know?

That's right, he said. It's almost dark, we should go.

Make something up.

It's not just thinking, Zach said. He stood and brushed off his seat and reached a hand down to help her up.

She didn't take it. What is it? she said.

Come on, he said, let's go.

She took his hand and he pulled her up and they walked over and stood by the mule who had not stopped eating the brown tufts of snake grass the entire time they'd been sitting. Zach leaned against Jenny's flank and looked at Anna. She was standing with her arms straight down along her sides and her fists were curled up in her sleeves for the cold and she was looking at him. Her skin looked almost blue in the last light to darkness and her expression was earnest to the point of protestation and her hair was blacker than anything he'd ever seen. It's thinking about thinking, he said. It's thinking about thinking about thought.

That's crazy, she said.

Yes it is.

Anna walked Jenny over to a boulder and mounted up and swung the rope around the mule's neck and tied the free end back to the halter. She sat forward. She held the mule steady and Zach mounted up behind her and took the rope and held it under her arms and touched his heels to Jenny's flank. As soon as they came down off the bluff it was too dark to see. By the time their eyes adjusted they were in the trees and all was shadow. They did not speak now; there was just the crunching of Jenny's feet and her breath and their breath. A little later the creek again over the stones in the dark and would that he could throw something anything some memento from his old life into the flowing stream and would that by the time it made alongside the house on the current he could pluck it from the water and see it tried and weathered and fortified by its cold dark passage over the ancient stones and would that he could stand there and by the power of its charge become the man he would yet be so that she would turn to him and see him and know him and trust him and not just this heart pounding into her back through how many layers of clothes?

An hour down the trail he looked up and saw stars. He let go of the lead and reached his hand around and tilted up her chin for her to see. When he took his finger away she stayed in the posture and her back arched slightly for the uplooking and he leaned back and looked at her softly churning hips so close so close and he wanted very badly to lift up her jacket and put his hand in the hollow and push her gently into an endless arch so that her throat gulped the very stars and he leaned forward and closed his eyes. Anna, he whispered.

Don't, she said. Don't say anything.

CHAPTER THIRTY SEVEN

That night he had the last dream and the last dream was heat and breath and flesh. Are you trembling? he asked her, Am I trembling? he asked her but she could not speak and she covered his mouth with her hand and she arched her back and pushed her finger against his tooth and lifted up off the bed and bit his lip as her breath rushed out and then he woke up and his mouth was bruised and he lay there with his hand on himself in awe of the world and in the dream he was talking his mouth was moving as he lay in his room and there was a storm outside which was the first night's storm down to the precise panescraping of the wintry branches but there was no storm without the dream and he lay on his back alone in his room and his mouth was moving with no referents it seemed to the words at all, moving without a correlative in the real world at all, so that he began to despair and to ask his body to live to please live because his body was leaving him in the dispersion of words which even he could not hear and she came into the room, opening the door slowly and walking in her bare feet with the long T-shirt over her body and her dark skin through it as if illuminated everywhere from a canting light so that through the very thread the very weave of the fabric her breasts rose her nipples rose and fell with her breath and her stomach plunged and her hips darkened down into that consummate darkness and her thighs pushed at the shirt and withdrew and pushed and withdrew like scents like aromas pulsing a curtain as she walked and she walked a long time and his sex throbbed to bursting and her feet were bare on the wood and I can't sleep, she said and I can't sleep, he said and she leaned there with her knees just grazing on the sheet's edge and looked down at him endlessly and slowly lifted off her gown and lay it like pooled water on the floor beside her and her hair was a heavy ink all about her unbelievable bareness and she lay down upon him crushed down so softly upon him and she cursed in his mouth and Again, he said and she cursed in his mouth and he turned her over and breathed her mouth's breath and Give me your spit, he said, Spit in my mouth and it was hot and he drank it and her nipples hardened on his chest and he held her hands in his hands and pushed her hard into the bed and she tilted up for him her overflowing wetness and no world no world was outside of her none and he pushed deeper inside her and I want, he said, and You are, she said, and he held her throat in his hand and like a bird it pulsed like a heart it pulsed and he could feel already the crescendo of her trembling and he was lost in her body and deep in her stomach and deep to her throat and she reached out her finger and caught it on his tooth and pushed it against his tooth and he could feel her trembling and Are you trembling? he asked her, Am I trembling? he asked her but she could not speak and she covered his mouth with her hand and she arched her back and pushed her finger against his tooth and lifted up off the bed and bit his lip as her breath rushed out and then he woke up and his mouth was bruised and he lay there with his hand on himself in awe of the world in awe of the world.

CHAPTER THIRTY EIGHT

The next morning when he came downstairs he didn't even look at her. She was grating beets at the counter and she was humming. He didn't even look at her back. He walked all sideways facing away from her like a man parting an oncoming crowd. He went out into the morning and fed Jenny. He shovelled manure into the wheelbarrow and dumped it on the pile near the herb beds and tined the pissripe wood chips to disperse them and spread new chips in the stall. He patted her on the neck and called her Cordelia which nickname had already stuck with some of the children. When he came back into the kitchen Anna was gone. He washed his hands at the sink and took two cans of pinto beans and four wheat tortillas in a napkin and put them on the counter. He went upstairs and came back down with his knapsack. He put a bottle of water with the food in the sack and slung it up over his back and walked out the door around the west corner of the house and ran smack into her. She had an armload of clay pots and they went tumbling and one of them broke on the ground. The three girls were with her, Patricia in the middle and July and Rene holding her hands, and July and Patricia laughed softly and Rene stared ahead blankly. Zach apologized and bent down and stacked the pots and handed them into her arms without looking at her and then he just walked past them and disappeared into the copse of blue pines and began to climb again toward Salt Peak.

The morning was crisp and blue and farther up the green pines were very green. The ground was cold and wet. An hour up the trail he knelt by the stream and drank and his teeth hurt down into his jaw for the cold. He stuck his face in the water and came up blowing and dripping. It tastes like sky, he thought. What do you know? he thought, What do you know about the taste of sky? He walked all that day. He stopped and beheld every species of plant or tree he could discern, the dark and light gradations along the rockwalled path where a thousand years of silt was a thumb's width of a shade apart from the millennium after and before. On the dry alluvial bar of the creekbed he knelt and sifted the fine mineral dust through his hand. He looked at the shapes of stones and held them until they were the same temperature as his hand and then he put them down where he'd found them and picked up another and held it the same. He squatted in the clearings and chewed the tough winter snake grass and studied the land. He studied the blue susurrations the distances made of the westernmost air.

He lunched in a high meadow and lay on his back with the sun on his face and the deer came upon him unknowingly. He lay very still. They came closer and still did not see him. There were two of them and then they were four and then five and then a sixth saw him immediately and bolted crashing through the trees with the others close at his highrumped tail in like terror and then he breathed.

When he made Salt Peak it was late afternoon as it had been before and he scrabbled up as they had before and he stood. He looked in each direction, south, east, north, and finally west and he tried to see clear to Arizona, to imagine it, and he could see nothing. He could not believe that he wasn't what he was, what he had been. He sat there on the stone and asked that his father and his mother come out of the rock of buried memory that he might see them, recognize them. He sat for a long time like some meditant while the light failed westward over the hills and they did not come. He stood and walked to the edge of the promontory. He said his name, Brannagan, and kicked a piece of shale into the abyss. He thought about blood. He thought what was blood, what? He looked at his sundarkened wrists and their veins and what coursed there, what had happened there, who had loved and warred and died and birthed there and what gesture, what tic in the eye or cadence of speech or even notion, what man, what Zachary long dead among the Dutch or the Dineh coursed there in his arm who perhaps had looked at the unfurling line of red rock against an endless blue sky and called it philosophy? In all his life he had not thought once about the inheritance in his bones the genius of which lay decomposite in the earth itself generation to generation and now impossibly he was part native to this land which earth he'd never once considered or perhaps only as the blind ingrate who just gloms the eighty some odd years of breath and strife and feeling and thought which earth engenders and which earth assimilates back and which earth he knelt on now of a sudden on the windy mountain bluff and implored with the palms of his hands without knowing what to ask of it, without knowing what it wanted of him or even what language it spoke.

Then it was dark. He ran. He ran in darkness and he barely walked to rest and when he burst in the door three and a half hours later he was breathing strenuously and his back was soaked with sweat and he could taste the salt on his mouth. The house was still. Then he heard them in the reading room and he walked through the kitchen and down the short hall and they all turned to look at him where he came and leaned heaving in the doorframe. He looked at Anna. She had the book of tales in her lap and the blind slobbering girl under her arm and he could not believe she had not come to him in the flesh and blood night of the flesh and blood world. Zach, Wahkim said, we're trying to cross the ocean.

That's not a problem, Zach said.

It is, Jonah said. There's a strait.

What's a strait? Chris said.

Strait! Edmund said.

How many are you? Zach said.

Neil looked at Raoul. Raoul looked at Anna. Anna looked at Zach and shook her head and smiled and arbitrarily thumbed open the book and arbitrarily catalogued the heroes of the journey at hand and then they all looked at Zach. All right, he said. Hold on a minute. Let me catch my breath.

CHAPTER THIRTY NINE

Anna had told Zach that Samuel slept only three or four hours a night. She had not known that he napped constantly during the day, like an animal. He was forever stealing away from the house and she had no idea where he went but it was clear to Zach now that he went to find a place to sleep. In the bushes around or in the low branches of trees or maybe, because Zach had seen them let him touch them, with the deer. He slept on the bicycle with his head against Zach's back and Zach listened to that gnawing dreamspeech upon his scapulae the way the blind conjure a face with the close tracing of their hand. The speech unintelligible, private, and midday when Zach sometimes strapped his jacket across the basket the boy's drool soaked his shirt cold in the wind the travelling made.

And usually he slept in camp after they'd eaten, sitting erect with only his chin slumping into his chest, the troubled sound of his breath under the crackling of the fire, for about half an hour. He'd wake and stay up most of the night looking at the sky or humming softly to himself or enacting one of his strange sibilated epic battles whereupon he wielded a branch for a sword and partook of both sides of this imaginary fray, whispering fiercely in a language all his own and sallying and retreating and advancing again and sometimes, in a boundless privacy, dying dramatically there with the branch stuck in his chest and then falling, finally, asleep. Now he stood and made a circle and sat back down again. What? Zach said.

Samuel didn't like it there. They were camped in a wash ten miles south of San Augustine. He looked around with eyes which Zach was sure could see farther and more clearly than his own and he wrapped the sweater farther around him and crossed his arms about his chest as if he was himself crossed, vexed at the very shadows and darkness and dipping trees and wind that portended whatever illness in the place. He stood and circled again and sat and looked into the fire with that effortless quality of vigilance. As if he wasn't going to let that fire go anywhere. As if he knew what was best for it.

Zach was eating their habitual meal of bananas in the hot bread with the melted chocolate chips. He offered a slice to Samuel and the boy shook his head no. Do you remember that night you swam out to the boat? Zach said, with his mouth full. You ruined the moment, you know. I almost kissed her, I almost kissed her that night. Do you think I should have?

Samuel levelled at him a look nearly castigating.

There was a moon, Zach said, in mock defense. She was cold. She wasn't really cold. She just let me wrap the blanket around her. She smelled like leaves.

He looked at the boy. Samuel was biting his lower lip and he was studying Zach and his eyes were dancing, or the firelight upon them was.

Have you noticed this? She smells like leaves. Like spring and fall at the same time. How can she do that? I had just put the oars up and we were just drifting like this—he floated his hands out softly over imaginary water—when here you come splashing up and drenched, flopping around in the boat like some fish trying to dry off. You're crazy. January and in the lake. You just wanted some attention. Samuel I believe you were jealous.

Samuel sprang up suddenly—Zach knew that he would—and

landed on his back and rolled around in his inimitable wheezing kind of laughter. When he finally stopped rolling and laughing Zach looked at him and said, Well, I'm asking you an important question. Do you think I should have kissed her? which sent the boy rolling and wheezing and laughing again, until he finally sat up hiccuping and holding his chest for the pain of it. When he had nearly subsided Zach said, You carrot headed maestro, take your herbs. Let's sleep. We're going to ride all day tomorrow.

The boy lay completely still, breathing in and out of his belly, soothing the mystery of his own exuberance as Anna had taught him to do. But he did not like it there in the wash and he would not sleep, valerian and passionflower or no, until morning, if he did sleep at all:

March 3

Walking with Samuel
in the woods for kindling—oil drum, pine cone,
Why my sadness
when everything he points to
has a name?

CHAPTER FORTY

Now it was the second week in February. Zach was standing at the counter watching Anna's knife slide down through the throat of a green pepper when he knew that for the first time in his adult life he was living in a body. I am in a body. He looked at his hands splayed on the marble block and he looked at her sunbrowned arm beside his. He had taken an onion out of the refrigerator. I am in a body, he thought. I am. The late afternoon sun was coming in the window and Anna's hair was wet and fragrant from a shower. There were children behind them drawing with crayons on the tables and his chest was hot in the sunlight and the faucet dripped on the soiled fresh roots in the sink and his own hands were sundark and his arms were strong from the work and he pressed his hands down into the cold marble slab and her knife cleared the throat of the green pepper and I am in a body. I've never heard of anyone to cut an onion just by looking at it, Anna said.

Zach laughed. I'm trying to be the first.

He picked up the knife. But he knew.

They worked and cooked together now regularly and not ordinary meals either but ones that Lazar himself might approve of and the children looked at the food Anna laid out before them on their plates and ate it as indiscriminately as if it were charred gristle cut from the corners of a pan. By now Zach knew the daily protocol of every child at The Lake down to the number of pellets or drops of a remedy or hydrotherapy they needed and he administered to them alongside Anna, the two of them silently handing bottles or implements back and forth across the reclined bodies and later on the porch or walking about the lake discussing prognoses like coevals of a medical ward.

On that day of construction several weeks before Zach had studied the lay and procedure of the run-in shed and particularly Canada's craftsmanship which seemed to him a veritable felicity and he'd studied him with an intensity that equalled or more likely surpassed the intensity with which he had prepared for his university thesis exams. And during the days now he and Samuel were building a new two-horse stall for Jenny equipped with a sun roof and a tack room alongside. Nate took the money out of Zach's wages (he was working Tuesdays and Thursdays now) and brought the wood out on the flatbed. When he tried to offer a hand Zach told him that this one he'd just as soon do on his own and Nate for once did not chide him but nodded his head one time and said surely and told him to keep him abreast of necessary supplies.

Evenings now Anna sat on the porch swing and not the hung tire and Zach sat with her, leaning most often up against the juxtaposed porchshaft, watching her foot gently pushing on the new porch boards, and they spoke with a quiescence that mirrored the decrescendo of the day and with circumspection they told each other about their lives. In truth he could not sit next to her. In truth his body charged with a voltaic current just to hear her bare footsteps padding on the floorboards of another room.

But it was the boy too. One afternoon Zach was kneeling on the gallery painting the new boards he and Anna had replaced with the leftover wood from the run-in shed. Samuel was sitting

on the banister with one shoe and sock removed and very carefully he was clipping his toenails and examining each shard as
if he'd just discovered the body's processes of autonomic regen-
eration and it amazed him so that he lined them up on the rail
like an exhibit for all to see. Roy was standing in front of the
steps and the ramp guarding the wet porch against the children's
footsteps and all manner of ruinous beasts that seemed intent in
his mind on marring the paint job. Anna was in the kitchen
cooking and he could smell onions and garlic and then the
swooning heaviness of sherry and cream and roasting duck.
Zach looked up at Samuel who was admiring his own foot.
That's very nice, Zach said. He indicated the little queue of removed nail. Maybe the Smithsonian will take those. In five hundred years people will come from all over the world to look at
the cuticle fossils of the great redheaded maestro, Buddhacus
Epilepticus.

Samuel stared at him and then shook his head as if Zach was
unfigurable. He put on his shoe and sock and took the like off
his other foot and bent again to his task as if Zach didn't exist
at all. They had of late begun this kind of banter (a banter half
silent, with of course only one party speaking between them,
but a banter nevertheless). Gradually betwixt them an uncanny
understanding had been growing that could only be called telepathic and it gave them what amounted to a kind of license with
each other which spanned from foolery as now to the woeful
and the serious and the sublime. Zach was already convinced
that Samuel was older than anyone in the world and so the vast
difference in their ages seemed some mere inconvenience of tem-
porality of no consequence whatever and they behaved with
each other as alter egos of a lifelong fraternity. Their intentions
were utterly plain to each other. Two weeks before Zach had
found a meadow five miles from the property which was protected from the wind by a promontory backdropping it to the
north and a dense cluster of trees on each side, east and west.
He'd hike to the place and sit in the sunlight and look out across
the southern slope. One afternoon he broke from the trail into

the clearing and at precisely the same moment in mathematical vis-à-vis Samuel broke through the wood on the other side and the two of them stared across the very same space of what they thought was their privacy and then Samuel fell down in the stiff grass laughing.

And if they had become inseparable physically they were even more so mentally. It had begun, like everything with Samuel, with sleep. One night Zach was sleeping when a great peacefulness overtook him so that he felt he had to rise so as not to let whatever it was pass unregistered from his conscious life and he'd woken up with an actual smile on his face and opened his eyes into those of the boy's whose face was no more than three inches from his own, breathing. Zach had not even been surprised. He had not said a word and they'd stayed like that for several barely blinking minutes and then Samuel had taken a blanket and folded it to make a bed for himself on the floor at the foot of Zach's bed. Zach didn't tell Anna this. Nor did he tell her that Samuel slept there almost nightly in the last weeks and that the boy for all his peacefulness had nightmares and that Zach would know and wake as if he himself was having them and rise and lean down over the twitching figure and put his hand on his head and speak quietly into the whorled mystery of the boy's ear until he ceased. He never told anybody that.

Now the boy followed him everywhere. When he chopped wood Samuel stacked it a piece at a time as if there was some law against leaving the cleaved pieces about the stump. Zach could not so much as wash a dish without Samuel coming up behind him with a rag. When he took his early morning walk Samuel came along immediately and it was clear that he'd been at vigil somewhere in the morning shadows waiting for him to leave the house. And when he did his calisthenics and swung his arms and opened his lungs for the crisp air the boy did the same, and without humor but in earnest, as if the two of them were training for some kind of event. Sometimes in the evenings they would chunk wood into the stove and just stare together for hours at the tinder leaping through the vents. The other children would come into the room and look at them like they were on exhibit in a museum installation on Early American Life.

One Tuesday morning the boy was sitting on the back of the motorcycle, sitting with mummified rigidity, and Zach of course did not dare lift him down and when he asked him what he was doing Samuel just looked at him and indicated with a motion of his head and a roadward look that they were going to be late. At Nate's he handed Zach tools while he worked and explored the intricacies of the place in such detail that Nate asked Zach if he had just come into the world and Zach said that he thought he had. The welding simply amazed him. Zach had to punch extra holes in the headband of the second helmet so that it would fit the boy's head and he wore the helmet nearly half the day, sometimes standing outside the garage for long periods of time, looking straight up at the sun.

At The Lake they walked in the woods for hours and now Samuel led the way and he would take Zach to a sequestered meadow or some kind of den or even sometimes just a particular log across a trail or athwart a creek. He would stand there pointing with a marvelous look on his face and Zach would look to where he indicated and half the time he had no idea what in all that bramble and molted foliage the boy was referring to. Their walks lasted longer each time and often they'd come back after dark or just in time to watch the day's last sunlight flare up and extinguish in the water. It was on one such evening that Zach's blood father came up out of the lake. They were sitting on the bank watching the sunlight diminish on the ripples of the eastern shore, the reflection at first a protracted scintillant column and then a funnel and then a final concentrating several points of light which snuffed out at once as if an actual cluster of lit matches hissed under the dun water and all was dark. Zach threw a rock at the place and then he was lying down, just flung back into the bank looking up at the sky and then his eyes shut and he was beside no lake but jostling in a pickup truck, his head resting in a lap, the lap, and the source of all male continuity and all belongingcalm and courage and even a chance at posterity, even the chance at being in the priceless wealth of a body that does continue and does not just die, not even after death itself, was driving quietly beside him, this father, with his mansmell all about him and his simple manhands on the wheel. And Zach knew that the child was himself. And he knew that the child was sickly. And he felt now with tremendous strain that he wanted it to live, wanted to succor it even from where he dreamt it because fate was undecided about it. He wanted desperately to convince fate to let it live, to feed and abet it, to breathe for it, in it. And more he knew that he had never in his life prayed, or that what he had thought had been prayer before he could no longer even pray anymore had been memory, that he had not pined for god but for this man, not because he was great or capable of any agency at all but because he was only, because he was him, he, and they were, and all the space in the universe between them was what he had called prayer. His hair was gray, his skin was leathery and sunburnt— his eyes, my god, were blue. And he strained to see the face of the woman in whose lap he lay but he could not. It was as if she evaporated increasingly upward until her torso began to disappear into sheer atmosphere. But he could hear her

you're drunk, Wyn, pull over I'm going to walk with him to hitch, you're drunk   *and I can feel his hand let go of the wheel and come toward me   and that is where I begin   why can't I see her feel her smell her see her?   where I will begin   all that time I thought I was praying   just touch me on the tiny shoulder   the little scapula, the little nascent wing of me   let it* stop the car, *she says   and he does, he stops the car*   I'm all right, *he says*   you're as bad as me, worse I bet, I'll bet you are, but suit yourself, get down   *the light is simply his hand bending around the car*   we would have been just fine, *he says   and the breath off him is burnt wood rained upon   the windows are down, the sweet sexualsmelling sage   and the car stops, and I cry, I, cry   I can hear it and the hand starts to come down toward me, upon me, bigger than my body, gently descending like sky   and there is no lap now, as if I'm nesting on air   I can barely hear her now*   stop the car, *she says*   it is, *he says*   no, *she says,* it isn't   look out the window at the fucking road, *he says*   you're drunk, Wyn   we would have been fine, he says   *the body turning, the strength pouring out of the hand, descending like blood out of a pitcher flooding my boy's sick veins   making me strong*

and then he opened his eyes. He looked over at Samuel sleeping. He looked at the darkening lake. He sat up. He bent his head forward and with both his hands he slid his fingers back through his hair, once, and looked up at the world. Good lord, he said.

February 17

*Three turtles still on the banks of the lake early this evening, July
with a nosebleed, walking toward me holding her head upward,
Neil and Raoul came down the stairs, one with a hole in the knee
of one pantleg, the other with a hole in the knee of the other
pantleg, three turtles on the bank of the lake early this evening—
motionless, the smell of bacon still in the walls from this morning,
a driving hammer on the loose pages on the desk, July whispering
in my ear something urgent in an inscrutable language, holding
her nose, What? I said, she whispered it again,
What? I said, she took me by the hand,
a craving for cognac, a pain in my right shoulder, a movement in
the leaves today that gave Jenny a fright,
and Neil and Raoul came down the stairs*

with the box in which the turtles hunkered down in their shells

and July pointed to them and they set the box down, the light was

lavender this evening,

on the lake it was almost lavender,

Jenny sniffing at the boards of her new stall, iron bread pans, a

rusty spade that broke in my hand, Samuel actually trying to put

it together as if his spit were glue, maybe, maybe, and they set the

box down and July took me by the hand and I picked up the box

and we carried it to the lake and her nose bled again and I wiped

it on my shirt and we washed it

in the lake

and she threw up a little in her hand

and I wiped it on my shirt

and we washed it in the lake

and we put the turtles back,

the sky was lavender, plantains in a huge ceramic bowl,

three turtles on the banks of the lake this evening,

and we sat,

she pushed the turtles into the water one by one like boats

and we sat,

with one finger she knelt and pushed them in,

and she whispered it again and I said, What language is that? and

she said, Is your name Zach?

and I said, Yes of course, laughing, Of course

and she said Shhh they'll hear us and I

said, Who? And she said Shhh, Shhh

and then I made

a deep wordless song that was the color

of the water and she fell,

she fell so soundly

asleep in

my lap.

CHAPTER FORTY ONE

Anna knew. Whether from some change in him or some telepathic similitude grafted off of him and the boy who could say. But she knew. One night Zach and Samuel came back long after dark and ate the cold plates Anna had left for them in the refrigerator. It was roast chicken and still lukewarm from the cooking and it was delicious and the whole house smelled for the rosemary and the rubbed sage. They ate in silence which is to say of course that Zach didn't speak and they ate as had become their habit, in the same manner and rhythm, tilting their heads to the side as they gnawed the bones like beavers at the same log. Their hands were filthy from the day but they licked their fingers regardless and silently Zach pushed the stool to the sink and washed the dishes and silently Samuel stood on the stool and dried them. He put his hand on the boy's head, still afire even in the darkness, and he went upstairs and the boy went no one knew where. On his bed was a note in her impossible hand and it said, Don't you think if you're leaving you should keep your distance. Then there was a space, after which, underlined and—as if it were possible—in a yet worse hand, it said, From him.

He knocked lightly on her door. He had never been in or even so much as looked in her room. He couldn't have said exactly why he'd never even opened the door but it was because the act seemed somehow irrevocable, as if the literal door was also a figurative one once passed through, even with so much as a glance, he could never return from again. She was awake; a thin knife of light under the door. He heard her shift her weight in bed and he heard her feet on the floor and she opened the door and stood looking at him in an old oversized tailored cotton shirt not unlike the mud- and whiskey-drenched one he'd ripped and the shirt covered her thighs almost to her knees and could have covered shorts and could have covered nothing at all. What? she said.

She had a book in her hand and her hair was some marvelous mingling of braided and not. On the spine it said, *Healing Plants of the Southwest and the Lower Americas*. She rotated the book on her hip and on the cover was a picture of some spindly plants foregrounding an endless crepuscular distance: orange and red striae across the bowing sky. He told her that he repeatedly dreamt that land.

What? she said.

Your note.

He wants to go with you.

Can I get out of the hall?

Hold on.

She was a little while coming back. When she opened the door she was stuffing the last of the shirt into the elastic waistband of a cotton skirt. He had never seen her in anything but jeans; she never wore anything else. How, he thought, can her legs be that color? He looked for longer than he thought to. He hoped she didn't notice, and then he hoped she did, and then he hoped again that she didn't. He walked by her and she barely moved out of his way and she was all bed warmth and loose hair and the aroma of olive oil. Thank you, he said. She shut the door.

He looked around the room. There was nothing in it save the bed and a dresser and, by the bed and next to the door, a plain whitewashed nightstand with a single drawer. On the dresser were several books on medicinal herbs and acupuncture and some strewn underwear and socks. On the night stand was a half eaten, torn loaf of molasses bread and a glass of water and the pipe and a small black and white picture of a tanned woman atop the shoulders of a young man standing in the surf. The woman was laughing with her head thrown back and the man was looking up at her, holding her hands. There was nothing at all on the walls. Above the bed a single bulb dangled from a cord looped around a cement nail and a handmade papyrus globe about a twisted coathanger for a substratum softened the light. It was the only light in the room. The bed itself was half the size of the room and it was old and ornate and made of brass with a towering headboard of brass columns the shadows of which lay crosswise and foreshortened on the bedding. She had hung a mosquito net from the ceiling and she had not taken it down for the winter. He could see the impression where she had lain. There were three large pillows and a down comforter and all were old and threadbare and fading to gray and discolored from sun and time but they were clean and she leaned against the bed in her white skirt and her white blouse with her sundarkened feet and her sundarkened neck exposed out from that blanched background like zones recondite and taboo. Her dark eyes. Her feral hair so incongruent in the uncanny comeliness around. He lost his bearings. The starkness of the room and the elegance of the bedstead and the lambent glow from the crude wickiup of a lamp and the hung netting amid the brass shadows like some baronial bedchamber felt more like a dream to him than any world one could be in and know. He leaned against the dresser. He picked up the book she'd set there and she said, You don't even know.

He put it down. He looked at her. She hadn't ceased looking at him from the time he crossed the threshold of her door. No man has ever been in this room.

Do you want me to leave?

No.

Tell me, he said. Tell me what I don't know.

You have no idea what can happen to him if he seizures. You wouldn't even know what to do. You wouldn't even know what—what do you think, what the hell are you thinking—do you think that you can just come in here like it was the toy department at Woolworth's and take your choice of the pick and put him in your pack three months later because you never had a father yourself and take him to Window Rock Arizona on a bus when you don't even know why you're going and who you're going to find and whether or not you even want to live at all and—

Anna, he said.

She closed her eyes. That is more than blinking, he thought.

I'm sorry, she whispered. He is a child. He may be a hundred and fifty years old but he's a child.

I'll tell him, Zach said. I'll just tell him he can't.

Her eyes were still closed. She sat like that for more than a minute and then she opened them. Don't tell him anything.

What?

She looked up at him—she placed upon him the soft wet smoldering coal of her eyes. So deep, so clear. He will do what he will do.

He saw her then, for a second, for a millisecond, for who she was: one who had already given away more than he'd ever had or could hope to have to relinquish, and luminescent in that darkness, apart, bereft even of the last hopeless bid to grace, powerful not by virtue of any personality which is merely to the soul what clothing is to the body but powerful for what she'd given away, for what had been taken from her and for what consolations she'd refused to receive or even hope for.

Anna, he said, I want to thank you. Thank you. I never would have been—

Just go Zach. She spoke in a whisper. Just go.

I'm not talking about the boy.

I know, she said.

What I'm trying to say—

What you're trying to say is you're a man. You're just what Kish said you would be.

Kish?

You come and fix fence and tell stories and sweetcharm all my charge and you're gone. You're telling me you're going, don't think I don't know you're already gone. It's what I told you all along. And you're going to take him too.

I haven't said a word to him.

Samuel is his own word.

Anna, I have no idea what I'm made for.

I do, she said.

What am I made for?

I'm not talking about you.

She pushed her toe into a worn knot of wood on the floor. I know what I'm made for. You have no idea what I'm made for.

What are you made for?

She laughed a little and looked up at him and then around at her room as if she wondered what was the use of it. Shit, she whispered. Then she looked up at him. I have good hearing.

Zach just looked at her.

I can hear the rain on the lake at night. I'm for that sound. And for singing. For singing them to sleep. For holding their broken bodies some of them for more than ten years not any three months Zach and for not crying—for not crying for them because they cried enough before they even got here. There was already enough crying. Before they were even born. And they're here just to be quiet now. To sleep off the crying. Because I already heard them crying, from before. Before you had a dream about any land I heard these children crying. Because I have good hearing. And if I can hear the first drop of rain fall I can go out and stand under the second. I can. And that is more than most people can say. I may be woods but I'm not slow.

Good god, Zach said, no one on earth could call you slow.

I'm not slow. I'm for dancing.

Dancing?

I can waltz.

You can?

I can waltz like you wouldn't believe.

Zach stood off the dresser. She pointed a finger at him, hard. Don't, she said. Don't stop me. Do you want to hear me or not?

I do.

Do you really want to hear?

Yes.

For telling my dead goodbye. For walking out into that field—she jerked her head southward indicating the meadow that bordered the east flank of the lake—and clapping my hands once above my head every day to let them know I haven't—for remembering. I can remember the sunset on the buttons of my father's shirt. I can remember the smell of sweat and whiskey on a thorn I pulled out of his arm when I was nine years old and we were sitting on the porch and the pine trees looked like they had maple syrup on them and I had just swum in the lake and I had on her jeans and her T-shirt with turpentine on the collar and I could smell spaghetti from the kitchen and there wasn't no one even in there cooking anything.

She looked at the flat, black, roomreflecting window. For talking to my mother. For watching her skirt float out there over the lake every morning because I'm to understand she wore the color violet every day and for cursing him for falling before I at least was a fullgrown woman damn you Zach why did you come at all until the day I die so he comes to me. He comes to me. And she does. And I lay down in the grass and I whisper her name and her voice is the only sleep I know. For that. I am made for that. Just go, she said.

You amaze me, he said.

Don't praise me.

He walked toward the door and before he even touched the knob she spoke to his back. Because I can put my body against stone or water and feel what you can never feel. I can feel the lake over the backs of the fish.

He turned. I know.

No you don't. You don't know.

I know.

What do you know?

I know what you're telling me. I've known it.

The dancing?

I haven't known about the dancing.

I have a sister, she said.

You do?

In my mind. I have a sister in my mind.

She jabbed her toe into the floor again and blew at her hair. Let me just shut my mouth.

I need to go there, Zach said.

And then what?

I don't know.

I may not take you when you want me. Only the world can do that. You'll have to feel the trouble in your bones, not in your mind.

I have.

You'll have to let me put back whatever I take from you.

All right.

You'll have to let me mark your body so you know where you live.

All right.

You'll have to. She was glaring hotly now and he had never seen her eyes so wide nor so wet nor the look in them now and the look in them was fear.

You will, she said.

All right, Zach said. I will.

CHAPTER FORTY TWO

The following morning when he came down the stairs he had Nate's knapsack over his shoulder. His hair was wet from showering and he'd combed it back off his forehead and shaved very closely. She turned and looked at him when he came in the kitchen and then she turned quickly back around. She was stirring eggs at the stove. Most of the children had already eaten but Wahkim was playing chess with Chris and Rene was sitting quietly at the table drooling. Zach slid into the chair next to her and immediately she began kissing his face and he just let her. Just sat there like a boy off to school under his maudlin mother's barrage. She stopped; she seemed flummoxed by his lenience, that he would finally just let her, and she turned and crossed her arms and scowled down at the floor on the opposite side of her chair. Anna came over and put a plate of eggs in front of him and Zach picked up his glass and started to rise to get his juice but she put a hand on his shoulder. She came back and poured his juice and said that there was ham that she could fry and he said that sounded good. She took the fry pan she'd already cleaned out of the dish rack and cut a piece of ham and laid it in the melting butter and called over the sound of the sizzle if he wanted more eggs and he said no thank you. When he'd finished his eggs he watched the boys for several minutes. Wahkim was more than good at the game. For every minute Chris took to decide upon a move Wahkim took about two seconds. He'd make his move and then look up and away superciliously as if it insulted his intelligence to even strategize with such an opponent. He slurred when he spoke due to some byproduct of his paralysis or his generally stunted growth (he was twenty one and he looked no more than thirteen) and his mind was supposed to be slow but Zach had observed his acumen constantly and he'd deduced that it was selective and that the boy dealt it out consciously and not without craft. And Wahkim knew it too, knew it of himself and knew that Zach knew it of him. When Zach smiled at his arrogance, as he did now, Wahkim would look slantwise at him as if he dared Zach to give him away.

Rene still wouldn't look at him but neither did she leave. She was studying the floor, a gossamer trail of spit descending steadily out from the corner of her mouth where her head was tilted to the left. He put his hand on her back, fraternally, not sensuous, and she shrugged it off and sulked. He pulled the board out of the boys' reach and put the plates of cold eggs and ham and tortillas which Anna had made for them an hour ago where the board had been. They looked at him sullenly and began to eat slowly, lifting the forks with mimed, immeasurable effort, and then they grinned at him of a piece and Wahkim punched him in the arm and said his name. Said it again and punched him. Anna came back with the ham and put it in front of him.

I'm sorry you had to dirty the pan again, Zach said.

It's not a problem.

Did you grain Jenny yet?

Samuel did way before sunup.

How's the bump on her leg?

The spavin?

I guess.

It's a little better. She's got the ringworm again though.

What's that?

Those patches on her skin.

I was wondering about those.

It's my own fault.

How's that?

Dirty blankets. It's a fungus. I'm going to hose them down later on.

I can do that, Zach said. I have time for that.

That's all right. There's a special soap and all.

Have you seen him this morning? Zach said.

For a second, in the paddock. He's in the shed.

This ham's delicious.

Doris brought it. They just butchered Wednesday. Do you want some more?

No, thank you.

There's plenty, I'll cut you some.

No, really, I'm full.

More juice? she said.

He just looked at her back. I've got a full glass, he said. Thank you.

In fact the whole time they spoke she had her back to him at the stove but the eggs were gone and the dishes were washed and there was nothing for her to do at the range. I'll take care of their dishes, Zach said. You don't need to wait for them.

You better go out to the shed, she said.

Zach picked up the boys' empty plates. They gave him challenging looks like kid pugilists and Wahkim pulled the board back in front of them glaring at Zach all the while. Then they bent to it again as intensely as before. Zach washed the dishes at the sink and laid them in the rack and stacked the other plates in the cupboards above though they were not yet dry. Then he stood next to Anna and just stood there. The two of them looking down at the spatula in her hand. With her fingernail she peeled some dried egg off the rubber. Her shoulders began to shake. She gripped the spatula very tightly and began to shake it as if she was mad at it, as if she was trying to wring some information out of it. Then she put it down on the stove. She reached into her back pocket and pulled out a small circular cosmetic mirror and held it in the palm of her hand and looked down at it with deliberate gravity. Then she held it up. She moved it up and down across her features, in small eddies and in large arcs, slowly taking in, part by part, her whole face. She held it at a distance and brushed at her hair with her fingertips and brought it back close and looked into her own eyes one by one, tracing with the end of a pinkie the curve of her lashes, and she angled the mirror down at her mouth and along the smooth sweep of her chin and she was crying. Then she was just crying. Doris lent me this from her purse. What have you done to me?

Zach put a hand on her shoulder. Don't touch me, she whispered. She was hardly audible.

I'm supposed to look at this? I'm supposed to look at this all the time now?

He said her name; he tried to. She whirled around and covered his mouth with her hand, stopping his breath at the last open vowel of *nah*. It's not going to be your back going down that road, she said. You think I'm going to stand for that? Watch me. You watch me.

She went out the door and down the steps. He watched her through the screen until she disappeared over the rise in the road, toward the lake.

CHAPTER FORTY THREE

Then he was in the shed. Standing just inside the doorway, looking down at the boy who must have known he was there but who was bent so seriously to his task that he appeared oblivious. He was humming an upbeat melody and Zach could have sworn that it was Vivaldi. Zach began to hum along but the boy's tune radically diverged and he turned around and looked at Zach crossly as if he'd disturbed the organics of a composition. Pardon me, Zach said.

Samuel squinted up at him, not because of any light or dust but out of scrutiny. He looked old. He looked like an older man looking at a younger one during a time of duress, wondering if the young one was going to fold. He was filthy. He was wearing one of Anna's jackets and there was grease all over it and there were smudges on his face and even a flat clot of it in his hair. His hands were nearly black. He got up repeatedly for some tool or rag and when he moved about the shed lost in Anna's coat he looked like some bellshaped dwarf floating a few inches from the ground. What are you doing? Zach said.

In the center of the floor was an all but dissembled girl's bicycle, upsidedown, balanced on its seat and handlebars. The rear wheel was on the floor alongside and the front sprocket was soaking in turpentine in a metal bucket, along with the chain. One of the pedals had been removed along with the ball bearings which were laid carefully in the lid of a coffee can. He'd clipped the brake cables and found some number three wire somewhere in the shed and he was threading it through the plastic sheath. Squinting down into it as if he could see when the wire was going to come out. Zach squatted down and leaned against the jamb of the door and watched him work. The humming and the wheezing. The tiny fingers moving so rapidly at the work, as if they had eyes each of them, in a hurry and not. Efficient to the point of art. As if they were indeed at a composing. He threaded the new cable into the brake lever and notched the end in the groove and screwed down the handle to secure it, then he fished in the bucket and examined the chain and put it back and took out the sprocket and shook it three times draining it and reattached it to the crank. He swirled the chain about in the solvent and pulled it out again and let it drip for a time and wiped it with a rag and laid it gently around the two sprockets, the smaller rear one first. Next he oiled the bearings in their casing and matched the ceiling to the capsule and sunk the apparatus on the spindle and reattached the pedal. He spun it. It didn't even slow down for a good twenty seconds. He spun it again. Finally he picked up the rear tire and examined it and frowned. He pumped it halfway up, then cradled it in the fork, walking around behind and closing one eye for balance, spinning it to gauge the wobble, and it wobbled considerably, and he frowned again. He tightened down the bolts with a wrench, alternating back and forth, and then he pumped the tire the rest of the way. Then he put his hands on the bars and looked at Zach.

Zach rose and helped him turn the bike right side up. Samuel put the kickstand down and reached behind him on the bench and took down a plank of wood to which he had bolted a stout metal rack. What time did you get up this morning? Zach said.

Samuel didn't even look at him. He held the wooden platform behind the seat, steadying it with his chest, and licked the frame quickly in an X with a utility knife in four places where the holes in the braces met the frame. Then he drilled the holes. With the power drill, right through the hollow steel, his whole body shaking but the auger steady enough. Zach shielded his eyes for the flying metaldust but the boy just closed his completely and angled the bit from memory and when he broke through three of the holes were perfect and one was off by an eighth of an inch. He marked the frame again and rolled the bit around the inner edge of the hole until it widened enough to disappear his mark. He put the drill on the bench and blew the residual dust from about the holes and then he began to cough. A dry, bottomless, grating cough. It lasted a full five minutes, his body heaving so violently, as if it wanted to loose its frame. He didn't like anyone to touch him when he coughed and Zach simply watched him, and when he finally ceased he just went about the work as if nothing had happened. He bolted the rack to the frame very tightly and then he walked out of the shed, turning and holding up an index finger to Zach admonishing him not to follow. When he came back he had cradled in his arms a large dairy crate. He put it on the plank and looked at Zach. He wrapped two stiff bungee cords through the plastic grating and around the rack and hooked them again on the diagonal. Then he put a hand on the seat and one on the rim of the crate and looked at Zach and then at the handlebars of the bike. Zach walked over and steadied the bars. Samuel stood on the pedal with one foot and the crossbar with the other and swung himself over the edge and settled gently into the crate. And sat there smiling. He smiled so broadly that Zach burst out laughing. What is that grin?

But instantly the boy grew serious. From where he sat ensconced in the crate he was looking out past Zach's shoulder, across the lot, toward the house. His face looked suddenly inconsolable, even tragic. Zach turned.

Outside the children were coming en masse across the yard, toward the shed. Anna was standing on the porch with her arms in a dead akimbo, staring out across the lot with a look at once proprietal and desolate, like a landowner surveying a failing crop. They came silently, in a ghostly flotilla, somber. The morning mist indeed rolling like fog over an ocean. Their unspeaking deliberateness out from that brume downright eerie. They gathered around the shed and stood toeing the ground or milling about as if waiting for a cue. They seemed both reluctant and purposeful, like citizens at a public arraignment convened to try one of their own. At first they didn't even look at Zach. Singly, or in pairs, they came to the door of the shed and looked in at Samuel. They stood there as only children can, with faces utterly expressionless yet full of meaning. Each in turn they looked at him for a long time. They seemed to be examining him, or committing him to memory. And Samuel, sitting cross-legged in the crate, stared back at them with that same fixity, yet his was a hollower, a hungrier look. Then one by one they shook Zach's hand. When the last child had quietly turned and walked back toward Anna and the house the boy just looked up at the man and his face was again calm, was in fact so calm it seemed washed of anything in the world. Zach looked at him. He looked at the bicycle. He looked at him again and then again at the bicycle. All right, he said. Fuck it. Just fuck it. It's no crazier than that damned bus. No crazier than walking down main street arm and arm with an iron skillet.

Samuel was watching Zach's mouth make the words as if he had suddenly gone deaf as well as speechless and was reading his lips. Then they locked eyes

*who was born knowing me   I who was born knowing you
then it is not eternal recurrence?   he is full of time, full of
birds   all those years with a whatness repeating: put your
index finger so infinitely on your other index finger?
yes   everywhere I laid my hand then, into towels, over knobs,
the terrible interrogatives   that sermon I heard as a teenager
about Peter weeping like no other man   I am my own Peter,
have been, if   they held my hands in their own hands   peace
be with you, peace be with you   what weights sunk my eyes
in the dream were Anna   and then the land which tells me
every night in sleep that I can live and burn and fly and con-*

tinue and disappear   that I will leave one thumbprint in that
friable light at dusk and thanks   I may not be worthy of
either of them   she reached out her hands under my eyes as
if to cup water   ladled out my eyes   quiet with the purpose
wait, I said, I need time   and I would teach those barely
younger than me the hows of thought but not the whys and
the wherefores? because maybe there is no wherefore or worse
if the wherefore is then the world is not?   is is is is   they
might not even be alive, she said   this child who knows me, I
who have always known him   that adrenaline of mind, that
endless pontificating talk which begins so bravely in window-
less university rooms and ends so far from bravery, could I say
cowardice?   the will dying as if death wasn't change?   how
could Nietzsche have thought even death wasn't change?   even
then he could not have believed it or else he would not have
wanted to die   do you have any idea how far Window Rock
Arizona is from here?   no more absurd than that red halo it-
self   whoever is in this child he is not alone   put your hand
on the fire of his head   tell him you are not a curse on the
possible   tell him you are possible   I am possible   even
though whither we are going   fuck whither are we going   if
you are really that calm   you Virgil, you sprite   she cried
for me   let time, let birds   endless morning saturated with
blue   dear god how I wanted to live

and it seemed as if Samuel sat waiting. It seemed as if he sat
listening. Then without taking his eyes off of Zach's he drew his
arms upward in a circle and slowly closed his cupped hands
over his ears.

Chapter Forty four

The fire had long died out. Zach's mouth was foul with festered chocolate and banana. Samuel was kicking his leg. Standing alongside him kicking his leg with a determined ferocity. Zach sat up and looked to where the boy pointed. A dozen or more trucks entrained were coming down the gravel drive that led from the main road. Their radios were blaring and some of the drivers were shifting down and gunning the engine and spinning the wheels on the gravel. Some were hollering obscenities out windows and fisting the sides of their doors. Illuminated by the rearward headlights were men piled in the beds of the trucks and Zach could see them pushing and shoving each other. One man actually went over the lip of the truck bed and rolled down the wash embankment and got up cursing and ran after the truck which sped up as if to leave him. When he caught hold of the tailgate he hung on and the driver stopped suddenly and he went flying in among the other men. They beat on him and then he stood in the center of them all and raised his arms and bellowed up at the night and all the men laughed and pulled him down and he toppled upon them.

The trucks pulled into the turnaround. Zach sat up and pressed the face light on his watch. It was twenty one minutes after eleven o'clock. The trucks made a circle and faced their lights inwards upon each other and then the drivers cut the engines but left the headlights on. The men were whooping and hollering. They leapt out of the trucks and stood around pushing each other. Wrestling. Spitting. Smashing their bottles down on the stones. The last radio was cut off and the men gradually grew quiet. As if they had been commanded by some greater authority over them all to hush. But for a door slam and a whisper the night was as silent as before they had come. Two men took off their shirts. From behind the seat of one of the trucks a man gave each of them a length of pipe. They walked out into the middle of the circle, the truck lights brightly on them. They stood stock still, staring at each other, holding the pipes. For a time the entire proceeding seemed frozen. Then one of the men in the crowd shouted, Pussies! The two men began to circle each other. Their breath visible above them where they crouched and stalked like cavemen brandishing torches. No one else had spoken; the men around stood silently, reverent in the manner of churchgoers. Some had climbed back up in the beds of the trucks the better to see and some were sitting on the hoods and others were standing about humbly with their hands crossed over their groins. The two men circled slowly. Now an unbelievable stillness, a viscosity, came over the scene. One of the men faltered. He wiped his brow. The other man struck without hesitation. The pipe whirling around unseen and striking the man on the left side of his head. He went down. The man stood over him and clubbed him viciously on the head, steady determined blows like a smithy at a forge, grunting each time, and the sound of the skull crushing was dull and then aqueous and then a further dull, a pointless beating of the earth itself. It seemed to Zach a sound entirely final, unreclaimable even to the air it traveled upon. Samuel, he said.

But the boy had already stiffened out of all hearing. He was kneeling beside Zach with his hands on his thighs and he was fixed on the scene but without looking at it anymore, or without registering it. Zach leaned over and looping his hands under

Samuel's arms from behind he picked him up and placed him between his legs and the boy didn't even break the pose, his body hardened like some nuclear piling, the current through him palpable and hot in Zach's hands. Several men went forward solemnly, with a bizarre dignity, and picked up the body and put it in the bed of one of the trucks. The other men broke from their poses and began talking again softly and then louder gradually until they were whooping and jostling again. They leapt into the vehicles. The engines started up and the music came on loud and dissonant and all was as it had been before. The trucks made their way up out of the wash and some of the drivers put their gears in low and revved their engines and spun their wheels on the stones. Samuel had begun to shake and spit was bubbling out of his mouth. Zach held him against his body. He began to sing, an unkempt song. Low, softly into the boy's ear, and he could not think of any words so he sang nonsensically in a language unheard of, a language perhaps forgotten.

But a truck was coming back down the drive. It made the corner into the turnaround and the lights swept across them and fanned out around the field. There were no men in the back nor in the passenger seat. The driver jumped down and lost his balance and nearly fell. He cursed. He picked something up off the ground and Zach saw that it was one of the pipes. He squatted and looked at something else there among the gravel and prodded it with the pipe. Then he got down on his hands and knees. He seemed to be smelling whatever it was. He got back into his truck and began to back up and pivot out of the drive. Then he stopped. He stepped out of the truck and unzipped his fly and urinated. It seemed to Zach that he urinated for a long time. It occurred to him that the man had been sent back to get the pipe and that those who had been in his truck had piled into one of the others. The man shook himself and zipped and climbed again into his cab. Zach heard the transmission lurch into gear but the truck did not go anywhere. For a long time. Lie down, Zach said. Lie down.

Samuel was blubbering and he would not lie down. As if he

had a coil in him that stood him up, an armature. Lie down, Zach whispered, fiercely.

The man got out of the truck. He walked to the edge of the gravel where the grass began and he looked out over the expanse toward them. He walked out a little farther. He went back to his truck and got in and turned the wheel and went forward slightly and back and forward again until the lights were trained directly toward their camp. He turned on his brights. He climbed out of the cab and now he had the pipe in his hand and he walked again to the perimeter of grass and gravel. He put his hand to his brow like a man looking out to sea, but the light was behind him and the gesture was pointless. He came forward.

Samuel, Zach said, I am going to put you behind that tree. I'm going to put you behind the tree now. You must stay there. Can you hear me? You must stay where I put you.

But Samuel was not at all coherent. Neither it seemed could he see. His eyes were nearly all whites, the pupils pitched back into his head, and his jaw was frozen upon itself and he was seething. Zach picked him up and carried him and placed him behind the tree and said in his ear with violent softness, Stay. Right here. Don't move.

Zach turned around. The man had stopped. He was about halfway to their camp. He came forward again. Who the fuck is that? he called out.

Zach didn't say anything.

Who the fuck is that?

Zach could tell from his voice and the way he walked that he was drunk. He looked around for some stick or rock but there was nothing. He thought that it would be better to walk toward the man. He thought that if he seemed preemptively friendly the man might lose interest and leave them alone. That he could at least in this way gain some distance from the boy. They came toward each other now as if some covert meeting had been arranged. I'm Zach, he called out. Just passing through.

The man didn't say anything until he was very near. He stopped ten feet away and looked at Zach, studied him. Then he walked close enough so that Zach could smell the liquor on his breath. His jacket was open and his shirt was unbuttoned down to his belly and even in the cold night air he smelled like sweat, fresh and old. Who the fuck are you?

I'm Zach. I'm just passing through.

Hah, the man said. Hah. He looked at the ground and then pushed Zach backward with his hand. You saw that shit, didn't ya? Didn't ya?

Yes. But it doesn't mean anything to me. I'm not from around here. I'm just passing through.

Sure you are. Who's that girl behind the tree. Is that Angie? Who's that girly you got hid behind the tree?

I don't know what you're talking about.

You want to see some brains? There's brains out there in the turnybout. Who's the girly. There's fuckin brains out there in the turnybout. Look like guts but it's brains.

I'm just camping. I'm on a bicycle trip. I'm on the way to Window Rock Arizona.

The man took three steps toward the tree and Zach stood in front of him.

You got Angie back there, don't ya? the man said, and he was laughing. He looked at Zach as if he was a curiosity. What are you anyway? he said. You doinkin Angie? Angie! he called. Angie!

He held the pipe straight out in front of him and he was grinning. He pushed the end of it into Zach's chest. Who's the girly. Show me her. Is she naked?

Leave us alone. It's my son. He's sick. Leave us, please.

Your son? What the fuck do I look like to you, Billy Cravins? You can bullshit Billy Cravins but you can't bullshit me. You greenbelly fucker. Huh? He jabbed the pipe hard into Zach's chest. Huh?

I don't know who Billy Cravins is.

He was just here. What the fuck is wrong with you? He was sittin right there in Boyd's truck. He jabbed Zach hard once more, lower, and Zach lost air and the man pushed past him and came around the tree and stood looking down at Samuel. What the fuck is that? he said.

Samuel was splayed in a strange sitting posture. One leg was angled awkwardly behind him with his knee twisted back and the other was tucked deeply into his groin. One of his arms was looped around his neck and the other hand was on his stomach. He looked like a kid yogi shot dead at some circus bazaar. That's my son, Zach said. I told you he's sick. Leave us alone.

Is he dead? The man prodded him with the pipe. Samuel didn't move.

He's dead, aint he. He prodded him again.

Shit for brains, the man yelled. He bent down and yelled in Samuel's ear. Hey shit for brains, are you dead?

Samuel reared up and a fluid came out of his mouth and he heaved and jerked violently and his body whipped forward and he arched back and froze and his eyes were only whites. The man leapt back and hollered, Jesus mother fuckin christ! and he raised the pipe high in both hands and swung it down with tremendous force towards Samuel's head. Zach tackled him and they rolled on the ground. He wound up on top of the man and sat on his chest and pinned his arms momentarily and in a voice he'd never heard before he yelled, Leave us! The man spat in his face. He kipped up with great speed and headbutted Zach and the world spun. He fell back and scrabbled upon the ground and knelt on all fours to get his bearings. The man rose and kicked him in the ribs. He fell again and rolled away and heaved for air and looked at the man and spat. He was walking toward him, the pipe in his hand. Light from the headlights a hundred yards away shone off the steel. Zach knelt, looking at the pipe. The man started to laugh. I'm going to kill you you wetback or whatever the hell you are.

Zach pushed himself to his feet and as he rose he stepped forward and hit him. Hard across the mouth. The man staggered back but he did not fall nor let go of the pipe. He grinned. He came forward again but before he could wind back to swing Zach lunged at him and stayed his arm. The man grabbed

Zach's shirt with his free hand and the two stood frozen there in a terrible embrace, breathing. He spat again in Zach's face.

And then Zach let go of him. For some reason he just exhaled and let his shoulders slump. Like a man resigning. He let go the man's arm and he bent his head down like a penitent and the man wound back and swung the pipe at Zach's head with all his body weight behind it. Zach ducked and the pipe wailed over him and he wrapped his arms around the man's waist and lifted him bodily and hurled him against the tree. He lost wind and dropped the pipe. Zach reached down and grabbed it and thrust it crosswise under his chin and into his throat. He pushed. The man reached up and tried to grab the pipe but Zach kneed him as hard as he could in the testicles and the man lost his grip. He pushed harder and the man started to choke. He reached for the pipe again but Zach kneed his groin brutally and he let go. He began to kick at Zach's shins but it felt like nothing, like so many grasses blowing about his legs. He pushed the pipe deeply into the man's jugular and when he started to feel him falter he pushed even harder. He looked into his eyes and pushed and an immense sadness came over him such that he saw pooled in duplicate in the pupils of those two swimming sicknesses the image of himself standing abandoned as a child in a windy arroyo with the sage at the crests whipping insanely in the gusts and the sky bloodred in a great beauty which was only sadness to him and a door hanging in the remains of some disintegrating structure banged on its jamb in that wind and he pushed harder into the man's throat and the banging door was as a great volume in his head and he felt such gravity in his hands and such strength as if he could wring the tree itself in two or as if by the power in his hands to crush even the bole of a tree the boy himself would be borne up away from the earth and rip through that perfect envelope of crepuscular beauty and then the man's head tilted forward and he slid, slowly, down the tree.

Zach laid the pipe down and looked at the top of the man's head. No breeze blew the hair. He picked up the pipe and hurled it into the thick cluster of rushes and walked to the other side of the tree and picked Samuel up in his arms and took him back to their camp. He lay the boy down momentarily and took his jacket which he used for a pillow and laid it out and wrapped the boy up in it and picked him up and began to walk toward the embankment which led up to the road.

Chapter Forty five

He scrabbled up the hill using only one hand for purchase and Samuel's head lolled about and he put his chin on it to anchor it. When he made the crest he held the boy in both arms and just stood. He didn't look at him. He looked down the western road. He looked east. He started walking east. Nothing but darkness, not a sound but his steps and his breathing which at first he didn't hear and then heard and swallowed and tried with his mind to tame. He walked for fifteen minutes before he heard the soft faraway whooshing of an approaching car. It was coming from the west but it took him almost a full minute to discern the direction; he wasn't sure until he looked back and actually saw the headlights in the distance. He hoisted Samuel up in his arms and walked and told the boy that they were going to get a ride and that the night was fine weather for walking and that there was plenty of traffic on the road and that he had a chocolate bar and some almonds in the pockets of the jacket wrapped around him if he got hungry and that they would get a ride and that he didn't mind walking and that the motion was good for his legs which were stiff from riding all day and that the air felt fine in his lungs and that he didn't mind walking at all. When the car was several thousand yards away he turned and stepped into the road and still walking only sideways now he shifted Samuel to his left arm and held out his thumb. The car angled toward him and then seemed to accelerate. It swerved once away and then served back toward him and at the last second swerved away again screeching the wheels and someone stuck his whole torso out the rear passengerside window and yelled, Faggot and Zach heard a bottle break and then another and then the taillights diminished and he squared his body to the shoulder of the road and walked on.

Then the night was so quiet. So clear. He could hear the rhythmic scraping sound his chinstubble made against Samuel's soft hair like a sandpipe tapping out the tempo of the striding. For another quarter of an hour not a single car passed. Then he heard again the distanced oceanic whooshing and this time he knew immediately that it was from the west and he did not even turn to face it until the sound of the tires grew loud and when he did turn he was surprised to see the lights still so far away and he told himself that he would walk until he collapsed if he had to, that it did not matter, that he would walk with the boy into the earth itself if it came to that and he called himself Zachary many times low and out loud and he told himself to walk well and then the car, the pickup truck, stopped just ahead of him and he came up alongside it. An elderly man leaned over and pushed open the door and said, Where you goin?

Zach stood with the boy in his arms. He looked east down the road. He looked back at the man. He was afraid of what his voice might sound like. My son, he said. He's had a seizure. He has epilepsy. I need to get him to a hospital.

For no more than two seconds the man studied them. I can take you as far as Vidrine. There's a twenty four hour station there and you can call for an ambulance. Hop in.

Thank you, Zach said.

He climbed into the truck and sat and pulled the jacket tight around Samuel's body and covered his head. They drove in silence for over an hour and then the man spoke, quietly, as if he was addressing his own reflection in the windshield. It looks like you been scuffling.

Zach didn't say anything. Forty five minutes later they pulled into the Stop 'n Go in Vidrine.

Thank you sir, Zach said.

You're welcome, the man said.

He stepped down and watched the truck pull away and waited thirty seconds and started to walk and stopped and told himself to count thirty more which he did and then he began to walk east again down the road.

There were more cars now, but no one stopped. People yelled things out the window. Threw cans. Once a couple in an old Chevy Impala pulled over and looked at them like they were advertising clothes in a storefront window and sped off again. Then the lights ceased. The night was as quiet as before. A car passed every ten minutes or so but he no longer stuck out his thumb. When he approached Bonita it was a quiet town, as quiet as the country around it. A beat-up white two-door Monte Carlo passed him and pulled over into the lot of the darkened post office and waited for him and as he approached a large overweight man got out and hoisted up his belt and asked if he needed a ride.

Yes, Zach said. We do. Thank you.

Where you goin?

Marjolaine.

Marjolaine! Shit, I can take you as far as Shirley.

I appreciate it.

They got in and he floored the accelerator and they screeched out onto the road. What the fuck do you do in Marjolaine?

Zach just looked out the window. The man kept looking over at him. Finally he asked Zach who the boy was and Zach said that it was his son.

The man was quiet for a moment and then he looked over at Zach again. You look a lot like a buddy of mine named Ricky. He was Apache or some shit. He was a crazy son. One time he was fuckin a girl in the cargo train and the train started up and Ricky thought he just had a wild one under him and when he'd done with her he looked up and he was clear over in Wilcox and he didn't even know he was movin the whole time.

The man laughed and rolled down the window and spat. Rolled it back up and hawked again and rolled it down part way and spat and missed. Mother fucker, he said. He wiped at the globule on the inside glass with the elbow of his jacket and the car swerved across the center line and back again.

The girl wasn't but sixteen and she started to bawlin on him and ran into the Texaco and called the cops when it was she who pulled the living man out of Bluejays herself and took him to her car cause I seen it with my own eyes. I was sittin right there next to him. I aint seen him since his first parole.

He looked at Zach. You aint even listenin to me, are you?

Zach didn't say anything.

A few minutes later the man said that the car was getting heavy and he pulled over alongside an expanse of alfalfa between two towns and Zach thanked him and opened the door and lifted Samuel up in his arms and climbed out. He walked. He walked through the tiny town of Omega where he and Samuel had lunched on the steps of the general store a hundred years ago and he passed the field across where the horses stood in absolute stillness sleeping with their heads bent slightly forward and their necks declining also so that they looked like they studied en masse something diminutive in the grass before them and they did not wake or so much as twitch as he passed and they looked like a sculpture garden of the horse with their noses converging on the selfsame hub and their bodies radiating around it as fleshspokes of a single becalmed wheel and then the cottonfields flattened out flank to flank and the miles stretched out darkly ahead. They were just east of Omega Creek when Zach heard another car coming from the west. He waited as before until the car sounded as if it was upon them and then he turned and stuck out his thumb. It slowed as it approached but it passed. Then it stopped. It reversed until it was about twenty feet from them and stopped. A young woman leaned out of the passenger window and asked if they were all right.

No, Zach said. This child. He has epilepsy. He's had a seizure. I need to get him to a hospital.

A man leaned clear across the seat and stuck his head out the passenger window and by the red taillights he studied them. We'll take you, he said. Climb in.

The couple was from Lufkin Texas and they were travelling to see family in Opelousas. They drove a Jeep sport utility vehicle and it smelled new and there was nothing at all in the compartments atop the dash or in the casing between the two front seats. There was also, superimposed upon or underneath the perfumed disinfectant of the manufactured vinyl and upholstery, the smell of gardenias and chocolate. They were travelling at night because they couldn't find a hotel on the way that wasn't grody, the woman said, and they had decided just to drive all night instead of bothering to stop in every town to search. They were recently married, recently returned from Maui. They held hands. Hers on top of his, his thumb making graceful rivulets along the ridges of her veins. She spoke of the resplendent greenery of the mountains and the fallow volcanoes and the snorkeling and the otherworldly fish and the endless buffets in the imperial hotels and the mules they'd rented to go down into the very center of one such volcano. Mary is allergic to dander, the man said, so we had to tie a bandanna around her mouth and nose the whole time she rode the horse—

The mule, Mary said. It was a mule.

Right, the mule, and it looked like we'd kidnapped her. He laughed heartily.

She did look pretty cute that way too. He laughed again and she said his name in mock embarrassment. Tom.

You should see his family, she said. Oh my god. She said it like there was a lot of space between the three words. Oh-my-God. She turned around and looked at Zach. She didn't seem to even notice the welt on his forehead or the shirt torn at the collar or the thin echelons of mud on the right side of his face.

His mother refuses to be called Hilda. Her *name* is Hilda. *Everyone* calls her Hilda, and she corrects them and says, Hilde-gard, it's Hildegard. And then she looks down at you over that long nose—she's taller than Tom—and I swear one of these days those glasses are just going to come skooching off the end of her nose, and she says, And I'd be *obliged* if you'd remember it. I'd be *obliged?* the woman said, as if the phrase was unheard of in the history of all discourse.

Mary's the only one who actually calls her Hildegard, Tom said, looking in the rearview mirror at Zach, stroking her hand.

He gave his wife an empathic look. *Her* mother's just great. Sometimes I think I should have married her instead.

Tom! Mary said, and slapped at his arm with the back of her hand. That's gross. Then she put her hand back in his and he stroked it some more and they looked at each other.

But Joey—

Oh god, don't tell him about Joey, Mary said. We don't even know him, Tom. He'll think we're weirdos.

Joey, Mary's brother, *is* weird.

He *is not* weird. He just won't go outside. What's wrong with that?

What's wrong with that? He's pale.

So, it's fashionable.

Says who.

Says Calvin Klein.

Oh god, Calvin Klein. It's also fashionable to look like you don't even have a gender.

Maybe he just likes his room, Mary said.

Mary, he's twenty. How good can a room be?

All right, he's weird. But don't pressure him.

Pressure him?

I mean don't ask him to play football or something.

What's wrong with football? Football's good. Maybe I could help him break through.

You're sweet, she said.

They were silent for a time. At some point the woman turned

around in the front seat and by the bleeding light of the dash she looked at them and asked Zach again if the boy was going to be OK. Zach nodded his head yes. This time she did see him. She just stared at him. Zach was clenching a large clump of Samuel's hair between his teeth. He could feel his own skin puckering randomly on the bones of his face and he was trying to make his face stay still but it would not stay still. Because the boy was cold. Zach had wrapped him tightly in his jacket and turned his face into his chest because he had known; even before Samuel's body began to cool against his chest he had known. He had known it when he came around the trunk of the tree and gathered him up in his arms. And now Samuel was cold. The little body rose and fell and the soft hair rose and fell underneath Zach's chin and he tasted of that hair but it was Zach's chest that rose and not the boy's. Outside the car the world was. The small towns in their hopeful clusters were. The stars wheeled in their immutable and cold exigencies of fire, sun upon sun upon sun, but the boy didn't breathe; hadn't been breathing; he had suffocated on his own vomit when the man raised the pipe to bash his skull.

They drove all the early hours of that morning and they passed through Rosevine and Milam and the man said that there ought to be an EmergiCare or some such satellite hospital in Many but he wasn't sure. Zach had to clear his throat three times before he could speak. I think he's going to be all right, he said. He's stabilized now. We live near Marjolaine and I'd like just to get him home.

The couple looked at each other. We'll take you there, the man said, talking to his wife as if it was she who needed transport. We'll take you to Marjolaine.

She put both her hands around his and held it tightly and looked at his profile and said his name. Said it again and stroked his hair. Tom.

He looked ahead down the road in the attitude of an explorer.

It's not too far out of our way, he said. Heck, we're driving all night anyway.

Thank you, Zach said.

He looked out the window at the rushing lights, the rushing darknesses, and he held Samuel's body very tightly and each lamppost, each tree, each store, each house seemed to be made for that place, for that land under it only and no other, and the land in between, the dark woods, the wide open spaces, even the minutiae of land, the median strip grass, seemed so softly, so generously, to coat the scabrous earth. And he thought of Anna and he knew that he loved her. He thought that he had to touch her, had to breathe her and lie with her pore to pore and tell her. He thought of Lazar and he marvelled at the existence of such a man on the earth. He thought of his parents, his self-absorbed and vacuous mother and his rapacious father and he knew that they had to be. And further he knew that he was who he was not only in spite of them but also because of them, blood or not because of them. He thought of the sheer sustenance they'd given him, the food and clothing and shelter all his young life which care seemed to him now an extravagant and unwarranted bounty, a grace, they who despite themselves had surely saved him from what ills and what sicknesses and even perhaps what death he would never know, and he thought that he must see them if only to thank them. And he thought of his blood parents and he knew that his mother was dead and that he would find his father eventually and that he would stand there and shake the man's hand across an unbridgeable gulf of shame and sorrow and that they would be.

By the time they got to Nate's the woman had been sleeping for more than two hours; the man meanwhile had tuned the radio on loudly to an evangelical talk show in order to stay awake. It was almost dawn. It was cold. Colder than it had been when he'd left. Colder than it was in the wash. And windy. When Zach unlatched the door and kneed it open the air whipped through the car and a newspaper folded in the crook of the windshield lifted up and set upon the man's face and veiled him for a moment and he grabbed at it in disgust and threw it down. It's March and it's still winter, he said bitterly, to no one.

Zach got out and walked around the front of the car and made himself look at the man over Samuel's shoulder as he thanked him. Tom cracked his window. Good luck, he said. The woman didn't wake up. Thank you, Zach said again. The car drove off. He sat on the curb of the gasoline island, the same curb on which Nate's son Bobbie had been sitting so long ago. He held the boy in his arms and he wept. There was no bottom to it and the sounds were not human sounds and the words not human words. When he looked up the eastern light was just paling the rooftops and the tops of the trees were naked in the light and the wind whipped them leafless as they were and they bent and dipped and righted for a moment and then surged again. He stood up with the boy in his arms and began to walk toward The Lake.

It was very early but some cars were already out on the road. A few beeped and one actually pulled alongside and stopped and a man leaned over and offered them a ride. From working at Nate's he'd become somewhat familiar in the town. He thanked the man and told him no and they entered the woods walking a half an hour later and the wind abated for the trees. He could hear his steps now and he could hear voices in the woods and voices it seemed in the expirations of his own breath. Voices under the soles of his shoes. In two more hours he'd crossed over the two bridges and the clay began to darken underfoot and the road bent southwest toward the bottom and The Lake. He realized that he was not even panting. The boy's weight was as nothing to him and his legs felt like they could walk forever. He took huge strides, as if with his walking he was eating and digesting the very clay of the road. He walked toward her with great determination, the steps beginning to falter now and not from weariness but from the determination itself, from the plaintive and guileless beginning itself, his body leaning forward toward the beginning so that he had to stride longer for the leaning, the corrupted road unskeining before him in a rushing, beginning to straighten under him even as he perceived its curving, and the voices in the woods called out to him a thousand unintelligibles, neither slander nor mockery nor caveat nor song, but more like gossip, called out quietly with the temper of senseless and benign gossip, as if in memory of their whispering, their now molted leaves, and he did not heed them. And then the soul left the body; or so it seemed; a final cold, a further dovetoned ash in the cherubic face. And the voices ceased, and if the air is the home of the soul it took the boy, bore him up, gave him back to the very breath we breathe.

The lake was visible now, and then the last bend in the road, the house through the last scarf of trees, and then Anna. She came down the gallery steps in a robe he'd never seen her wear, running barefoot across the gravelly dirt, windmilling, her limbs flailing outward and saying something which Zach couldn't hear. He is not sleeping, Zach said, but she already knew it. She came running, her mouth mouthing something, and He is not sleeping, Zach said. Then he could hear her, the high pitched keening, the mouth an emptiness of mouth, the voice itself already the voice of his own new heart. What have you done? she cried. What have you done with the garden I trusted to you?

Chapter Forty six

He carried the boy in a wool blanket up to Bull Clearing. He wrapped him yet tighter in the wool and leaned the bundle against the bole of a tree and walked back down the short trail to the property and he went to the shed and took from the wall the two spades the one of which was broken on the bladepoint and he climbed the trail again and began digging. Spade unto earth. The singular sound of it like a reaper's blade scything through the barely budding clusters of the treelimbs. The ground was hard from winter. It took him over four hours. He dug it nearly six feet deep and five feet around and when he was finished he climbed out of the hole and looked at it and sunk the blade in the mound and traversed the hillside to the creek and lay down and put his head entire into the freezing runoff and drank. He drank in gulps until he could no longer swallow and then he surged up heaving for air and rolled onto his back and lay breathing on the bank. Then he stood and walked back to the clearing. He sat leaning against the tree and put the boy between his legs, against his chest, and waited. He waited all afternoon. It was dusk when he heard her feet coming up the trail. She came out of the wood and she walked to the grave and looked down into it for a long time and

then she turned around and slid the pack off her shoulders and
Zach stood and gathered up the boy. He carried him to the edge
of the hole and handed him to Anna and she took him in her
arms and he climbed down into the grave and she knelt and
leaned over and handed down the bundle and her hair brushed
so briefly against Zach's face and Zach laid Samuel down carefully and climbed out. Go away, she said.

From The Lake?

There was a long silence.

No, from here, from the grave. I want to be alone with him. I
have some things of his to put in there that I don't care for you
to see.

Zach stood looking down into the grave. He started to turn.
I'm coming back, he said.

Go, she said. I want to be alone with him.

I'm coming back. I'm not leaving.

Go away.

I'm not leaving.

I know. Go away.

Anna, I'm not leaving. Don't think that I'm leaving you.

I know.

I'm not leaving Anna.

I know. It's all right.

It's not all right. I'm not leaving you.

I know, she said. I know.

You have to know. This is where I am. You—

I know Zachary. Let me be with him a while. I'll call for you.

He turned again to leave and then hold her, he thought. Hold
her. Now. And if not now then never. Then nothing and never
and never. Now the last light is coming low through the trees
and now the boy will never look again on this living world and
now that hawk and then another and another now dipping
earthward over the branches and now the faint lakefed breeze
and the tangent fire in your palms if you would just turn them if
you would just lift them and if you do not hold her if you cannot so much as hold her if you do not hold her then it is not and

all is not and there is no light and no hawk and no breeze and no palm and no man and no woman and if there is no woman then there is no world and if there is no world then you are what you were before and you are not what you were before so hold her. He turned and before he even faced her she was hitting him, her fists raining down on his shoulders and his chest in deep speechless thuds and he made no effort to block them. He said her name and walked slowly into her wilderness until his body smothered her blows. And then he held her. She made a sound he would never hear again his whole life. It was inside an exhale but it was falling and it was a groaning and a weeping and cooing and a prayer and it was soft in his ear and then it was over and never to be again and her breath was warm and steady. After a time it was dark. He let her go. He put the shovel over his shoulder and walked into the trees.

ACKNOWLEDGMENTS

Kären, who alone in all my life believed in me absolutely.

And I thank Bay Anapol for her passionate encouragement at the beginning of this prose fiction; Joanne Meschery, the benevolent phantom over the enterprise; Barbara Grossman, who was determined that Viking publish the book; my editor at Viking, Molly Stern, for her verve and insight and commitment, nay, loyalty, to the book; Walter Donohue of Faber and Faber for his dignified approach to publishing and his carefully measured suggestions; and not without Molly Friedrich, who throws open doors, and the hard working Paul Cirrone, also of Aaron Priest.

ff A selected list of titles available from
Faber and Faber Ltd

In case of difficulty in purchasing any Faber title through normal channels, books can be purchased from:

Bookpost, PO BOX 29, Douglas, Isle of Man, IM99 1BQ

Credit cards accepted. Please telephone 01624 836000, fax 01624 837033
Internet www.bookpost.co.uk *or* email bookshop@enterprise.net for details.